DAUGHTER OF MOTH

DAUGHTER OF MOTH

THE MOTH SAGA, BOOK IV

DANIEL ARENSON

CHAPTER ONE
AN UNPLEASANT ENCOUNTER

The creaky, horse-drawn cart trundled across the bridge, taking
Madori away from her homeland and old life.

Here it is, she thought and took a shaky breath. *The border.*

The Red River flowed beneath Reedford Bridge, beads of
light gleaming upon its muddy waters. The cart clattered over the
last few bricks, rolling off the bridge and onto the western
riverbank. Madori looked around her, expecting more of a
change—a different landscape, a different climate, at least a
different shade of sky or scent to the air. Yet the grass still rustled
on the roadsides, green and lush as ever. Elms, birches, and
maples still grew upon the plains, and geese still honked above. A
wooden sign rising from a patch of crabgrass, a crumbly old
fortress upon a distant hill, and a twinge to her heart were the
only signs that they had left Arden behind, entering this kingdom
of magic and danger named Mageria.

Magic and danger? Madori thought, raising her eyebrows. She
had heard tales of dark sorcerers, brooding castles swarming with
bats, and creatures of both nightmares and fairy tales. Sorcerers?
She saw only two distant farmers toiling in a turnip field.
Brooding castles? The fort upon the hill—a mere crumbly old
tower—looked liable to collapse under a gust of wind. Wondrous
creatures? Madori didn't see anything wondrous about the cattle
that stared from the roadside, lazily chewing their cud and flicking
their tails. When Madori twisted in her seat to look behind her,
gazing across the Red River to the eastern plains, she couldn't
even distinguish between the two kingdoms—this new realm of
magic and her old homeland.

And yet . . . and yet this *was* a new world. She knew this. She felt it in her bones, even if she couldn't see it. It wasn't in sorcerers or castles or creatures—it was in the chill that filled her belly, the tremble that seized her fingers, and the tightness in her throat.

I'm leaving my home forever, she thought as the cart trundled onward. *I will find magic here. I will find a new life. And I don't intend to return.*

Sitting beside her in the cart, her father patted her hand. "Excited, Billygoat?"

Madori rolled her eyes. She hated when he called her that. Her name was Madori Billy Greenmoat—"Billy" after Bailey Berin, the great heroine of the war whose statue stood outside the library back home. "Billygoat" was just the sort of groan-worthy pun her father would come up with.

"No." She stared forward over the head of their horse, an old piebald named Hayseed. "I don't get excited about things. And *please* stop calling me that."

Her father smiled and Madori groaned. It was a smile that practically patted her condescendingly on the head.

A sigh ran through her. She knew that her father was something of a legend in both halves of Moth, this world split between endless day and eternal night. He was Sir Torin Greenmoat, the famous war hero, the man who had fought in— and eventually ended—the war between day and night. The man who had made day and night cycle again, then broke the Cabera Clock, once more freezing Moth between light and darkness. The world saw him as a great warrior and peacemaker. But to Madori, he was simply her dull, boring father with his little quips and infuriating smiles.

She looked at him. Torin didn't even look like a hero. At thirty-eight years of age, the first wrinkles were tugging at the corners of his eyes, and hints of white were invading his temples and beard. He wasn't particularly tall, handsome, or muscular. He wore a simple woolen tunic and cloak, and he drove a humble cart pulled by Hayseed, an old horse no more impressive. Despite being knighted years ago, he wore no jewels, and soil hid under his fingernails. He didn't seem a warrior, a hero, a knight—simply a gardener, which was how Madori had always known him.

She knew the tales of Torin fighting in the great War of Day and Night, but that had all happened before her birth. Madori was sixteen now, the war was long gone, and to her, Torin Greenmoat was no hero but the most annoying man in both halves of the broken world.

"Are you sure?" Torin said, still smiling his little smile. "You look a little nervous. You're traveling into a new kingdom. You're going to try and gain admission to Teel University, the most prestigious school in the sunlit half of Moth. You're leaving everything you've ever known behind. You—"

Madori groaned. "Father! For pity's sake. Are you trying to get me to kill you? You're worse than Mother."

His eyes widened. "What? Never!"

"Mother scolds me nonstop, but you just smile and hint. That's a lot worse."

Torin grunted. "If your mother were here, she'd have spent the trip berating you about your clothes, your haircut, and your Qaelish lessons. You know that. Be thankful I'm the one taking you on this journey."

Madori had to admit he was probably right. Father was perhaps more embarrassing than britches split down the backside, but Mother was a terror. Koyee of Qaelin was as much a legend as Torin, and *she* actually acted like it.

While Torin was a Timandrian—a man of sunlight, his hair dark, his skin tanned—Koyee was an Elorian, a woman of the night. Her hair was long and white, her skin pale, her lavender eyes as large as chicken eggs. Koyee stood only five feet tall, but Madori thought her more terrifying than any warrior.

"Why do you wear this rubbish?" Koyee would say, tugging at Madori's clothes. "Why don't you wear proper Elorian dresses? And your hair! I've never seen a young woman with nonsensical hair like that. And your Qaelish—stars above, you've been neglecting your lessons. This turn you will read your Qaelish poetry books until you memorize them."

"I'm not Elorian!" Madori would say. "My hair is black. My skin is tanned bronze. I don't want to dress or talk or look like an Elorian, all right, Mother? Now will you—"

That's about as far as Madori would ever get. A slap usually silenced her, followed by screams, tears, and finally long hours in her bedroom, forced to study the language of the night.

Sitting on the cart, far away from her distant village near the darkness, Madori shuddered. She looked down at her clothes, which she had sewn herself. She wore a violet tunic over purple leggings, and leather boots heavy with many buckles rose to her knees—clothes strange in both day *and* night. Her hair, she knew, drew even more perplexed stares. She cut it herself, shearing it so short she could barely grab the strands between her fingers. She left only two long strands on top, both sprouting just above her forehead; they fell down to her chin, framing her face.

"I already look strange because of my mixed blood," Madori would often tell her mother. "I might as well have strange clothes and a strange haircut."

The argument never worked, but Madori thought it apt. Even if she wore proper Timandrian clothes—a skirt and blouse—or proper Elorian clothes—a slim, silken *qipao* dress and embroidered sash—she'd look out of place. She had inherited some Timandrian traits from her father. Her hair was black, not white like the hair of Elorians, and her skin was tanned, not pale like a child of darkness. But nobody would mistake her for a full-blooded Timandrian. Her Elorian blood—the blood of darkness—was clear to all. She was slim and short, barely standing five feet tall—normal perhaps in the darkness, but diminutive in the daylight. Most obvious were her eyes—they shone a gleaming lavender, large as owl eyes in her small, round face. A tattoo of a duskmoth—one wing black, the other white—adorned her wrist, a symbol of her two halves, of a soul torn between day and night.

A mixed-child. A child of both daylight and darkness. Perhaps the only one in the world.

And so I will seek a new home, Madori thought, throat tight. *A place where I'm accepted.*

The taunts rang through her memory, cutting her like icy daggers.

Mongrel!

Freak!

Creature!

As old Hayseed pulled the cart along, leaving their homeland behind, the pain still lingered inside Madori. She lowered her head and clenched her fists in her lap. Fairwool-by-Night, her old village, lay in the daylight near the border of darkness. Grown near the shadows, its people feared the night. Fairwool's children had spent years shoving Madori into the mud, spitting onto her, and mocking her mixed blood. Madori never told her parents—a father of sunlight and a mother of darkness—about how the other children treated her. She knew it would break their hearts.

And so now I'm leaving that home, she thought, and her eyes stung—those damn eyes that were twice the size of anyone else's here in daylight. Fairwool-by-Night was a backwater, a forgotten village full of ignorant fools; the entire kingdom of Arden was a land of fools.

But Mageria...

Madori looked down the road, and a tingling smile tugged at her lips. Ahead, the plains led to misty hills and a hidden world of wonder. Here was a new kingdom—only another kingdom of daylight, it was true, but a land of magic nonetheless. People here were educated, unlike at home, and they would accept Madori. At Teel University she wouldn't be simply a mixed-breed from a humble village. At Teel she would learn the secrets of magic. She would become a mage. She would grow strong.

She noticed that Torin was watching her, his eyes soft. He patted her knee. "Whatever happens at the trials, my daughter, I'm proud of you. Whether they accept you to the university this year, or whether we have to return for new trials next year, I love you. More than anything. To me you are magic."

She blew out her breath and rolled her eyes. "Oh, Father, you are such a horrible poet."

And yet tears filled her eyes, and she leaned against him and hugged him close. He kissed her head, lips pressing against the stubbly top.

"Even if your hair is too short," he said.

She managed to grin and tugged the two long, black strands that framed her face. "This part is long. It's good enough."

Torin groaned. "It looks like a damn walrus mustache is growing from your head."

For the first time since leaving her village long turns ago, Madori laughed. "Excellent. That's what I'll tell Mother next time she harasses me—that I simply have a head-mustache."

She was still laughing, and even Torin smiled, when hooves and horns sounded ahead.

Madori looked up and her laughter died upon her lips. She reached into her boot where she hid her dagger.

"Trouble," she muttered.

A convoy of armored riders—a dozen in all—was heading down the road toward them. Since leaving home, Madori had seen many travelers along this pebbly path—farmers, pilgrims, peddlers, and soldiers on patrol. But she had never seen anyone like the riders ahead. Each man wore priceless plate armor, the steel bright and gleaming in the sunlight. Their horses too wore armor—and these were no old nags like Hayseed but fine coursers, each more costly than anything and everything Madori's family owned. As the convoy drew closer, Madori tilted her head and squinted. She was well versed in heraldry—one of the few fields of study she enjoyed—but she didn't recognize the sigils on these riders' shields and banners. The symbol showed a golden disk hiding most of a silver circle—the sun eclipsing the moon.

Hayseed nickered and reared, raising the cart and pushing Madori and Torin back in their seats.

"Easy, girl, easy . . ." Madori said. Despite her calm words, she clutched the hilt of her dagger. These riders ahead were no good; she could smell it on them.

Raising dust and scattering pebbles, the convoy reached them, its formation not parting to allow the cart through. Torin had to tug the reins, pulling Hayseed to a halt. The riders ahead halted too, staring through eyeholes in their helmets.

Torin raised a hand in a friendly gesture, though Madori saw the tension in his jaw, heard the the nervousness in his voice.

"Hello there, fellow travelers!" he said. "Lovely day for a ride."

They stared down at him. A few riders gripped the hilts of their swords, and wondrous swords those were—the scabbards filigreed with silver motifs, the hilts wrapped in black leather, the pommels bearing gemstones.

The lead horse, a magnificent beast of snowy white fur, snorted and pawed the earth. Slowly, his gauntlets creaking, the horse's rider pulled off his helmet. The man had a cold, hard face, one that could have been handsome were it not so aloof. Wavy blond hair crowned his head, the temples streaked with white.

Chin raised, the rider gazed down with icy blue eyes. Disgust filled those eyes like coins filled a rich man's coffers.

"Torin Greenmoat." The rider sneered. "So the rat has left his gutter."

Sitting in the cart, Torin glared up at the rider. "Hello again, cousin. I see the snake has left his lair."

The snowy horse sidestepped, and its rider clenched his fist around the hilt of his sword. "Yes, technically we are cousins." The man's voice was smooth and cold as ice around a frozen corpse. "Your mother's sister had the sense to marry into a proper, blue-blooded family, sense you clearly lack. But you will address me as all in Mageria do—as Lord Serin."

Madori had spent the trip here thinking her father the dullest, most insufferable man on Moth, but right now, she thought Torin Greenmoat a true hero. She leaped to her feet in the cart, drew her dagger, and pointed it at the riders.

"Get out of our way!" she said. "Ride your pretty little horses through the mud and let us pass, or by the stars above, we'll soon see how blue your blood truly is."

"Madori!" Torin hissed, pulling her back down into her seat. "Be silent."

The riders ahead snickered. Lord Serin glared at Madori like one would glare at dung upon a new boot. He raised a handkerchief to his nose as if Madori's very scent offended him.

"Learn to control your mongrel of a daughter," the lord said. "It's bad enough you bedded an nightcrawler, begetting a deformed half-breed, but you can't even keep the beast muzzled."

Madori stared, mouth hanging over. She could barely breathe.

Nightcrawler. It was a foul word, a dirty word for Elorians, the people of the night—the name of a lowly worm. She winced, remembering the names children in Fairwool-by-Night would call her. *Half-breed! Mongrel! Creature!*

All those taunts—years of them—pounded through Madori now, and somehow Serin's words were even worse. This was Mageria, the land of her dreams, not some backwater village. These were noblemen in fine armor, not peasant children.

Her eyes watered and Madori screamed. She leaped from the cart, ran across the road, and waved her dagger at Lord Serin.

"Draw your sword and face me!" she shouted. "I'm not scared of you. I have no muzzle and I can bite. I—"

"Madori!"

A hand gripped her wrist and tugged her back. Torin was pulling her away from the lords and onto the muddy roadside. Madori struggled and kicked, but she couldn't free herself from her father's grip. The riders roared with laughter.

"She's a wild animal, cousin!" Lord Serin said. He spat toward Madori; the glob landed on her boot. "She doesn't belong in Mageria. Mongrels belong in cages."

With that, the armored lord spurred his horse. The animal cantered forward, hooves splashing mud onto Torin and Madori. The other riders followed, spraying more mud.

"Send your nightcrawler wife back into the night!" Serin shouted as the convoy made its way around the cart, heading east down the road. "The Radian Order rises in the sunlight. The creatures of darkness will cower before us."

With that, the riders turned around a bend, vanishing behind a copse of elms.

Madori stood on the roadside, mud covering her clothes up to her chest. She clutched her dagger, fuming, and spun toward her father.

"I could have slain them all!" Her fists trembled. "Let's go after them. We'll leap up from behind. We'll—"

"We'll ignore them and keep traveling to our destination," Torin said calmly.

Madori raised her hands in frustration. "You'll just give up? I thought you're a war hero! I thought you fought in battles. How could you just . . . just . . . ignore them?"

She expected her father to scold her, but Torin sighed and lowered his head. Madori was surprised to glimpse a tear in his eye.

"Father . . ." she whispered, her anger leaving her.

He pulled her into an embrace, and she let her dagger fall into the mud.

"Yes, my daughter, I fought in battles. I still fight them every night in my dreams. And I don't want this life for you." He placed a finger under her chin, raised her face toward his, and stared into her eyes. "I want you to follow your dream of becoming a mage—not a warrior like I was. We'll keep traveling to Teel University and forget about those men. You will achieve greatness on your terms, not letting others drag you into the mud."

She gestured down at their filthy clothes. "We're already in the mud." She laughed softly and hugged her father. "All right, Papa. We keep going."

They climbed back onto the cart, and Hayseed resumed walking, taking them down the road. Madori had spent the past few turns dreaming about Mageria, this kingdom of magic and enlightenment, the home of the great University. She spent the rest of the turn in silence, staring ahead, a cold pit in her stomach.

Mongrel.

Beast.

A creature for a cage.

She lowered her head, clutched her hands together, and missed home.

CHAPTER TWO
THE TOWERS OF TEEL

After traveling by cart for almost a month, Madori saw the splendor of Teel University ahead. She gasped and tears stung her eyes.

"It's beautiful, Father," she whispered, clutching the hem of her shirt. "It's so beautiful."

He nodded thoughtfully, bottom lip thrust out. "The gardens aren't bad."

She punched his arm. "I don't care about the gardens!" She had to wipe tears from her eyes. "I've never seen anything like this."

When Madori had been a child, her mother would read her fairy tales of castles, their white spires touching the sky, their banners bright. Madori had always thought the stories just that— stories. Yet here before her was a fairy tale come to life.

She didn't know where to look first; her eyes wanted to drink it all in at once. She forced herself to move her eyes from the bottom up, admiring every bit in turn. Down the road, past green fields and a pond, sprawled a town of a hundred-odd buildings, their roofs tiled red, their walls built of timber foundations and white clay. Beyond the town, dwarfing even the tallest of its roofs, rose ivy-coated walls topped with merlons and turrets. Behind the walls rose four great towers, taller than any temple or castle Madori had ever seen; they seemed to scrape the sky itself. Between the towers rose a great, round building ringed with columns. A dome topped the building, looking large enough to easily contain all of Fairwool-by-Night with room to spare.

"Teel University," Madori whispered, her fists trembling around folds of her shirt.

A place of knowledge. A place of acceptance. Perhaps back in her village she was a mere creature to scorn. Perhaps ruffians along the road mocked her mixed blood. But here, finally, was the place Madori had always dreamed of, a center of enlightenment.

Torin pointed. "The dome is the Library of Teel. I've seen it illustrated in books. They say it's the largest library in the world." He pointed at the towers next. "Each of the four towers contains its own faculties of magic."

Others were traveling the road around them, heading toward the university. Madori saw thoroughbreds with braided manes pulling fine carriages, and behind their glass windows—real glass, a material as expensive as gold!—Madori saw youths dressed in finery, jewels adorning them. Parents spoke animatedly, and they too wore costly, embroidered fabrics.

"Ah, when I was a lad, I studied in Agrotis Tower," said one man, riding by upon a destrier. A samite cloak hung across his shoulders, and he patted his ample belly with a pudgy hand heavy with rings. "Of course, back in those days, I weighed a few stones less. Climbing all those stairs would be harder now."

The man's son, a scrawny youth of about sixteen years, nodded silently and nervously coiled his fingers together. Golden chains hung around his neck, and his sleeves alone—puffy things inlaid with rubies and amethysts—probably cost more than Madori's house back home.

She suddenly felt very plain, what with her humble woolen leggings and shirt—garments she had sewn herself—and muddy boots heavy with buckles. She owned no jewelry, and her prized possession was her dagger with the antler hilt, hardly the weapon of nobility. Her father looked just as humble, clad in a simple tunic and breeches. Madori had known that only noble children could attend Teel University, and officially she *was* highborn; her father had been knighted after the war. But riding here upon her cart, she realized that—despite the technicality of her highborn blood—she was as far removed from true nobility as lizards were from dragons.

Twisting her fingers in her lap, she looked at her father.

"They're probably just as nervous as you are," he said.

Madori bit her lip. "Their clothes are nicer than mine."

"Everyone's clothes are nicer than yours, Billygoat. That's what happens when you don't listen to your mother."

She snorted. "Mother wants me to dress in Elorian silk. Then I'd really stick out like a frog in a fruit bowl." She sighed. "Papa, when you went to the war years ago, were you ever scared? I mean . . . suddenly just so scared you didn't think you could do it?"

His eyes softened and he patted her shoulder. "All the time."

She looked around at the other youths with their rich clothes and jewels, then up at the university towers. "How did you go on? How didn't you run home?"

He mussed the cropped hair on the top of her head. "You're not going to war, little one."

"I know." She gulped and nodded. "But I'm still afraid."

He looked ahead at the rising walls of the university, seeming lost in thought. Finally he spoke softly. "I'll teach you a little trick I used back in the war—when I was afraid, when I was in danger. I told myself: To survive, you only have to breathe the next breath. That's it. Just the next breath." He took a deep breath, then slowly exhaled. "And then another breath. And another. I tried not to think too far ahead—just on taking that next breath, and every time that air flowed down my lungs, I realized that I'm still alive. I'm still going. And I could go a little longer and I'd survive that too. Some people say that you achieve great things step by step. But sometimes it's not even about moving—it's about living a little longer and realizing that you're still around, that you'll be all right."

She nodded and took a deep breath. "I like that, Papa." She leaned over in her seat and kissed his cheek. "Thank you."

Hayseed walked onward, pulling the cart into the town of Teelshire. The road was cobbled here, lined with houses that rose two or three stories tall, their roofs tiled, their windows filled with glass. Madori saw shops selling fabrics, pottery, sculptures, and books. An inn pumped out smoke from four chimneys, the sign above its door displaying a wolf in a dress and the words, "The Dancing Wolf." Everywhere she looked, she saw the other applicants—highborn youths with darting eyes. And among them . . .

Madori gasped. "A mage," she whispered. She tugged her father's sleeve. "Look. A real mage."

The man walked ahead, clad in a black cloak and hood. His eyes gleamed from the shadows. With a flourish of fluttering robes, he stepped into a shop with no sign, vanishing into the shadows.

Torin grumbled. "I've seen mages like him in the war—the black robed ones. Nasty folk. Your mother still has a scar along her arm from their foul magic." He winced. "Madori, are you sure you want to do this?"

She nodded vehemently. "Yes! Not all mages wear the black robes. Not all practice the art of war. I will practice the magic of healing." She thought back to that horrible year—the year her mother's belly had swelled, the year her little brother or sister had died in the womb, leaving her still an only child. She nodded. "I will do this. I will pass the trials. I will gain admission. And I will become a healer."

Because healers were respected wherever they went, she knew. Healers were not mongrels or monsters. Healers were beloved.

Past shops, around a pond, and along a road lined with cottages, they reached the walls of the university. An archway loomed here, its bronze doors open, tall enough that a cherry tree could have stood within it. Guards flanked the entrance, clad in burnished breastplates, red plumes sprouting from their helmets. A potbellied, mustached man stood in checkered livery, ringing a bell. His hand was coned around his mouth.

"All applicants to Teel University!" he cried out, bell clanging. "All applicants step through these gates! Parents shall wait in the town. All applicants—step through!"

Torin watched the portly crier. "His mustache looks a bit like that thing that's growing off your head."

Madori nervously tugged the two long, black strands that framed her face. "You sound like Mother. Now go—I saw a tavern farther back. Wait for me there. Swap war stories with the other fathers."

She made to hop off the cart, but he held her shoulder.

"Wait, Billygoat." He tapped his cheek.

She rolled her eyes, but she dutifully gave him a kiss. After climbing off the cart, she gave dear old Hayseed a kiss too, then gulped and began walking toward the gates.

"Good luck!" Torin cried behind her.

Madori dared not even look back at him. If she looked back and saw him waving, saw dear old Hayseed, saw all those memories of home, she thought she wouldn't dare keep going.

Breath by breath, she thought. *Like Father taught me.* She inhaled shakily and walked forward. *Just survive the next breath.*

Chin raised and legs trembling, she walked through the gates, entering Teel University.

* * * * *

Torin watched his daughter vanish into the university, then stood for a long moment, staring at the gates. Finally, with a deep sigh, he turned and headed back into the town of Teelshire.

"Good luck, Billygoat," he said softly, walking along the cobbled street.

A part of him, however, didn't wish her luck. That part, perhaps petty, wished that Madori failed at the trials. If she gained admission to the university, Torin would travel the road home alone. His daughter would remain here among these walls for four years—a journey of many turns away from Fairwool-by-Night.

I'd miss you, Torin thought. *Koyee would miss you too.*

Madori often clashed with her mother—the two would argue over everything from Madori's clothes and hairstyle, to her disdain of Qaelish lessons, to the tattoo on her wrist—but Torin knew that the two women deeply loved each other.

Women? Torin frowned. Since when had Madori become a woman? It was only recently that Torin was changing her swaddling clothes, teaching her how to walk, and delighting whenever she learned to speak a new word. And now—in a blink of an eye—she was a woman?

He sighed.

You became a woman somewhere between Fairwool and Teelshire, he thought. He was both proud and terrified of how fast she had grown up. Maybe he was scared to let her walk alone in the world. And maybe he simply missed the child she had been, a child who had depended on him.

He didn't know how long the trials would last, but he saw many other parents ambling about the town, finding bookshops, teashops, and mostly alehouses to wait in. They were typical nobles, he thought, men and women adorned in embroidered fabrics, sporting bright jewels for all to see. Torin was the son of a knight, and after returning home from the war—a hero known across Moth—he had received his own knighthood. Yet he sought no castles, no riches, simply the humble life of a gardener. He knew that his simple peasant's garb, the dirt beneath his fingernails, and his humble demeanor dreadfully embarrassed Madori whenever they visited the courts of Arden—and even here in Mageria. Torin smiled grimly.

Good. It's a father's job to embarrass his children.

The houses and shops rose three stories tall around him, their windows displaying wares from across Mageria—rich woolen fabrics to rival even those from his village of weavers, statues and paintings of landscapes, armor and weapons, and all manner of books and scrolls. The shops were doing good business this turn; Torin guessed that the Turn of Trials was their busiest of the year, a time when the wealthiest parents across the world came to wait nervously . . . and spend.

Finally Torin passed by The Dancing Wolf tavern again. He decided that more than he cared to shop, he'd like to drown his worries in a big mug of ale. Worrying for Madori always gnawed on him—he hadn't stopped worrying about her since her birth—but now a new concern had risen. The encounter with Lord Serin still weighed heavily upon him. His cousin's warning echoed in Torin's mind.

The Radian Order rises in the sunlight. The creatures of darkness will cower before us.

Torin grimaced. He had heard similar rhetoric years ago. Last time, such hate-mongering had led to a war across the world. Torin had feigned indifference around Madori, not wanting to worry the girl, but now his belly twisted. The memories of that war years ago—the fire in the night, the blood on his sword, the countless dead around him—still haunted his dreams, and now those memories flared even here in this peaceful, sunlit town.

Shaking his head grimly, he stepped into the tavern.

A large, warm room awaited him. His usual haunt back home—a cozy little tavern called The Shadowed Firkin—was a place of scarred oak tables, a scratched floor, and commoners boasting about the size of their squashes and the longevity of their sheep. But here Torin found a tavern that looked almost as luxurious as a nobleman's hall. Tapestries hung on the walls, depicting scenes of hunters and hounds under a sky full of birds. Actual tablecloths covered the tables, revealing cherry-wood legs engraved in the shapes of horses. Armchairs basked in the heat of two roaring fireplaces, and sunlight fell through stained-glass windows. Casks of ale and wine rose along one wall, and a bar stood gleaming with polished brass taps. The tavern was still half-empty, but every moment the bell above the door rang as more parents shuffled in.

Nodding at a few other fathers—their cheeks were already red with ale—Torin made his way to the bar. He sat on a stool, placed a few coins on the counter, and ordered a dark brew.

He raised the drink in the air, silently making the same toast he always did—a toast to old friends. To Bailey. To Hem. To lost souls, old memories.

"It's been seventeen years, friends," he said, his voice too low for anyone to hear. "I still think about you every turn."

He drank for them, thinking of home, missing that old tavern near the dusk, missing his old friends.

Snippets of conversation, rising from the armchairs by the fireplace behind him, reached Torin's ears, interrupting his thoughts.

"Now the Radians!" one man was saying. "There are some folks with sense to them, I say. Proud. Get things done. They're doing some good work in Timandra."

A second voice answered. "I've been saying it for a while, I have. Can't trust the nightfolk. Damn 'lorians moving into the sunlight now—I saw some myself, right here in Teelshire! You let in a few, soon they'll swarm. Let the Radians deal with them."

Torin twisted in his seat, glancing toward the hearth. Two noblemen sat there, holding tankards of ale, their cheeks ruddy and their bellies wide. They noticed his glance and raised their tankards.

"Oi, friend!" said one of the pair, his yellow mustache frothy. "You agree with us, don't you? You're a man of Arden; I can tell from the look of you. Right on the border with the night, you lot are." He nodded. "The Radians will protect you. They'll protect us all from this infestation of filthy Elorians."

Torin winced. *Filthy Elorians* . . . His wife was Elorian. His daughter was half-Elorian. He had fought and killed to save Elorians from the cruelty of daylight.

The ale tasted too bitter in his mouth. He turned away from the men and faced the bar again. His heart sank.

Did I make a mistake? he wondered, throat tightening. *Should I have truly brought Madori here into the wide world—a world that is hostile toward her?* Part of him wanted to race outside, barge into the university, grab his daughter, and drag her home to safety. Madori would shout, claiming she was old enough to seek her own fortune. Even Koyee would insist that they could not shelter Madori forever. But how could Torin let his little girl go alone into this world—a world full of hatred and ignorance, a world that would hate her simply for her blood?

Torin stared at the suds in his mug. Before Madori's birth, he and Koyee had fixed the Cabera Clock. For a year, the world had spun around its axis, night and day cycling. For a year, the world had seen Timandrians and Elorians as one. With peace restored, Torin and Koyee had broken the Cabera Clock again; Koyee still wore a small Cabera gear around her neck. The world was frozen again between endless day and night, and now—only a generation later—hatred was returning.

Should we have never broken the clock? Torin wondered. *Should we have never restored Moth to the way it was, the way its people wanted it?*

A stool creaked as a cloaked, hooded man sat down beside Torin. After ordering his own mug of ale, the stranger spoke in a low voice.

"You're right to ignore those fools." He turned his head toward Torin, though his face remained hidden in the shadows of his hood. "You can't fix stupidity, only hope to avoid it for a while."

The stranger's voice seemed familiar, as did his slender, short frame. Torin leaned closer, squinting, trying to see into the hood's shadows.

"Bit warm in here for a hood and cloak," Torin said.

The man received his mug of ale, took a sip, then leaned closer to Torin, letting some light fill his hood. "Warm but safe."

Torin's eyes widened. He nearly choked on his drink. "Cam?"

His friend—Camlin, King of Arden—smiled thinly and pulled his hood further down, letting new shadows hide him. "Hullo, Torin old boy. I thought I saw you in the crowd outside. You stick out like a black sheep with those ridiculous clothes from home."

The weight instantly lifted from Torin's shoulders. The world was dangerous, his daughter was leaving home, and hatred lurked only several paces behind him—but his friend was here, and things suddenly seemed a little brighter.

"*I* stick out?" Torin said. "Look at your clothes." He pointed at Cam's shabby old cloak.

The slender man sipped his ale. "That's different. I'm in disguise." He dropped his voice to a whisper. "I can't just walk around without this cloak and hood. People would mob me. I'm the King of Arden after all."

"King consort," Torin corrected him. "Queen Linee is the real monarch."

Cam groaned. "Will we ever have a single conversation without you reminding me of that fact?"

Torin grinned. "Depends. Will your head ever shrink back to its previous size?" He grabbed his friend's shoulder and squeezed it. "It's good to see you, old friend. When's the last time we met? It's been... Merciful Idar, a year now. Not since last summer when Madori and I visited the capital. What are you doing here in Mageria?"

Cam glanced around the tavern, but it seemed like all the other patrons were busy speaking among themselves, bragging of their children's prowess and making wagers on who'd gain admission to Teel. The diminutive king turned back toward Torin.

"Tam's here—trying out for the university."

Torin's eyes widened. "Your son? The Prince of Ard—"

"Shush!" Cam glanced around, eyes dark. "He's here in disguise too. I begged the boy to stay in Arden. We have fine schools there as well, but the lad wanted to study magic. In fact, I blame you." He gave Torin a stern look and jabbed his chest. "It's your daughter who put that nonsense into his head. Turns out last summer, when Madori and Tam were taking all those walks in the garden, they weren't having a secret romance as we feared. Oh no. It was much worse than that. Madori was telling my boy all about how she wants to be a mage someday, and well . . . Tam hasn't stopped talking about magic since." He gulped down ale and sighed. "It can't have been easy for Tam, growing up in the palace, only several moments younger than his twin. Imagine it, Torin! Robbed of a birthright by a moment in time. The twins are identical—Idar, I can barely tell them apart!—yet one is heir, the other not. I suppose I can't blame Tam for wanting to find his own way, to find his own power. But I'll miss him. This isn't his home. Honestly, I don't know if I wish him to succeed or fail and return to Arden."

Torin nodded glumly. "I feel the same way. Children. They ruin your life, don't they?"

Cam groaned. "You're getting rid of yours soon! I still have one at home." He drained his ale and ordered another drink. When the serving girl had left, he spoke in a lower voice. "Torin, there's another reason I came here. I knew you'd accompany Madori here, and I wanted to speak with you."

Torin raised an eyebrow. "How did you know it wouldn't be Koyee taking Madori here?"

The king snorted. "I saw Madori and Koyee interact enough times; the two would kill each other on the road. No. I knew it would be you here. Torin, there's trouble. Trouble back home. Trouble here. Trouble all over the sunlit half of Moth."

Torin blew out his breath. "Tell me about it. We ran into some trouble on the road here. Radians." He grimaced; the word tasted foul in his mouth. "I crossed paths with Lord Serin, my cousin. He's one of them."

Cam barked a mirthless laugh. "*One* of them? Torin, my boy, he's their *leader*. His fort rises right on the border with Arden, and his disciples are spreading through my kingdom, spewing their bile. They opened a chapter right in Kingswall—in the capital, Torin!—just a short walk from the palace." Cam placed down his mug as if the ale had turned into mud. "The words they speak . . . by Idar, they remind me of you-know-who."

Torin nodded. "I was thinking the same thing. I thought we got rid of that rubbish in the war."

Cam sighed. "Pluck one weed, another rises. If I've learned anything from sitting on the throne, it's this: Fighting ignorance is like fighting weeds—an eternal battle." He clasped Torin's arm. "My friend, I came here to warn you. Koyee is in danger. Madori is in danger, maybe even within the walls of Teel. You're in danger; the Radians see you too as an enemy. By the Abyss, we're all in danger from these fanatics."

A chill ran down Torin's spine. "Idar's Beard, how serious are these Radians? Will they turn to violence?"

"They already have." Cam winced. "Last month in Kingswall. A convoy of Elorian merchants entered the city, selling silk and silverware. The local Radian chapter hung them dead from trees and burned their wares, accusing them of stealing work from honest Timandrians. I found the Radians who did it; those bastards rot in my dungeon now. But more keep crawling across the kingdom. Torin, this is serious. And I need you to listen carefully." Cam leaned closer, staring at Torin. "Send Koyee into the night for now. Madori too, if you can talk sense into her. But you, Torin—I need you with me in the capital."

Torin laughed mirthlessly. "The capital? Cam, you know I don't belong in Kingswall."

"I know. But neither do these Radians. Many in Kingswall respect you, the hero of the war, Sir Torin Greenmoat. I need you to stand at my side, not a gardener but a great lord. I need you to preach peace and acceptance and counter Serin's rhetoric."

Torin had thought his spirits couldn't sink any lower. He stared glumly into his drink. "We've had peace for seventeen years, Cam. But now . . . this feels like the old days."

Suddenly he missed Bailey so much it stabbed his chest. If his old friend were here, she'd know what to do. She'd shout, pound the bar, and probably rush out to find and kill Serin right away. She had led their little group in the last war. If violence flared again, how would Torin fight it—older, his dearest friend gone, his own daughter in peril?

"Will you come with me, Torin?" Cam said, not breaking his stare. "I need you—not in your gardens by the dusk but in the heart of our kingdom. I can't face this alone."

Torin closed his eyes. He hadn't seen Koyee in almost a month, and he missed her so badly he hurt. How could he send her into the darkness while he stayed in the light? Again Serin's words echoed in his mind: *The creatures of darkness will cower before us.*

Torin opened his eyes and nodded. "Of course, Cam. Of course."

CHAPTER THREE
SON OF SHADOW

They rode through the sunlit forest, three people of darkness upon three black panthers.

Jitomi tugged the hood lower over his head, his eyes darting. Mottles of light fell between the trees, stinging whenever they hit his skin. His cloak was heavy, his hood was wide, and the forest canopy was thick, but still the light hurt. It baked his back and stung his eyes—large Elorian eyes the size of chicken eggs, eyes made for the shadows of endless night.

Not for this place, he thought. *Not the eternal daylight of Timandra.*

He grimaced, stroked the panther he rode on, and looked at his companions. His sister, Nitomi, wore tight-fitting black silk— the outfit of the dojai, assassins and spies trained in the night. Over them she wore a cotton cloak and hood, a garment purchased in the daylight. Two straps crisscrossed her chest, and many tantō daggers hung upon them. More blades hung from her hips, and throwing stars were clasped to her legs. A diminutive woman—halfway into her thirties but still small as a child—she looked at him, her large blue eyes gleaming, and grinned.

"Are you excited, little brother? I bet you are. I bet you're so excited you can't even talk so much, because the excitement is squishing all your words in your throat, but I don't have that problem! I'm so excited for you too, so much I can hop!" She hopped upon her panther. "Soon you'll be a real mage with real magic! Unless you want to turn back. We can turn back if you like, go back into darkness, and you can become a dojai like me, an assassin of shadows. We don't have magic, it's true, but—"

"We keep going," Jitomi said, interrupting her. He had been living with Nitomi for all his sixteen years; the only way to converse with her, he knew, was to interrupt a lot. His sister was twice his age—she had even fought in the great War of Day and Night alongside the heroes Koyee and Torin—but still had the heart of a child. "We don't turn back."

And yet a part of him did want to turn back. A part of him feared this land of daylight. He had been only a babe when the Timandrians had invaded his homeland of Eloria. The sunlit demons had marched into the shadows with blades, with torches, and with dark magic. Jitomi had grown up seeing the scars of that magic upon the warriors of Ilar, his island homeland in the darkness.

His nine sisters—Nitomi the eldest among them—were either dojai assassins or steel-clad warriors in Ilar's army. Yet what use were blades against magic? In the war, so many Ilari soldiers—brave, strong men all in steel—had fallen to the sunlit mages. His father had hoped that Jitomi—the family's youngest child and only boy—would become a great warrior, an heir to their fortress. But Jitomi had disappointed his father, had spat upon the family tradition, had left their castle in the darkness and journeyed here into the light . . . to find Teel University. To find the secrets of power.

"Qato blind," said the third rider, voice plaintive.

Jitomi turned to look at the man—if a man he was. His cousin, Qato, seemed more like one of the mythical giants of ancient days. While Nitomi was small—shorter than five feet— Qato stood seven feet tall, wide and stony as a cliff face. His panther, the largest of the beasts found in Ilar's wilderness, grunted under the weight. Normally bare-chested, even in the cold of night, here in daylight Qato wore a thick robe and hood, hiding himself from the sun. A massive katana, large as a pike, hung across his back. His eyes were narrowed to slits in the daylight, even this mottled daylight of the forest.

Jitomi rode his panther closer to his cousin. He patted Qato's knee. "We're almost there. Then you and Nitomi can return home. Soon you'll be back in the darkness."

Of course, home lay a two moons' ride away, but Qato needed all the encouragement he could get.

As for me, Jitomi thought with a sigh, *I won't be returning home for a while, not if I'm admitted to Teel.* He looked up at the sky, wincing in a beam of light that fell between the branches. *The university studies are four years long . . . four years in this strange light of endless day and heat and life everywhere.*

As much as the light seemed strange, the life that filled Timandra was even stranger. Eloria was a land of rock, water, and starlight, but here—here the entire landscape was made of life. Blades of grass grew under the panthers' feet, tiny creatures that survived even when stepped upon. Trees grew from the soil, giant creatures with rustling green hair. Birds and small furry animals crawled upon the trees like parasites, scuttling, crying, squawking. Jitomi had been in Timandra for two moons now, and while he was starting to get used to the sunlight—he could tolerate it with his cloak and hood—seeing life everywhere still seemed so strange. He had learned that not all these creatures were animals; many of them were called "plants," and they had no thoughts, no feelings, no sense of pain—much like the mushrooms back in Eloria but far taller and grander. Eloria had no plants, and still Jitomi struggled to distinguish between them and the strange animals of this place. To him it was all a surreal dream, an endless menagerie—life beneath, around, and above him.

He passed his fingers along his neck, up his cheek, and over his brow. A dragon tattoo coiled there, rising from collarbone to forehead. Jitomi could not see the tattoo, but he could imagine that he felt the inked scales.

Protect me here, Tianlong, black dragon of Ilar, he thought. *Lend me some of your strength.*

"Qato homesick," moaned the giant dojai.

"Me too, cousin," said Jitomi with a sigh.

Little Nitomi bounced in her saddle. "Not me! Not at all. I was so bored back in Eloria. It's so boring in the darkness what with all those boring shadows and boring stars and boring . . . well, that's all there is in Eloria, isn't it? Shadows and stars. That's why it's so boring! I love the daylight. It's an adventure! I love adventures. I once went on an adventure with Koyee, have I told you? We went to a distant island of secrets, and we saw a monster—a real monster with four arms!—and there were giant weaveworms who boiled their babies, and—"

"Qato knows!" moaned the giant.

Jitomi nodded. "Yes, sister, you've told us that story ten times this turn already."

"I can't help it!" The little woman was still hopping. "It's the best story I have, and—"

"Sister, look." Jitomi pointed between the trees and down a hillside. "I think we're finally here."

They rode a little farther, and the last trees parted. Grassy hills rolled in full sunlight toward a valley and farmlands. Past flowery meadows lay a town of many houses, a columned temple, and a walled complex containing towers and domes.

"Teel University," Jitomi whispered.

The panthers bristled and growled; creatures of darkness, they still feared open daylight. Jitomi dismounted and stroked his beast.

"Qato, will you stay here with the panthers?" he asked his cousin. "They're strong and noble animals, but they still fear the daylight. Let them remain in the cover of the forest."

The giant nodded. "Qato stay."

Jitomi smiled thinly. In truth, he worried more about Qato than the panthers; he had never seen his cousin so miserable.

Nitomi bounced off her mount. "I'm not staying! I'm going right with you. I bet we'll find another adventure down there. Do you think they have weaveworms? Do they have weaveworms in the daylight? Did I tell you about the time I traveled to the island with Koyee, and we saw weaveworms, and we saw a *real* monster with many arms, and—"

Jitomi placed a finger against her lips. "I think we better not speak of weaveworms and monsters here. The locals might think we're strange."

She nodded knowingly and clamped her palms over her mouth. She spoke in a muffled voice. "Okay!"

Leaving Qato and the panthers, the siblings began to walk downhill, their hoods pulled over their heads, their cloaks shielding their skin from the light. Jitomi sighed. Even without his sister prattling on about giant worms, the siblings seemed strange enough in this land. Jitomi had seen many Timandrians over the past two moons of travel: they were a tall, wide people, their skin bronzed, their hair dark, their eyes small. Jitomi was an Elorian, born and bred in darkness; his skin was milky white, his hair silvery and smooth, his eyes large and gleaming, his ears wide, his body thin.

I'm as strange to Timandrians as trees, grass, and sunlight are to me, he thought. He had to crush an instinct to turn back, to race home to Eloria. He had come this far, seeking the secrets of magic; those secrets lay in the valley below. He would be strong. He would not turn back. If he ever returned to Eloria, it would be as a mage.

They walked down the sunny hillside, found a pebbly path, and took it through the meadow. Many flowers—Jitomi wished he knew their names—swayed on either side, and small animals—

furry creatures with long ears—raced away from his feet. When they finally reached the town and Jitomi stepped onto its cobbled streets, he lost his breath.

Towns in Ilar, his island of the night, were places of stone and fire, their black pagodas rising into the starry sky, their braziers crackling, their banners streaming in the moonlight like birds seeking flight. They were places of silence, of dark dignity, of a solemn beauty like crystal caves or underwater ruins. But here, in Teelshire, he found a town that spun his head—a place of endless color, sunlight, and life. Flowers bloomed in gardens. People wore not the dark silk of his homeland but colorful tunics and robes of cotton, wool, and fur. Stained-glass windows glittered upon the houses, and red tiles shone in the sunlight.

"It's beautiful," Nitomi whispered at his side, for once not launching into an endless stream of words.

He nodded. They stepped deeper into the town, heading toward the walls of the university.

As they walked, Jitomi's sense of wonder soured. At first it was a little boy who saw them, gasped, and fled. Past another street corner and a shop selling honeyed cakes, it was two women who pointed, muttered, and spun away on their heels. In a courtyard with a marble statue rising from a fountain, three men spat, and one shouted, "Nightcrawlers go home!" before storming off into a tavern.

"We're not very popular here," Jitomi said to his sister. He couldn't help but admire the ingenuity of the slur—nightcrawler, the name of a worm and, supposedly, the children of night.

The little woman was bouncing about, gaping at the many shops, taverns, statues, and gardens. "So what? Let them stare. Let them mumble. Jitomi, we are the children of a great lord! I'm a dojai and you're almost a mage already. They've just never seen an Elorian before. I bet they've never seen weaveworms either. Do you think we might still find weaveworms here? Maybe in the mountains up there, or—"

"Sister, hush. Let's go quickly. I want to reach the university and get off these streets."

A few men were glaring at them from a roadside ale-house. One held a knife. Another wore a strange brooch upon his lapel—it looked like a sun eclipsing a moon. The men spoke in low murmurs, and Jitomi caught something about how "Serin will send the creatures back into the night." He walked on, moving to another street.

The siblings hurried onward, and even Nitomi fell silent for once. Jitomi was too young to remember the great War of Day and Night, but his older siblings had told him many tales of those days. The fleets of daylight had sailed against Ilar, the great southern empire of the night. Those ships had smashed against the walls of Asharo, and many Timandrians—sailors and soldiers—ended up in chains, whipped, enslaved to their Ilari masters.

Yet now we're the foreigners, he thought. *Now we're nothing but creatures in a strange land.* He took a deep breath. *The war is over but hatred remains.*

They were near the walls of Teel University, walking across a courtyard, when they saw the demonstration.

A couple dozen Timandrians stood outside the university gates, raising banners with the same eclipse sigil. An effigy of an Elorian hung from a lamp post between them, formed of straw and wood—a twisted creature, its eyes cruel, its fingers clawed, its fangs red. The Timandrians chanted together in their tongue, which Jitomi had been studying for the past few years. He understood these words and they chilled him.

"Radian rises!" the people cried. "Radian rises! Elorians go home!"

One of the demonstrators, a young woman with long golden hair, rose to stand on a box. Cheeks flushed, she shouted, "Hear me! I am Lari Serin, a Radian warrior. Teel University is tarnished with the filth of nightcrawlers. Send all Elorian students home! Keep all magic in Mageria! Send the creatures back into the darkness."

Jitomi froze in his tracks, staring. So there were other Elorian students at Teel? That both comforted and worried him. He had hoped to fade into the shadows here; if other Elorians had come to study magic, and if tensions were rising, would he find himself caught in a racial war?

"Radian rises!" shouted Lari—the young, golden-haired woman. She saw Jitomi and his sister, pointed at them, and her voice rose even louder. "More creatures of the night walk among us. Nightcrawlers will burn!"

With that, Lari brought a candle to the hanging effigy. The Elorian of wood and straw caught flame. The demonstrators cheered, cut the burning effigy down, and stomped upon it. Their banners rose higher, and their voices cried out for Radian. Whether Radian was a god, movement, or leader, Jitomi didn't know, but whatever the case, the word meant danger.

Until now, Jitomi had been fighting the temptation to turn back, to run home to the night. Strangely, now he found himself clenching his fists, squaring his jaw, and marching forward with renewed determination. Nitomi walked at his side, silent for once, her eyes darting.

Leaving the protestors behind, they finally reached the university gates. Towers flanked a stone archway, its keystone engraved with two crossing scrolls, sigil of Teel. Guards in particolored livery stood at the open doors, their helmets plumed. When Jitomi peered inside, he saw a cobbled cloister, a towering elm tree, and columned halls. Many other applicants already stood within; some were fellow Elorians, hooded and cloaked.

Teel University... center of learning, wisdom, and magic.

Jitomi turned toward his sister. She stared at him, her large eyes damp, her lips quivering.

"It's time to say goodbye," Jitomi said softly and held her hands.

She nodded and sniffled. "I'll miss you, baby brother. I'll miss you so much. It won't be the same at home without you. Please do well here. Please become a very powerful mage very quickly, then come back to Ilar. I'll think about you every turn. I promise." She unclasped one of her many daggers from the strap across her chest. She handed it to him. The tantō was curved, the hilt wrapped in silk, and the sigil of Ilar—a red flame—was engraved onto the blade. "Take this. It's good steel and it will protect you here. It's the only gift I have to give."

He took the dagger and slid it into one of his cloak's deep pockets. He was about to turn and leave when Nitomi leaped, wrapped all four limbs around him, and hugged him tightly.

"Goodbye, brother," she whispered.

"Goodbye, sister."

Tears filled his own eyes. He turned to step through the archway, leaving her there—wishing he had more to say, wishing he had more time with her. He felt stiff, awkward, afraid. He dared not look back.

If I pass these trials, I won't leave this place for four years.

He entered a cobbled cloister surrounded by columned galleries. Towers soared at all sides, and a great dome—large as a palace—rose ahead. Blinking furiously, struggling to keep his eyes dry, he stared at the elm tree. Its leaves rustled against the blue sky, and Jitomi thought of the stars of his homeland.

CHAPTER FOUR
FRIEND AND FOE

Head spinning, Madori took a deep breath and stared around at the fabled Teel University.

She stood in a sprawling cloister surrounded by porticoes. The place seemed large enough for an army to muster in. Many other youths walked around her, all highborn. All were better dressed, better bred, and quite a bit taller than her. Born to an Elorian mother, Madori stood barely five feet tall; women of the night rarely stood taller. Full-blooded Timandrians, children of eternal daylight grown on hearty sunlit fare, dwarfed her. As she moved among the crowd, Madori saw them stare at her, mutter, even point.

"An Elorian?" one boy whispered, gaping her way.

His friend shook his head. "Hair's black, skin's tanned. Half-breed, I reckon. I heard of those."

Madori sneered. She was about to march over to the two boys and clobber them—how dared they talk of her as of some animal!—but her father appeared in her mind. She could hear his damn voice again.

You will achieve greatness on your terms, not letting others drag you into the mud.

Madori grumbled. Father invented stupid puns, told jokes only he'd laugh at, and was overall a huge embarrassment, but he was also the wisest person Madori knew. Fists clenched, she walked away from the two slack-jawed boys, heading deeper into the cloister.

"Country bumpkins, they are," she muttered under her breath. "They'll never pass the trials."

She kept moving, worming her way through the crowd. She thought she caught glimpses of a wooden stage ahead. Used to being the shortest person around, Madori knew she'd have to step close if she wanted to see any speaker who might appear.

As she walked, she passed by some of the strangest youths she'd ever seen. Most applicants seemed to be local boys and girls, Magerians in cotton robes, their eyes bright and their hair golden. But many foreigners crowded the courtyard too. Some applicants seemed to be from Arden, Madori's homeland; they wore leggings, tunics, and tall leather boots. Others hailed from all over the daylight realms: jungle dwellers clad in tiger-pelts, their hair flaming red; northern Verilish youths, hulking and wide, wearing bear furs; southern desert children, their skin deep bronze, their tunics white; and even some dwellers of the distant savanna island of Sania, their clothes formed of many beads, elephants embroidered onto their cloaks.

Diverse as they were, all of them were Timandrians, Madori realized with a sigh. All were children of Timandra, the sunlit half of this broken world men called Moth. The day never ended here; these children had never known darkness. She, Madori, would always be a stranger among them—a girl born to a mother of darkness, an Elorian from across the dusk.

Her eyes stung. *Will I be an outcast here too?*

She was nearing the stage when she saw another group of applicants; these ones huddled close together, clad in robes and hoods. Madori tilted her head, squinted, and stepped closer.

Her heart burst into a gallop.

"Elorians," she whispered, a tremble seizing her.

Madori had seen many Elorians before. Her village was near the border with the night, and her mother often took her into the darkness. Madori had spent many hours admiring the stars and moon, feasting upon mushrooms and glowing lanternfish, and playing with Elorian children under the dark skies. Yet aside from her mother, she had never seen other Elorians in the sunlit half of Moth.

They were a slender folk, their skin milky white, their hair long and smooth and the color of starlight. Their ears were large, thrusting out, meant for hearing every creak in the deep darkness. Their robes were made of silk, embroidered with dragon motifs. Their most distinguishing feature, however, was their eyes. Those orbs were twice the size of Timandrian eyes, oval and gleaming blue and lavender. Madori herself—though tanned of skin and dark of hair—had those eyes.

Eyes for seeing in the dark.

She took a deep breath, sudden hope lifting inside her. Here in the sunlight, she was a curiosity, a girl for others to gape at. She was no more Elorian than Timandrian, but perhaps among the children of the night she could find some acceptance. After all, they too were curiosities here; Madori saw how the others stared and pointed at them. If Madori and these Elorians did not share the full bond of race, they shared the bond of alienation.

One of the Elorians noticed her. He raised his eyes and stared her way. His large, gleaming eyes were deep blue. A tattoo of a dragon crawled up his neck and cheek, finally coiling over the eyebrow. Strands of hair fell across his forehead, milky-white, and a silver ring studded his nose. He didn't speak, didn't step toward her, merely stared, his gaze penetrating. Slowly, the others in his group turned to follow his gaze, and Madori saw the confusion in their eyes. Like everyone, they too were trying to decide what she was—a girl with Timandrian hair and skin, her eyes large as an Elorian's.

She took a step toward them, needing that comfort, that acceptance, that security of a group. But before she reached them, she paused.

No.

A voice spoke in her head again, but this time it seemed to be her own voice, not her father's—a voice from deep within her.

This is not the path to acceptance.

She was in Timandra now, about to apply for admission in a university full of Timandrians. She had to make a choice how to live here, which side of hers to embrace. If she chose to mingle with Timandrians, perhaps she could still find some acceptance in the sunlight. If she chose to live as an Elorian, she would forever be an outcast here—just one more outsider, a misfit among misfits.

She caressed her own tattoo—a small duskmoth upon her wrist, its one wing white, the other black. Duskmoths were creatures shaped like the world, torn between day and night. They were creatures like her, forever halved. Madori tore her gaze away from that strange, tattooed Elorian boy and his comrades. Leaving them, she walked toward the wooden stage.

Several men and women stood upon this stage, clad in flowing robes. *Mages*, Madori knew—each from a different school. One mage, a stern looking man with cold eyes, wore the black robes of offensive magic—dark spells used in warfare. Several other mages wore white, green, and red robes, though Madori did not know what those colors signified; her father had met only the dark mages in the war. She wondered which of these professors could teach her healing; it was the skill she had come here for, the skill she refused to leave without.

One mage, an elderly woman clad in blue robes, stepped toward a podium on the stage. She was a frail little thing, barely larger than Madori, her hair white and her skin deeply lined. The woman raised her arms, and when she spoke, her voice boomed out, loud as a crashing oak. Applicants started and gaped as the thundering words pounded out of this dainty woman's mouth. Already they saw magic at work.

"Welcome, applicants, to the Teel Trials!" The mage gazed across the crowd. "I am Headmistress Egeria. You've traveled here from many lands to prove your mettle. I see applicants from across Mythimna. I see boys and girls from our homeland of Mageria." Cheers rose from the crowd at this; most here were local Magerians. "And I see applicants from the pine forests of Verilon, from the plains of Arden, from the cold arctic isle of Orida, from the jungles of Naya . . ." As the headmistress named every sunlit nation, its applications cheered. The old woman continued. "I see students from the swamps of Daenor, from the desert of Eseer, from the savannah of Sania." She cleared her throat and fixed the round glasses that perched atop her nose. "And, for the very first time in Teel University history, I am proud to see that Elorians—children from the dark half of Moth—have chosen to cross into the sunlight to join our quest for knowledge."

At those last words, the crowd fell silent. Madori cringed. The headmistress had spoken with good intentions, but looking around, Madori saw that the applicants weren't as pleased with the prospect. Some students glanced at one another; others gaped openly at the group of Elorians who stood clustered not far from Madori, hidden inside their silken robes.

One applicant, a golden-haired girl who stood not far from Madori, snickered. "What's next, letting pigs apply?" she said— too softly for the professors on the stage to hear, but loud enough for Madori to turn red.

A few of the girl's friends stifled laughs.

"Truly, Lari, you think Elorians are pigs?" said a boy, addressing the girl. He grinned. "Pigs smell better."

Lari tossed back her golden tresses. "Rotten pig carcasses smell better than Elorians. My father says they're lower than maggots."

Again the friends laughed.

The headmistress was speaking again, but Madori was paying no attention. She glared at the group of snickering youths. There were several of them—Magerians by the looks of them, all tall, golden of hair, and blue of eyes. They wore fine clothing of rich, embroidered cotton, and golden jewelry adorned their wrists and necks. They all wore the Radian sigil upon their lapels—a sun eclipsing the moon.

Madori ground her teeth. "Radians," she muttered.

The lead girl—Lari—seemed to hear her. She turned toward Madori, tilted her head, and narrowed her eyes.

"And what have we here?" she asked.

Madori clenched her fists. Lari was everything Madori was not. She had perfect clothes, perfect hair, a perfectly beautiful face—the kind to make boys trip over their own tongues. She was taller than Madori, obviously better bred, and about a thousand times wealthier. If Madori were a plucky little mutt, here was a prize racehorse.

"Somebody who'll punch your perfect little teeth out of your perfect little mouth," Madori said, raising a fist. "So I suggest you shut that mouth if you don't want this fist shattering it."

Lari laughed—a beautiful, trilling sound like rain upon leaves. "Oh my. Oh dear. This isn't an Elorian, my friends. This is . . ." She gasped and covered her mouth, feigning surprise. "A *mongrel*."

Her friends grimaced. A few made gagging noises.

Madori leaped forward. She barely stood taller than Lari's shoulders, but she didn't care. "A mongrel who'll bash your—"

"*Applicants!*"

The voice boomed across the crowd, louder than thunder. Madori froze, her fist inches away from Lari's face. She spun to see Headmistress Egeria glaring from the stage. The elderly woman was pointing at Madori. Around the headmistress, the professors stared at Madori, eyes boring into her.

"Is there a problem, applicants?" the headmistress said.

Madori forced herself to lower her fists, though she still fumed. Grinding her teeth, she stared back at Egeria and shook her head.

At her side, Lari pouted, a picture of innocence. The girl leaned closer to Madori and whispered, "Oh sweetness, such temper . . . truly you mongrels are rabid beasts. Someday we Radians will put you all down."

The headmistress was still staring at them; so were thousands of curious applicants. Madori forced herself to take several steps away from Lari and her friends.

We'll settle this later, Lari, she thought, her cheeks hot. *You might be a perfect little lady, but I'm a farm girl, grown up wrestling boys in the fields, and I can bash you and your friends to bits.*

After clearing her throat, the headmistress continued speaking to the crowd.

"As I was saying: Teel University accepts only the very brightest, the very strongest, the very wisest of all youths to learn the secrets of magic. Every year, we can admit only two hundred students to our school. Over two thousand of you have gathered here this turn." The headmistress raised her chin. "Most you will soon return home."

Grumbles rose across the crowd. Madori looked from side to side, judging the others' reactions. Some students seemed confident; Lari and her friends stood smiling, hands on their hips, sure of their victory. Other students looked worried; one boy wrung his hands, while another actually whimpered.

Ninety percent will go home, Madori thought. *But I won't. I lived my life an outcast, a misfit, a creature to be scorned or pitied.* She squared her jaw. *I will pass these trials, and I will become a mage. I will become powerful.*

"To weed out the chaff," Headmistress Egeria boomed out, "you shall partake in three trials. A Trial of Wisdom. A Trial of

Wit. And finally a Trial of Will. Only those who pass all three trials shall attend Teel University. Your names will be called out one by one. When you hear your name, you will enter Ostrinia Tower." The headmistress pointed at an archway beyond the stage; it led into the base of a brick tower that scratched the clouds. "There your trials will begin."

With that, the headmistress stepped back. A young mage stepped forth to replace her, unrolling a scroll that dangled down to his feet. He began to read out names one by one. As each name was called, an applicant walked toward the tower.

Madori chewed her lip. She hadn't registered her name anywhere. How would they know to call her? She looked around, seeking somebody—perhaps a professor or other university member—to talk to. She cursed herself; how could she have missed signing up! As she scanned the crowd, she saw the Elorian boy—the one with the dragon tattoo and pierced nose—staring at her again.

Madori froze and narrowed her eyes, staring back, but the boy wouldn't look away. His eyes seemed to stare deep into her, his face expressionless, and something about him unnerved Madori. She had seen many Elorians before—after all, her mother was Elorian, and Madori spent many turns in Oshy, a village of the night—but never one like this, one so . . . the only word she could think of was *intense*.

She took a step closer toward him, intending to insist he explained his stare or she'd stab his eyes. Before she could take a second step, however, a hand reached out and tugged her sleeve.

"Billygoat?"

She spun around, for an instant sure that her woolhead of a father had stepped into the university grounds, the only parent here to utterly humiliate his child. But it wasn't her father who stood there, holding her sleeve. Madori's eyes widened.

"Tam?" She rubbed her eyes. "Prince Tamlin Solira?"

It was him. The Prince of Arden himself, her best—her only—friend in the world, stood before her.

Madori's father had spent the war fighting alongside the king and queen—his dearest friends. Madori spent half her summers in the darkness of Eloria, the other half in Kingswall, the capital city of Arden, spending time with the king, queen, and twin princes. The adults spent most of their time in dreadfully dull conversations, telling old war stories and discussing politics; so did Prince Omry, Tam's twin and heir to Arden. Meanwhile, Madori and Tam—bored senseless with the court—would sneak out into the gardens to chase butterflies, explore secret paths, and pretend to be adventurers.

Of course, they were older now, almost adults themselves. Tam was seventeen, a year older than her, and quite a bit taller. Brown, curly hair fell across his brow, and his smile was bright. Madori had always known him to dress in the finery of a prince, but here he wore simple woolen garments, clothes no finer— though perhaps more traditional—than her own.

"Hush!" His voice dropped to a whisper, and he winked. "Don't say my name here. At least not my full name. I'm sort of, well . . . undercover."

Madori grumbled. "And don't you call me Billygoat. You know I hate that stupid name. I am Madori Billy Greenmoat." She glared at him for a moment, then felt her eyes sting. She pulled him into an embrace. "What are you doing here, Tam?"

He grinned and mussed her hair. "Same thing you are. Trying out for Teel. Remember how we'd talk about becoming mages someday?"

She tilted her head. "I also remember talking about slaying dragons, forming a juggling troupe, and training elephants to play oversized musical instruments." She punched his chest. "For pity's sake! Why would you come here? I need to gain some power. You're already powerful. You're a damn prince and—"

"Billygoat, hush!" When she punched his chest again, he grimaced. "All right, all right—*Madori*." He rubbed his chest, wincing. "Look, my father is worried about you. There's been talk of . . . enemies. And, well, I couldn't let you come here alone. So here I am." He gave a little bow. "Your protector."

She rolled her eyes and snorted. "Last time we met, I was the one protecting you from the evil bumblebees."

"Those little buggers were nasty, and there's worse than bumblebees here." He leaned in close, whispering. "There's this fellow, a lord, his name is—"

"Serin!" The voice boomed across the crowd of applicants, interrupting Tam. "Lari Serin!"

Madori craned her neck, peering around Tam. The professor on the stage was still summoning applicants; Madori had blocked out most of the names, but this one sent shivers down her spine.

Lari—the girl who had called her a mongrel.

Serin—the name of the cruel lord on the road, her father's cousin.

The two names, in tandem, felt like mixing poison with flame.

She's a Serin. Madori almost gagged. *She's a relative.*

Her chin raised, the sunlight gleaming upon her golden hair, Lari Serin strutted through the crowd, spreading smiles every which way. Other applicants clapped as she passed by; some even bowed. Obviously the girl was noble among nobles. Madori's belly soured and she gritted her teeth.

Lari caught her eyes, and the girl's grin widened. While walking toward Ostrinia Tower, she made a point of passing by Madori.

"Good luck at the trials, mongrel," she said and patted Madori's cheek. "Maybe they'll teach you to sit like a good little dog."

Madori growled, slapped Lari's hand aside, and leaped forward, intending to give the young lady two black eyes and a bloody nose. But Tam—damn the boy—grabbed her and held her back.

"Madori, no!" he said, dragging her away from Lari. "Let her go."

Lari laughed. "Keep her on a leash, boy! She's a wild one."

With a wink, Lari left them, heading across the cloister and into the tower.

Madori struggled and kicked in Tam's grasp. "Let go of me."

He refused and Madori cursed her small size; she didn't have the physical strength to free herself from his grasp, another reason why she had to learn magic, to gain power.

"Madori, listen to me," he hissed into her ear. "Do you know who that is?"

"A pretty little cockroach I'm about to stomp on."

"A pretty little cockroach who's the daughter of a very big, powerful cockroach. Her father is Lord Tirus Serin, the wealthiest man in Mageria—possibly in all eight sunlit kingdoms of Timandra." Tam sounded grim. "Not a person you want on your bad side."

Madori grumbled. "I think it might be a little too late for that."

Her fists were still clenched, but inside she trembled. The encounter on the road returned to her, and her eyes burned. She had fled the ignorance of villagers; now she found the same hatred even among the lords and ladies of sunlight.

Did I make a mistake leaving home? she thought, blinking away sudden tears. *Is there any home for me here—a girl of mixed blood, my Elorian eyes forever marking me a foreigner?*

Tam released his grip and she turned toward him, still held in his arms. She looked into his brown eyes and saw the same fear in them.

"What kind of place have we come to?" she whispered.

Before her friend could answer, the professor's voice boomed across the cloister again.

"Madori Greenmoat!"

She started. She wasn't sure how her name had ended up on the list—was magic at work here?—but she pulled away from Tam's arms.

"Good luck, Billygoat." A smile broke through the fear on Tam's face like sunlight through rain.

She nodded. "You too."

Leaving him, she walked through the crowd, heading toward the tower. As other applicants had walked this walk, their friends had clapped, cheered, patted them on the shoulders. As Madori walked, silence fell across the cloister, and thousands of eyes stared at her. She felt like a freak on show. She raised her chin high and squared her shoulders, forcing herself to walk with pride.

My parents are war heroes, she thought. *I am strong, wise, and determined. I am not a creature. I will pass these trials.*

She reached the tower. Jaw clenched, she stepped through its doorway and into the shadows.

CHAPTER FIVE
TRIAL OF WISDOM

Madori stepped into a round chamber, probably the oddest applicant Teel University had ever seen.

My clothes are strange and my hair is stranger, she thought. *My mixed blood is a curiosity.* She raised her chin and stared at the professors who sat ahead. *But I will pass this trial.*

They sat at a table upon a dais—three professors in robes, all staring at her. She could barely see them in the shadows; they seemed like hulking vultures looming above prey. A beam of light fell from a window, illuminating a circle on the floor. Madori stepped into the light, blinked, and stared up at the professors, feeling like a prisoner at a trial.

One professor, a little old man with a bald head and white mustache, cleared his throat.

"Hello. I am Elixior Fen, Professor of Basic Magical Principles." He thumbed through a booklet. "You are . . . Madori Billy Greenmoat, yes?" His voice was scratchy and high-pitched. "From Fairwool-by-Night, in the kingdom of Arden. Daughter of . . ." He adjusted his half-moon glasses, peering into the book. "Daughter of Sir Torin Greenmoat, son of Sir Teramin Greenmoat. Oh my." He raised his eyes in surprise and peered down at her. "Your father is something of a legend in these parts—I wager, in all parts of Moth."

Madori raised her chin, pride in her father swelling in her. But another professor spoke, quickly crushing her rising spirits.

"Torin Greenmoat is a fool, not a true noble. I remember him from the war. I do believe we fought in the same battle once;

of course, he was fighting for the wrong side. He is an insult to the purity of highborn blood."

Madori turned to look at this new speaker. Seeing him, her innards crumpled like old parchment.

This professor not only loomed like a vulture but looked like one too. His neck was long and scraggly, his nose was hooked like a beak, and his eyes were dark and glittering. His scalp was bald, and strands of oily, dark hair hung from his head in a ring like putrid feathers. He wore the black robes of warfare, the cloth dusty and tattered, and upon them gleamed a brooch of gold and silver—the Radian sigil.

A dark magician, Madori thought, anger bubbling inside her. *The kind father fought in the war. And a Radian to boot.*

"My father," she said, chin raised, "killed mages like you in the war."

The hooked-nosed Radian leaped to his feet, sneering. His fists clenched upon the tabletop.

"I would watch my tongue if I were you, *mongrel.* Your father spat upon the pure blood of Timandra, mixing it with Elorian filth." He snorted. "We see the result before us—an impudent, feral little—"

"Professor Atratus!" said Professor Fen, slamming his book shut. His white mustache bristled, and lines creased his bald head. The little old man seemed barely larger than Madori, but he spoke with authority. "Please, Atratus. We've not invited Madori here to discuss her parentage. Whatever happened between you and Sir Greenmoat during the war ended many years ago. We're here to judge young Madori, not any supposed crimes her father may or may not have committed." The diminutive professor cleared his throat and pushed his spectacles up his nose. "Now then, Professor Atratus, would you reoccupy your seat so we may begin?"

Never removing his withering stare from Madori, Atratus sat back down. His fists remained balled, and his lip curled.

The third professor, who had remained silent so far, finally cleared her throat. Clad in blue robes, she was younger than her companions—not much older than Madori's parents—with a head of bushy brown hair and olive-toned skin. A milky film covered her eyes; those eyes stared blankly over Madori's head.

She's blind, Madori realized.

"My name is Elina Maleen, Professor of Magical History," the woman said. "I will quiz you first, followed by my two colleagues. We desire for only the most learned youths to attend our university. Our questions will determine whether you are proficiently educated." The blind professor smoothed her robes. "You must answer *all three* questions correctly to pass to the next trial."

Madori gulped. Proficiently educated? She had grown up in a village, surrounded by farms. She had never gone to any school. All she knew was what she had read about in the village library. There were hundreds of books in that library, all donated by Queen Linee of Arden; Madori had mostly just read the books of epic tales and ancient deeds of valor. How would those help her at a school for magic? She wanted to object to this entire test. She wanted to tell Professor Maleen that she had come here to *become* educated. But before words could leave her mouth, the young, bushy-haired professor spoke again.

"Now, child, please tell me: What is the ratio of a circle's circumference to its diameter?"

Madori blinked.

What? she wanted to blurt out. How did that have anything to do with magic? Circumference? Daiameter? Only masons and shipwrights knew such things; she was from a village of shepherds and farmers!

She opened her mouth to object, to demand another question, but Professor Maleen leaned forward expectantly, and for a moment Madori lost her breath.

I don't know, she thought. Cold sweat trickled down her back. *I came here ill-prepared. I'll be among the ninety percent of applicants going home this turn.*

She froze. *Wait!* spoke a voice inside her. Percentages—she knew about those. She had just *thought* about them! Where had she learned about percentages?

She racked her mind, thinking back to Fairwool Library. When she closed her eyes, she imagined herself walking through that library again, passing by shelves of many books. In her memory, she reached out to one particular book, a dusty old tome with blue leather binding. She had loved its illustrations of stars, moons, and many graphs and geometric shapes.

A book of mathematics. Yes. She had read this book!

She opened her eyes, took a deep breath, and blurted out from memory, "It's a number that cannot be expressed in words or digits. It's roughly . . ." She mumbled under her breath for a moment, struggling to remember. "About twenty-two divided by seven. Three and a little bit." She nodded, hoping that was close enough. "Old Master Loranor, a mathematician from Eseer, referred to it as The Cosmic Number."

She took a deep breath, staring at the professor, and her heart pounded. For a long moment Professor Maleen was silent, and Madori barely dared to breathe.

Finally Maleen nodded. "Very good! Very good, child. You are correct."

Madori breathed out a sigh of relief. She managed a shaky grin and even gave a little curtsy.

Before she could catch her breath, however, Professor Fen rose to his feet. He was so short he actually dropped in height once sliding off his chair. He straightened his half-moon glasses, stroked his mustache, and passed a hand across his large, bald head.

"Now then . . ." he said, thumbing through his little book. "A question, a question . . . ah! Here we go. A very good question indeed, this one is." He smiled at Madori. "Listen carefully, child. Many years ago, both halves of Mythimna experienced both day and night, an alternating dance. Why is one half of Mythimna now always in daylight, the other always dark?"

Madori blinked. "Well, that's easy! It's because . . ."

She trailed off, frowning. Why *was* one half Mythimna—this world men called Moth—always in sunlight, the other always dark? She had always assumed that was simply the way of the world, that there wasn't any particular *reason* to it. This was like asking why the sky was blue, why mountains were taller than valleys, or why trees grew upward instead of down. She tilted her head.

"Well, it's . . ." she began, tapping her chin.

"Yes?" Professor Fen asked.

She chewed her lip, thinking back to the stories of the war. Her parents had told her this story! They had told her the story a thousand times, but Madori had always blocked it out, upset about her mother's latest lecture or her father's latest bad pun. Yet now she clawed at the memory. Her parents had been to Cabera Mountain, the heart of the broken world. They had fixed Moth. They had made day and night cycle again, only to freeze the world once more, what with Elorians blinded in the sunlight and Timandrians stumbling around in the dark. How had her parents done it? How had they made Moth turn again, then stop—

Turning!

"Because Moth no longer turns!" Madori blurted out, remembering. She nodded vigorously. "My parents told me that. Moth—well, Mythima is the world's real name—is round. A big sphere that floats in the sky, circling round and round the sun.

And, well, Moth once used to turn around its axis—many years ago—letting day and night cycle." She did a little pirouette, mimicking the world. "But the world stopped spinning around itself." She stood still, facing the professors again. "So one side now always faces the sun, the other faces the darkness. Were the world to spin again . . ." She gave another spin. ". . . day and night would cycle again."

Professor Fen smiled and slammed his book shut. "Correct! Very good, young Lady Greenmoat."

I did it! Joy spread through Madori. She had answered another question correctly! She grinned and rocked on her heels. "Thank you, Professor."

Professor Atratus, clad in his flowing black robes, rose to his feet. His glare shot daggers at Madori.

"Do not be so quick to grin, girl." He sneered, upper lip twitching. "It is my turn to ask you a question." Fists upon the tabletop, he leaned forward like a bird of prey about to tear into her flesh. "My colleagues asked you simple questions of basic mathematics and cosmology, the answers to which any half-wit child would know. But I ask you a question of . . . zoology." He leaned even further forward, bones creaking. "List three examples of how the Elorian race—that subhuman species of darkness—is inferior to the purity of Timandrian blood."

The other two professors tsked their tongues.

"Professor Atratus," Fen ventured, his mustache twitching, "perhaps a different ques—"

"She will answer that question," Atratus said firmly, straightening and squaring his shoulders. He stared down his beaked nose at her. "Answer me, Madori." He made her name— an Elorian name—sound like an insult. "Speak—or are you ignorant?"

Rage flared in Madori. She sneered right back up at him.

"Very well," she said. "I will list why Elorians are, as you say, inferior. First of all, Elorians are less talented at warfare. They have a lower penchant for violence, leaving them inferior at killing, looting, and conquering." The professors sucked in their breath at this, but Madori plowed on. "Secondly, Elorians are less proud of their heritage. They do not claim to be superior to others. Their humbleness, their lack of hubris, is probably why they remain in darkness rather than invade other lands." She spoke louder. "Thirdly, Elorians are inferior to you, Professor Atratus, because they lack your marvelous buzzard's beak of a nose which you thrust proudly in all directions."

She stood panting, her heart thumping so loudly she thought it could crack her ribs.

For a long moment, only silent shock filled the chamber.

Professor Atratus began to tremble. His face turned red. With a sudden jerk, he pounded the tabletop and screamed.

"Impudent little maggot! Your words are folly, but they show to all the answer to my question. Your insolence, your lack of respect, and your crass effrontery to science prove you are inferior! Your very presence here shows the baseness of your Elorian blood, of—"

"So I answered the question correctly," Madori said, smiling thinly. "You just admitted it."

Atratus sputtered, for a moment lost for words.

Professor Fen cleared his throat and stroked his mustache. "Oh my, Professor Atratus, I do believe she is right. You did just confess that she answered correctly. Did you hear it too, Professor Maleen?"

The blind woman nodded, a thin smile on her lips. "Yes indeed, Professor Fen. I do believe young Madori has answered all our questions correctly."

Professor Atratus looked ready to burst. He pounded the table again, cracking it. "This is rubbish! This subhuman mongrel is not fit for a fine academic institution such as this. She—"

"She has passed this trial," Professor Fen said firmly, his mustache drooping with his frown. "Or do you wish me to summon Headmistress Egeria to judge?"

Professor Atratus froze in mid-sentence, his mouth hanging open like some wall-mounted fish. The other two professors merely looked at him, blinking, eyebrows raised. Atratus sputtered, unable to speak, spraying saliva. He pointed a shaky finger at Madori, his cheeks red, then spun around. Robes fluttering, he stormed out of the chamber.

Madori exhaled a shaky breath of relief. "I passed the trial," she whispered.

The two remaining professors nodded, smiling warmly.

"You have passed the Trial of Wisdom," said Professor Fen, his mustache rising with his smile. "Step through that back door, child. It will take you to a new place where you will partake in the second trial—a Trial of Wit."

Madori suddenly couldn't stop trembling.

I passed. I passed the first trial.

Tears budded in her eyes.

"Thank you," she whispered, curtsied, and ran through the backdoor.

CHAPTER SIX
TRIAL OF WIT

When Madori stepped through the back door, she expected to find another chamber or cloister. Instead she found herself in another world.

Blackness spread all around her; she felt as if she floated in the night sky. She stood on a stone bridge that spread over the chasm. A door stood before her—not encased in a wall but simply standing on its own. When Madori leaned sideways, she could peer around it. Many more doors rose along the bridge like battlements along a castle wall.

A contraption of ropes, wooden circles, and metallic rings hung upon the door. The jumble was connected to the doorknob, blocking Madori from twisting it. She jangled the hodgepodge, listening to the metallic rings clink and the wooden circles knock together.

"A riddle," she said. "An elaborate knot."

So, she realized, the Trial of Wit involved opening door by door—each one posing a riddle. At a summer festival once in Kingswall, Madori had seen a trained parrot that could solve elaborate puzzles, opening doors to get a treat. It seemed that now she would have to play parrot.

She stuck out her tongue as she often did when deep in concentration. She spent a moment trying to fit the wooden balls through the metal rings, twist the ropes, and undo the construction. She managed to free one ball, only for the ropes to tangle through a metal ring, blocking the process.

She sank an inch.

Madori blinked, stared down, and saw that the bridge had become less substantial beneath her. The stone suddenly looked like thick smoke; it swallowed the soles of her boots. She raised one foot after another, then let each sink back into the bridge. It felt like standing in mud.

Shaking her head, she returned her attention to the puzzle on the doorknob. After a few juicy curses, she managed to remove two metal rings, which she tossed aside.

Her boots sank another inch. Madori grimaced and looked down. The bridge beneath her seemed like thin smoke now; she could see the chasm below.

"So there's a time limit," she muttered.

She returned to the riddle. She freed another metal ring. Her boots sank deeper; she was now down past her ankles. Two wooden balls came free; she tossed them into the chasm.

She sank down to her knees. Her feet dangled over the pit.

With a curse, she tugged open a knot, freeing the last metal ring. The contraption fell off the doorknob.

The bridge vanished beneath her.

Madori grabbed the doorknob, clinging as she dangled over the pit. She twisted and tugged, and the door swung open.

Heart thumping, she climbed through the doorway. The next segment of the bridge was still solid stone. She stood upon it, knees shaking.

If I had failed to solve the riddle, would I have fallen to my death? She cringed.

A new door stood before her. Already the bridge beneath her feet, solid stone when she had first stepped onto it, began to fade. Biting her lip, Madori looked for a doorknob but found none, only a little hole in the door where a doorknob should be. Instead, many bits of metal—hooked, curved, circular, and spiky—lay scattered at her feet. She knelt, lifted the pieces before they could sink into the vanishing stone, and jangled them in her palm.

"It's the doorknob," she whispered.

She narrowed her eyes. Yes, she saw a doorknob here—a few round pieces that could snap into its shell, a few narrow shards that could fit into the door.

Her boot heels sank, the bridge dissolving beneath her. She cursed, spat, and got to work. Some pieces refused to connect; others snapped into place, only to block another piece from entering its proper slot. Her fingers were shaking and her boots had sunken past her ankles when finally she had assembled the doorknob. She snapped it into the door an instant before the bridge vanished beneath her. Once more she dangled. She swung the door open and climbed onto the next level.

A third door faced her; many more waited behind it. Madori twisted her lips, sucked in a deep breath, and got back to work.

One door had no knob at all but a panel of sliding, metal squares that had to snap into place for the door to open. Another door was engraved with a great wooden labyrinth; she had to slide a key through the maze as the bridge faded beneath her, bringing it to the keyhole fast enough to unlock the door. Another door lay in pieces, a great wooden jigsaw on the floor; an invisible field blocked Madori's passage farther along the bridge, and she could only step through after assembling the broken door and opening it. Every level the riddles became harder. Every level more sweat covered her, and she began to think her tooth marks would forever dent her bottom lip.

Briefly, she wondered where the other applicants were now. Were they too locked in great, black chasms, moving along their own bridges? If they fell, where would they end up? Would they magically appear outside the university, or would they fall forever into black death? But she had no time to consider this carefully, only solve puzzle by puzzle, opening door by door, moving ever

closer toward the end of the bridge. Soon she could see it
ahead—the end of the chasm. A brick wall loomed there, a golden
door waiting within it.

Finally, weak and shuddering, Madori crossed the bridge,
reached the great wall, and stood before the golden door.

She grabbed the knob and twisted it.

It was locked.

She looked down at the last segment of bridge, seeking
jigsaw puzzles, hidden buttons, something—she found nothing.
She returned her eyes to the door, looking for a knob, a lock, a
maze, some puzzle to solve.

"Nothing," she whispered.

Musical symbols on the door glowed, then vanished.

Madori tilted her head.

"Do it again!" she said.

Again little musical notes glowed upon the golden door—
different ones this time—vanishing as soon as she stopped
speaking.

"Is there a password?" she said. Her voice made other notes
glow, but the door would not open.

The bridge began to fade beneath her. She sank down to
her ankles and winced.

A password . . . no. Not a word. Notes denoted a song.
Music. But what music?

"What do I sing?" she said. Notes glowed and vanished.

Madori tugged the two strands of hair that framed her face.
Music, music . . . she thought back to the lessons her mother had
given her; she could still read notes. But what song could she
possibly sing here to open this door? All she knew were old
Qaelish tunes.

Her boots sank another inch.

She grimaced and began to sing softly, an old song villagers would sing back in Oshy across the dusk. A few notes glowed again, soon fading, and Madori tilted her head.

Wait! she thought. Some of the notes were glowing gold, but others shone a bright blue.

She sang the tune again. Again—some notes glowed gold, others blue.

"I have to sing the blue notes?" she asked the door.

A few golden notes glowed, their light softer. The blue notes were brighter, larger; it seemed those were the ones to sing.

Her boots sank down to the ankles.

"Damn it!" she shouted. Golden notes glowed.

She cursed and began to sing the practice scales her mother had taught her, rising from a deep baritone to a high soprano. A gold note. Another. Another. A blue note! Gold. Gold. Blue again. She tried to memorize each note, but how could she possibly read this music like this? She had trouble enough reading the sheets her mother would give her.

Think, Madori. Concentrate. Save the blue notes in your mind. Ignore the gold ones. Write them down inside your thoughts.

She took a deep breath, blocking out everything, and sang the scale again. She ignored the golden notes. They didn't exist. They were nothing. She forced herself to see only blue, to write down the score in her mind. After singing a few more scales, she had it.

"It's the song 'Darkness Falls,'" she whispered.

She knew that tune. She knew it! Her mother had taught her to sing this song.

The bridge faded to mere mud. She sank down to her knees.

Wincing, Madori sang her song.

It was a sad tune, an old tune of darkness covering the land of Eloria, of hope fading, of a distant ray of light shining to guide lost souls home. As Madori sang, the blue notes glowed upon the door, one after the other, no golden notes between them. In Madori's mind, she was a child again, back home, singing with her mother.

She sang the last note—a sad, soft sound.

All the blue notes began to glow together, the song 'Darkness Falls' etched in light.

The last door swung open.

The bridge vanished beneath Madori.

She leaped through the doorway and into shadows and light.

CHAPTER SEVEN
TRIAL OF WILL

Her legs still trembling and her mind foggy with exhaustion, Madori stepped into a towering hall, ready to face her final and greatest challenge.

"The Trial of Will," she whispered.

After the bridge, she had expected something fantastical—a dragon to tame, an ogre to slay, maybe a gauntlet full of spinning blades and swinging pendulums to knock her into rivers of lava. But she simply saw a columned hall—roughly the size of a large barn—full of other applicants.

An elderly professor stood at a podium across the hall. He wore red robes, and his white beard flowed down to his feet. His nose was so long and curved, it drooped past his upper lip.

"Welcome, Madori Greenmoat!" the elder called out. "The last applicant to emerge from the Trial of Wit. I am Professor Yovan. Welcome, Madori, to the Trial of Will."

Madori blinked, rubbed her eyes, and took a closer look, sure that dragons and ogres would still leap out at her. The chamber was simple but well built—the columns carved of solid limestone, the ceiling vaulted and painted deep blue. Many tables stood in neat rows, and upon each lay a strange device; it looked like a wishbone carved of iron. Two chairs stood at each table.

"Billygoat!" The voice rose from the crowd of other applicants. "I mean—Madori! Thank Idar."

Tam wormed his way through the crowd, coming to stand beside her. He grabbed her hands and smiled shakily.

"Tam, what's going on here?" she said.

He brushed back a strand of her hair which fell across her left eye. "I thought you wouldn't make it this far. You're the last one through."

She bristled. "Of course I made it!" She looked around her at the other applicants. "Idar's bottom, those last two trials weeded out quite a few."

From two thousand applicants, she doubted that more than four hundred remained. They stood clustered between the columns, talking amongst themselves, laughing nervously and discussing their ordeals. Most were Magerians, but there were some foreigners too, even a few Elorians. The latter stood in the shadows far from the windows—their natural habitat—and spoke amongst themselves in low voices. Madori saw that the strange boy with the dragon tattoo stood among them. Again he was staring at her, his eyes intense, boring into her as if peeling back the layers of her soul.

A chill running down her spine, Madori tore her eyes away from him. But as she kept scanning the crowd, her heart sank deeper. She cursed to see that Lari Serin—looking as pretty, prim, and proper as always—had made her way to this last trial. She stood among several other youths with Radian brooches, basking in sunbeams that fell through a window, laughing as if these trials were no more challenging than a garden stroll. When Lari noticed Madori, her eyes widened. She smiled and waved, her face oozing honeyed poison. It was the face a sweet-talking traitor gives his master before thrusting the blade.

Bearded Professor Yovan cleared his throat—a squeaking sound—and raised his arms, letting his sleeves roll down to his shoulders. He spoke again.

"I shall now divide you into pairs! As I call each name, step forth and sit down upon the glowing chair."

Madori narrowed her eyes and tilted her head, seeing no glowing seats. The other applicants all turned to face the professor, their conversation dying. The old man unrolled a scroll, leaned toward it, and called out the first name:

"Tam Shepherd!"

Tam—going by his father's old commoner's name, rather than his secret royal styling—gave Madori a little smile and pat on the shoulder.

"Good luck, Billygoat," he whispered and stepped toward the professor.

A seat began to glow, and Tam approached it and sat at the small table. When the professor read another name, the seat across from Tam glowed too, and another applicant approached to fill it.

Professor Yovan kept reading names from the scroll, and slowly tables were filled—two applicants at each. Upon every tabletop lay the iron wishbone.

"Madori Greenmoat!"

She stepped forward dutifully, made her way toward the next glowing seat, and sat down. The table was small, just large enough for two chairs. She stared at the item on the tabletop, finally getting a good look at it. The metal wishbone was as large as a lyre, its surface craggy; she couldn't guess its purpose. The seat across from her was still empty.

"Lari Serin!"

The seat across from Madori glowed.

Oh wormy sheep hooves.

Madori had not thought this turn could have gotten any worse. When Lari approached, a small smile on her lips, Madori's heart sank down to her hips. Lord Serin and her father were cousins; Madori felt ill to think that she and Lari shared blood.

Her hair a perfect fountain of golden locks, Lari neatly swept her skirt under her legs and sat down, knees pressed together, her back straight. She smiled sweetly at Madori.

"Hello, mongrel," she said, voice pleasant.

Madori leaped to her feet, clenching her fists. "I don't know how you made it this far, but you're failing this trial. You—"

A sharp clearing of the throat interrupted her. Professor Yovan came shuffling forward, nearly tripping over his beard.

"Is there a problem, Madori Greenmoat and Lari Serin?" he said, brow furrowing.

Lari blinked innocently, a sweet smile on her lips. "Not at all, Professor. I was simply telling Madori what a pleasure it was to meet one with such . . . famous parents." She gave Madori a little wink. "I see she's inherited much from them."

The professor seemed to miss the implied scorn. He tossed his white beard across his shoulder. "Very well then. But please, girls, you can be friends later. Now the trial is about to begin." He hopped back toward his podium and raised his hands. "Applicants! The Trial of Will begins. Please, every pair grab your iron wishbone, each applicant holding one side."

Madori lifted the wishbone, holding one side. The iron was rough and cold in her palm. Lari grabbed the other side, then suddenly yanked the wishbone toward her, tugging Madori forward in her seat, forcing her to lean across the table. Madori found herself only inches away from Lari; the two's noses nearly touched.

"You're going home soon, half-breed," Lari said, all the sweetness gone from her voice. There was nothing but malice in her eyes now.

Madori sneered, clutching the wishbone. "Tell me, my lady, when you inform your father you've failed the trials, will you cry?"

"Next time I see my father," Lari said, "I'll tell him how I made a little mongrel child burst into tears. I think he'll enjoy that story."

Professor Yovan was still speaking from the podium. "Four hundred of you are holding onto two hundred wishbones. You may not rise from your seat. You may not kick, punch, bite, or do anything but sit neatly, holding the iron. Whoever drops his or her wishbone first shall return home. Whoever remains holding the wishbone . . . will become a student at Teel University."

Madori blinked. Was that it? That was all she had to do? Hold onto the wishbone? She tilted her head. That seemed too easy. Were there no puzzles here, no questions, no challenges at all?

"Get ready to scream, little one." Lari smiled wickedly. She leaned forward in her seat, her fist tight around her side of the wishbone. "I'll enjoy hearing it."

"I bet you'll scream when you fail," Madori said. "I bet—"

She bit down on her words, frowning. The wishbone was tingling in her hand—a strange, tickling heat like a thousand tiny jabs.

Lari gave a mocking pout. "What's wrong, mongrel? Does your widdle hand huwt?"

Her hand *did* hurt. The tingling intensified, becoming a prickly heat. Madori ached to drop the wishbone but only gritted her teeth and tightened her grip. When she looked around the chamber, she saw other applicants wince, curse, and one girl even yelped.

"My hand feels fine," Madori said, returning her eyes to Lari. "You look a little pale, though."

Madori was lying; her hand did not feel fine, not at all. It was as far from fine as wine from poison. The pain intensified, almost intolerable, and Madori took deep, ragged breaths. She tightened her grip. The iron began to crackle, and little sparks like lightning raced across it.

At the table beside Madori, a boy yelped and dropped his half of the wishbone. His opponent whooped in triumph, the wishbone glowing in his hand. He raised the metal instrument like a trophy. At another table, a girl burst into the tears and dropped her wishbone; her opponent laughed, her admittance to Teel won.

Madori returned her eyes to Lari and glared. Lari stared back, a single bead of sweat upon her brow, the only sign of any pain she might be feeling. Madori's hand was trembling now around the wishbone. The pain blazed, racing up her arm to her shoulder. Her very teeth buzzed and shook in her jaw. Years ago, Madori had read a book about the charred victim of a lightning strike; she imagined that this felt similar. Her hair crackled, her hackles rose, and goosebumps appeared upon her arm. Her very clothes seemed to burn.

All across the hall, applicants were crying out and releasing their grips. One by one, failed applicants trudged dejectedly out of the room while victors stepped toward Professor Yovan, rubbing their sore hands.

"You look like a dying rat," Lari said, sneering now. More sweat beaded on her brow. "Will you squeal before the end?"

Madori's entire arm shook as she clutched the wishbone. She whispered through a clenched jaw, the pain nearly blinding her. "I won't let go. I—"

The pain burst out, doubling in intensity. She gasped and nearly dropped the wishbone. She saw the same look of surprise on Lari's face; the girl's eyes widened, showing white all around the irises, and she emitted a little cry. Across the hall, dozens of applicants screamed or whimpered, dropping wishbones.

Madori gritted her teeth, tears in her eyes, and held on. Lari sneered like a wild animal, clinging to her end.

"I won't let go," Madori hissed, barely able to speak, barely able to remain conscious. "I'll hold on even if my hand falls off. I—"

The pain flared again, growing even stronger, so strong Madori thought her skull could crack and her jaw could spill her teeth. Lari screamed but clung on. Lightning crackled along the wishbone and raced up Madori's arm, raising smoke. Sweat and tears mingled in her eyes. Through the veil, she saw the last few applicants drop their wishbones.

Only Madori and Lari were now still competing.

"Give up, mongrel!" Lari shouted, tears streaming down her cheeks, her face a rabid mask.

The wishbone emitted a whistle like steam from a kettle. Welts rose along Madori's arm.

"You can do it, Lari!" Madori shouted. "Hold on longer! I love seeing you suffer."

The other youths all gathered around them, forming a ring around their table. They were pounding fists into palms, cheering, chanting.

"Lari, Lari!" most cried out.

"Let the mongrel burn!" somebody shouted.

"Hold on, Lari!" another youth cried. "Hold on and watch her burn!"

Madori was weeping, trembling, screaming, but she held on. The iron wishbone burned red, trembling in her grip. The pain was a crashing sea.

A single voice cried out from the crowd—Tam's voice.

"Madori! Madori!"

A few other voices joined his, and now some in the crowd were chanting for her. Madori could now see only smudges, but she thought she saw the Elorians cheering for her.

Her hand slipped.

She nearly dropped the wishbone.

It was too much. Too much pain. Too much agony. It was lightning, it was fire, but it was also the pain of her mixed blood, of her childhood, of endless taunts, endless doubt. It the pain of a girl torn between day and night, and she wept.

I have to let go.

Before her, Lari was snarling, teeth bared, face red.

She won't let go. I have to. I have to.

She ground her teeth.

No.

She screamed and tightened her grip.

No. I will hold on. No matter how much it hurts. Because I know pain. I was born into pain. What is more agony? Pain has always been my companion.

Lari was shaking, her hair standing on her head.

"Enough!" Professor Yovan shouted. "Girls, enough! Let go!"

But Madori would not. Lari would not. They clung on and the wishbone burst into fire . . . then shattered in their grip.

Madori fell back, her chair flipping over. She slammed down onto her back. She clutched half the wishbone in her smoking, seared hand. It still crackled in her palm, driving fire through her. She would not release it.

She blinked.

Did I win?

She raised her head.

She saw Lari still holding her own half of the wishbone. The girl struggled to her feet, then came leaping down onto Madori.

"Feel this pain drive into your heart," Lari hissed, shoving her half of the wishbone against Madori's chest.

Pain exploded like thunder.

Madori screamed.

The agony drove through her chest, coiling around her ribs, wrapping her heart in fire, and she kicked and thrashed and—

The pain vanished.

I'm dead. She trembled. *I died. The pain is gone and I float now in the afterlife.*

"Madori!" The voice seemed to echo from miles away, from a different world. "Madori, can you hear me?"

She opened her eyes. Through a veil of mist, she saw a wrinkled, bearded face gaze down upon her.

Is this Idar, god of the sun?

She pushed herself onto her elbows.

"Madori!" A wrinkled hand touched her cheek. "Child, can you speak?"

It was Professor Yovan, she realized. When Madori sat up, her legs shaking, she saw the greybeard holding Lari back with one hand. Both wishbone halves lay on the floor, the heat and lightning gone.

"What happened?" Madori whispered. "Did I drop it?"

Professor Yovan wiped tears from his eyes. "In the name of sanity! I've never seen anything like this. I had to cast a spell. I had to stop the magic. You two would have died, my children. Oh dear . . ."

Madori rose to her feet, trembling. Sweat soaked her clothes, and her hand was blackened and swollen. When she looked around her, she saw the other applicants gazing in shocked silence. Tam stood among them, eyes wide and mouth wide open.

When Madori looked over to Lari, she found something new in the girl's eyes—not scorn, not pain, but unadulterated hatred, a rage as pure as the pain of the iron wishbone. Welts ran up Lari's arm, and her hair stood in a tangled mess, but she never removed her glare from Madori.

Professor Yovan, shaking his head in wonder, raised the broken wishbone halves and placed them back onto the table. He wiped his brow.

"For the first time in Teel University history," he said, his voice shaking, "we have a Trial of Will tie. Both Lari Serin and Madori Greenmoat shall attend Teel!"

The crowd erupted into cheers.

Madori swayed, nearly collapsing, but managed to grin.

"I passed," she whispered and rubbed tears from her eyes. "I'm a student of Teel."

Professor Yovan, still pale and trembling, opened the doors to the hall. It was like opening a floodgate. Hundreds of concerned parents spilled into the room, calling out for their children. Mothers embraced proud young students. Fathers patted sons on their shoulders. A few flunked applicants still lingered in the hall; their parents scolded, embraced, or awkwardly tried to comfort their embarrassed offspring.

When she saw her father, Madori gave him a shaky smile. Torin's eyes widened and his face paled. He rushed toward her.

"I passed," she whispered. "I passed, Papa. I'm a student of Teel."

Torin grabbed her wrist and examined her burnt hand. Ignoring her words, he spun toward Professor Yovan.

"What is the meaning of this?" the gardener said, voice harsh. "What kind of institution are you running here? I sent my daughter to trials; you return her to me with a burnt hand?"

Madori winced, feeling her cheeks flush. Several other students were snickering.

"Father, please!" she whispered. "You're embarrassing me."

Torin seemed not to hear her. He grabbed the professor's shoulders, demanding answers. Old Yovan mumbled something about how he'd never seen anything like this, and how their wishbone must have been faulty, and how he would send Madori straight to the infirmary and deliver a honey roasted ham to Torin's tavern of choice.

A tall figure moved through the crowd. A smooth, genteel voice interrupted the conversation.

"Ah, and so the humble gardener, the man who slew so many of his own countrymen, cannot bear to see a scratch mar the flesh of his little mongrel."

Madori growled, hackles rising. She looked up to see the man from the road.

"Lord Tirus Serin," she muttered.

He turned toward her, raising both chin and eyebrows, and stared down his nose at her. He had replaced his armor with a rich, cotton doublet and a jeweled belt. A samite cloak framed him, the fabric shimmering with golden thread and gemstones. A Radian amulet hung around his neck, a golden sun eclipsing a silver moon. His golden hair shone almost as bright, scented of rose oil.

"We meet again, little one," the lord said, and something new filled his eyes, something not only scornful but hungry, lustful. "I hear you've been accepted into Teel." He reached out, grabbed her wounded hand, and squeezed so powerfully she winced. "Allow me to congratulate you. I'm sure my daughter will give you the proper attention."

Madori tugged her hand free, glaring at the man. "I'm sure we'll be inseparable."

Lari walked up toward them, slung her arm around her father, and gave Madori a smile full of sweetness, innocence, and the promise of vengeance. "I'm sure we will be, dear cousin . . . I'm sure we will be."

CHAPTER EIGHT
MISFITS

Torin sat in The Dancing Wolf tavern, staring at his daughter over his gift of a roast ham.

He forced himself to swallow the bite he had just taken. Professor Yovan's gift—as if any gift could undo the welts on Madori's hand—tasted like ash.

My daughter is wounded, Torin thought. *Radians rise across the sunlight. My king wants me to leave my home and fight them. And I'm supposed to feel good about a honeyed ham.*

If Madori shared any of his concerns, she was displaying none of them. The young woman—by Idar, she had been only a baby last time Torin had checked—was digging into the meat, trying to speak while chewing lustfully.

"And would you believe Tam's here?" she said, stuffing another bite into her mouth. "The boy somehow passed his trials but—" She paused to swallow. "—but if you ask me, he had to cheat or something, because he's a bigger woolhead than you. Oh, and—" She gulped down cider and wiped her mouth. "—and I saw magic! Real magic. Lots of it. Magical bridges and doors and glowing seats. I'm going learn to make our chair at home glow." She grinned and bit off a chunk of ham so large a wolf would choke on it. She spoke as she chewed. "Would you like a glowing chair for home? I wonder if it'll work on animals too. Or even people. I could make our rabbits glow."

Torin said nothing, only sighed.

I have to break my daughter's heart, he realized. *I have to place her in danger or shatter her soul.*

He took a deep breath. He could no longer listen to her words; every one stabbed him.

"Madori," he said softly.

". . . and did you see how long Professor Yovan's beard is? Idar! Down to his feet! I wish I could grow a beard. Maybe I can grow a magical one. Why don't you grow your beard too? I—"

"Madori," he said again, "I can't let you stay here. You have to go into Eloria with your mother."

". . . and they asked me about mathematics, and—" She paused and tilted her head. Very slowly, she placed down her fork. She spoke even slower. "I . . . what?"

Torin figured the best approach was to blurt it all out at once. "It's too dangerous. Radians are rising across the land. There's a Radian professor here at Teel—one Atratus—and Lord Serin holds sway; apparently he built a good chunk of the university. It's too dangerous for you here. It's too dangerous for you anywhere in Timandra right now. I'm moving to Kingswall to help Cam deal with this threat. You will go to Eloria with your mother."

Madori leaped to her feet, letting her chair crash backwards. Across the tavern, patrons froze over their meals and stared.

"Like the Abyss I am!" she shouted. "Are you crazy, Father? Are you absolutely mad? Go home—now? After all this?"

He reached out to her. "Madori, please. Hush. Sit. Listen."

"I will not!" Tears budded in her eyes. "You always do this to me, Father! You always let me . . . let me build up my hopes, and then you destroy them. It's like when you told me we'd go visit the desert, and you changed your mind at the last minute, and we went on a damn fishing trip instead." The tears were now streaming down her cheeks. "I can't believe you. I can't! I wish Mother had taken me here instead. I'm going to Teel and you can't stop me."

She turned and ran, making a beeline for the door.

Torin cursed. He slammed coins onto the tabletop and
made to run after her. He stumbled over a chair, cursed again, and
steadied himself in time to see Madori bolt outside. When Torin
finally made it to the door and stepped onto the street, she was
gone.

"Madori!" he cried out, seeking her.

People on the street—shoppers, villagers, students and their
families—turned to stare at him.

"Madori!" he shouted again, but she didn't answer. He
couldn't see her anywhere.

Well, that went splendidly, he thought.

He began to trudge down the street, peering into shop
windows, seeking the damn girl. Why did she have to make things
so difficult?

"You used to be easy to be around," he muttered.

What had happened? Madori used to be his best friend—
the girl he'd rock on his knee, tickle, laugh with, spend so many
wonderful hours fishing, playing, and reading with. And now?
Now Madori always found some other reason to think him the
most horrible troll this side of darkness. He only wanted to
protect her. How could she not see that?

He kept walking down the streets of Teelshire, seeking her.
Where would the damn girl go? Would she have run into the
university grounds? Perhaps into another tavern, or maybe she hid
in an alleyway somewhere?

He groaned. Of course. *She went where she always goes when she's
angry at me,* he thought. *To read.*

While Torin found comfort in gardening and Koyee in
music, Madori's escape was reading. She spent many hours in
Fairwool Library, delving into hundreds of books. Torin enjoyed
reading books on botany on occasion, and Koyee enjoyed old
tales of Qaelish lore, but Madori consumed books of adventure so
quickly she had to order more from Queen Linee every year.

Torin spun around and walked toward the town's bookshop—an old little building whose sign bore the words, "The Bookworm's Banquet." He stepped inside, entering a dusty, crowded chamber chock-full of books. The leather-bound volumes stood upon shelves, rested on tables, and rose in tilting towers. Beams of light fell through stained-glass windows, gleaming with dust.

Madori sat between two bookshelves, her knees pulled to her chest, her head lowered.

Joints creaking, Torin sat down beside her. She would not budge.

He took a deep breath and spoke softly. "You know, I lost my parents when I was only a child."

She said nothing. She wouldn't raise her head.

He kept speaking. "I remember my father's last words to me. As he lay dying, he spoke not of himself, not of fearing death. He spoke of me. He was afraid, he said, that he wouldn't be here to look after me. When I had you, I finally understood his words." He smiled wistfully. "When you're a parent, you never stop worrying for your child. Being a parent is to always worry. Even when you're afraid for yourself, it's because you're afraid of abandoning your child."

Finally she raised her head. She looked at him, her eyes rimmed with red, tears spiking her lashes.

"Well, maybe you have to finally let me grow up." She wiped her eyes. "I'm sixteen, Father. Mother was my age when she sailed off to war. I think I can handle a university."

Torin sighed. *If it were only handling a university,* he thought. *But war again threatens to engulf Moth.*

"If I let you stay here," he said slowly, "you must promise me you won't pick fights with Serin's daughter."

"I never pick fights."

Torin snorted. "I've seen you beat up Kay Chandler's boy a dozen times back home."

She bristled. "He keeps touching the library books with greasy fingers!"

"And if I let you stay," he continued, "you must promise you'll stay near Tam at all times. At *all times*. He'll look after you, and I will talk to him, making it clear that if *anything* dangerous happens, he's to take you to Kingswall at once."

"Father!" She rolled her eyes. "I'm not a damn child."

"You are. You always will be. To me at least." He glared at her. "Promise me, Madori Billy Greenmoat. You make a promise now, or I swear *I* will enroll at Teel University myself so I can watch over you."

"Father!"

He pointed at her sternly. "Promise me. If you think your mother is the evil parent, you haven't seen me in action. Promise or you will."

She groaned so loudly she blew back both strands of her hair. "Fine! I promise. I promise I'll stay away from that pretty little toad. I promise I'll stay near Tam. I promise I'll hide away in the corner and barely squeak so that no trouble can find me."

"And . . ."

She rolled her eyes. "And I promise that if any trouble does find me, Tam and I will join you at Kingswall. Fine? Now will you please stop latching onto me? I swear someday you're going to sprout an umbilical cord and try to lasso me with it."

He wrapped an arm around her and pulled her close. She objected at first but gradually relaxed in his embrace.

"I don't need a lasso," he said. "I just need to hug you."

She leaned her head against his shoulder. She spoke softly, a tear on her cheek. "I love you, Papa."

He kissed the top of her head. "I love you too, Billygoat. No matter what happens, I always will, and your mother and I are always somewhere out there for you—even if we're half a world away."

She nodded and her voice was choked. "I know."

He closed his eyes.

And so I leave her in a viper's nest. And so I will always worry. Perhaps that's the price of letting your children fly. He sighed. *Cam will call me a fool, but haven't we always been foolish?*

He rose to his feet. "Now come on, let's go buy you some school uniforms. You can't walk into class dressed like a purple scarecrow."

They left the bookshop together, his arm around her.

* * * * *

Madori stood under the tree, gazing at the road that wound south through grassy valleys, heading toward misty plains. She waved, watching the cart roll into the distance.

"Goodbye, Father," she whispered. "Goodbye, Hayseed. I'll miss you."

She thought she could see Torin twisting in his seat to face the town, waving at her too. But with every wave he grew smaller, and soon the cart, horse, and rider were but a speck upon the horizon, and then they faded into the mist.

Madori blinked, her eyes damp. She had always thought her father infuriating, but now she missed him already, and her throat tightened. She longed to race down the road, to hug him one last time, to pat Hayseed, to beg them to stay, maybe even to go home with them.

She rubbed her eyes. *But I won't do that. I'll stay. I'll become a mage.* She nodded. *I'll be strong and I'll be amazing.*

She turned away, facing the town again and the university that loomed above it. A gust of wind blew, whipping back her two strands of hair and fluttering her robes. She looked down at her new garments. Instead of her old leggings and shirt—items she had sewn herself—she now wore flowing green robes. It was a color she detested—she detested all colors other than black and purple—but all first years were required to wear the green. At least she kept her boots; the leather creaked as she walked, and the many buckles jingled. Her pack hung upon one shoulder, full of the scrolls and books her father had bought her along with her new robes. She wasn't sure how Torin had been able to afford all this; a gardener, he had never been a rich man, and parchment cost a small fortune. She suspected that Tam's father—King Camlin himself, come in disguise to see off his son—had footed Madori's bill.

When she had crossed the town and stood at the gates of Teel University again, she paused and took a deep breath. Only last turn, she had stepped through these gates for the trials, but somehow now this seemed an even greater boundary to cross.

"Once I step through now," she whispered, "my old life is gone. Father. Mother. Hayseed. Home. Once I enter these gates now . . . this will be my new home for four years."

She stood for a moment, hesitating, fingers trembling, resisting the temptation to run after her father. Finally, with a deep breath, she took three great paces forward and entered the Teel cloister.

The first time she had entered this cobbled courtyard, she had seen thousands of applicants. Now only two hundred stood here, the lucky new class. Four columned walkways rose around them, enclosing the cloister within a square, and the four Towers of Teel rose at each corner. An elm tree rustled in the center of the cloister, and clouds drifted across the blue sky above.

As always, Lari stood with her group of cronies, all wearing their Radian pins. A jeweled tiara topped Lari's head, and golden embroidery adorned her green robes. While Madori's robes were secondhand, shabby, and shapeless, Lari's robes were obviously custom-tailored, fitting snugly and sporting golden hems. The young noblewoman was busy telling a story while her friends laughed, and Madori caught snippets about how "the mongrel burst into tears . . ." and how "her gardener father had to save her." Ignoring the group, Madori looked at the other students, her new classmates. A couple dozen Elorians stood under the elm, seeking the shadows, their hoods pulled over their heads; unlike Madori, who had inherited Timandrian skin that could tan, these pure-blooded Elorians had pale skin they dared not expose to sunlight. Finally, between the Radians and Elorians, sprawled a mass of unorganized students. Most were local Magerians, but many were from other sunlit kingdoms, their eyes more hesitant, their hands clasped together nervously.

Madori wasn't sure where to stand. Certainly not near Lari and her friends, but neither did she crave Elorian companionship; if she aligned herself with the Elorians, she would forever be an outsider here. If she embraced her Timandrian blood, perhaps she could still find a larger group of allies—obviously not among the Radians, but perhaps among the largest group, those Timandrians still unaligned.

She saw Tam stand in the middle group, and Madori felt some relief. The brown-eyed prince, now wearing green robes, was a welcome sight, a little bit of her old life, of comfort. She walked forward and stood beside him.

"Hullo, Billygoat," he said.

She raised her fist. "Don't make me punch you."

He rolled his eyes. "Fine! Greetings be upon you, Lady Madori Billy Greenmoat the First." He bit his lip. "Better?"

"No. But you got lucky. Punching your thick skull would probably cripple my hand, and one of my hands is already injured."

Tam grimaced. "Save your fists for you-know-who." He glanced aside. "I have a feeling you might need them."

Madori followed his gaze and saw that Lari and her friends were tossing a doll back and forth. The doll was a crude, ugly representation of an Elorian—its fingers ending with claws, its mouth sprouting fangs, its large eyes red. When the effigy fell into the mud, Lari made a point of stomping onto it. The young noblewoman raised her eyes, saw Madori, and gave her a little wink.

"You're next," she mouthed silently.

Madori was about to rush forward and attack the weasel. Before she could take a step, however, Headmistress Egeria emerged from the southeastern tower and marched toward the new students, her robes swaying. The elderly woman's hair was collected into a neat bun, and the sigil of Teel—two silver scrolls—hung around her neck.

"Students of Teel!" the headmistress announced. "Welcome. Welcome to the university."

The students all turned toward the woman. Lari gave Madori another wink before kicking the doll behind the elm tree. When everyone faced her, the headmistress continued speaking.

"Two hundred of you have passed the trials. Now you stand here before me in your uniforms, your books in your packs. You may think the hard part is behind you, that your education is now guaranteed. *But!*" The headmistress pointed to the sky, her sleeve rolling down to reveal a knobby arm. "You are mistaken. You are not yet safe. Many of you—perhaps most of you—will still return home. It is not uncommon for only half our students to successfully complete their first year. Many more flunk during their second, third, and fourth years." Egeria narrowed her eyes, staring from one student to another. "If more than fifty of you become true mages, I would be very surprised. *Now!*" She cleared her throat. "You will spend your first year in groups of four. Your quartet will be your most basic, important unit of university life. You will sleep four students to a room. You will sit four students to a table. Every quartet will have a name, a symbol, a leader, and a sense of pride. Perhaps more than any other decision you will make at the university—or in life!—will be who to choose for your quartet. No time is better than now to decide. And so, students—please, arrange yourselves to groups of four!"

Madori cringed. Choose three other students—others who'd be her constant companions for years?

She glanced around her. "Idar's bottom, I don't even want to spend four years with you, Tam, let alone any of these strangers."

He grabbed her arm and tugged her close. "Too bad, because you're stuck with me . . . and two others, if we can find them." He looked around him. "Say, Billygoat, you know anyone else here?"

She nodded. "I know Lari. Fancy inviting her to join us?"

"Oh, certainly! I'd also like to stick my head into a crocodile's mouth."

Near the elm tree, Lari had found three friends—twin girls and a tall golden-haired boy, all sporting the Radian brooches. A second quartet of Radians joined together beside them. Slowly other quartets were forming—four Ardish students here, four Verilish ones there, four Elorians in the shadows, and others.

Grouped by nations, Madori thought, her heart sinking. *But who'd join a half-breed like me?*

A voice spoke beside her, soft and dangerous as flames about to spread.

"Madori?"

She recognized that accent—it was the accent of Ilar, an Elorian nation south of her own moonlit homeland of Qaelin. She spun around to see the Elorian boy with the nose ring and intense eyes. His dragon tattoo stretched up his neck and coiled over his eye; it seemed to stare at her too. His white hair fell across his brow, and his hood and cloak were pulled tightly around him.

She turned away from him. "I don't join Elorians."

His voice was soft but still carried a hint of danger. "You are Elorian."

She spun back toward him, glaring. "I'm mixed. You know that." She tugged her two strands of hair. "You see my black hair, don't you? Go join your fellow Elorians, the pure ones."

He glanced toward where other Elorians were forming quartets, then looked back at her. He shook his head. "No. I did not travel into sunlight to stay in shadows. In this school, who you know matters. That is how you survive. I cannot stay in darkness." He looked at Tam. "He is Timandrian. He is with you. I will be too. I will learn your ways, Madori the half-Timandrian." He bowed his head toward her. "I am Jitomi of Ilar."

Tam raised his eyebrows and thrust out his bottom lip. "Might as well," he said to Madori. "It's not like we've got too many options left."

Madori grumbled. The young prince was right. Most other students had already formed quartets; many seemed to have known one another from before the trials.

She cursed and jabbed a finger against Jitomi's chest. "Fine! But you remember something, Jitomi the Ilari. I am half Qaelish. I have nothing to do with your island of Ilar, even if both our empires lie in the darkness. And I won't speak to you about anything Elorian—not the old foods of the night, not the starlight, not anything. We'll be quartet-members, but we will not be friends."

He nodded and spoke with his thick accent. "I join you, Madori, because you are of sunlight, not because you are of darkness too."

She sighed. "Lovely trio of misfits we've got here so far. But we need one more."

She looked around her, biting her lip. Only a handful of students were still unsorted. One among them caught Madori's eye. She squinted and tilted her head.

A tall Daenorian girl was walking around the courtyard, looking from side to side, trying to join different groups only for them to snicker and move away. She was the only Daenorian here and seemed to stick out just as badly as Madori. The girl wore a necklace of animal teeth, and beneath her green robes, she wore armor molded to look like crocodile hide. Under her arm, she held a steel helmet shaped like a crocodile's head, complete with a toothy visor. A sword hung at her side, its pommel shaped as another one of the reptiles. The girl had dark skin and smooth, black hair that hung down to her chin. Her lips were full, her eyes bright and eager, and Madori thought her very pretty—certainly pretty enough that Madori herself felt plain, scrawny, and homely as a true billy goat.

And yet, despite the Daenorian girl's beauty and bright smile, every other student she approached quickly moved aside, laughed, scoffed, or even cursed the girl.

"They're real crocodile teeth," the Daenorian said, showing her necklace to a group of Ardish girls with blue eyes and golden hair. "If you let me join you, I'll give you some teeth."

The girls grimaced and turned away.

Never losing the brightness in her eyes, the tall Daenorian turned toward another group, this one of local Magerian boys. "Do you like my sword?" she asked. "My father said it has magical powers. Do you think magical swords exist?"

The boys only rolled their eyes and turned away from her.

"Foreign freak," one muttered.

Madori sighed. She looked at Tam. "You did say you'd like to stick your head into a crocodile's mouth. I think I found the next best thing."

Her heavy boots clanking, Madori walked across the courtyard toward the Daenorian.

"Oi! Crocodile girl!"

The Daenorian spun toward her, and her eyes widened in delight. Her mouth opened into a bright smile. "Oh, aren't you tiny and cute! Do you like toffy? I have some toffy somewhere in my pocket, though it's a bit squished. You can have some if you let me join you."

The girl reached into her pocket, fished around, and produced something flat, dusty, and covered in lint. She held it out toward Madori.

Madori struggled not to cringe. "There's no need for that. I'm Madori. Who are you?"

The girl's grin widened. "I'm Neekeya! I'm from South Daenor. Remember that. *South* Daenor. Not the north part where people live in castles, wear ribbons, and pretend they're all proper and fancy. I'm from the swamps. We're real warriors there. My father says I'm the best warrior in the kingdom, and he gave me this sword, and it has magical powers. Do you believe in magical swords?"

Madori bit her lip. "I suppose so. Would you like to join our quartet?"

Neekeya gasped and tears budded in her eyes. She leaned down and pulled Madori into an embrace. She stood quite a bit taller than Madori, and her embrace was warm, and though the girl was odd—her armor strange, her accent heavy—there was kindness and comfort and goodness to her.

"Thank you!" Neekeya breathed. "I'd love to. You're very kind. Would you like a crocodile tooth?"

Madori shook her head. "No thank you."

The four stood together: A girl torn between night and day, her eyes too large, her hair cropped short except for two long strands; a prince in disguise, a son of privilege masquerading as a commoner; a son of darkness, tattooed and pierced, in a land of light; and a swamp dweller of strange armor, eager eyes, and a smile that it seemed no darkness could crush.

"The headmistress said every quartet needs a name, a symbol, and leader," Madori said. "So what are they?"

Tam grinned. "That's obvious. You're our leader, little one. And our symbol is a duskmoth, like the one inked onto your wrist; after all, we're of both daylight and darkness here. As for our name? We will be known as Madori's Motley."

"No, Tam," Madori said.

But Neekeya grinned and hopped excitedly. "Madori's Motley! I like it. I like toffy too. Do you want some toffy, Tam?" She offered him a piece.

Jitomi too nodded. "Madori's Motley. I accept this name."

Madori only sighed. She had come here seeking acceptance in Timandrian society; now she found herself among a group of outcasts and misfits.

I suppose, she thought, *this is where I belong.*

With all the students in groups of four, Headmistress Egeria spun on her heel and led them toward a tower. Quartet by quartet, the students of Teel followed, beginning their life at the university.

CHAPTER NINE
CASTLE AND SCROLL

She stood by the grave of her father, staring up at the fortress that bore his name.

Salai Castle rose upon the hill, a pagoda three tiers high, its roofs tiled blue. A bronze dragon statue stood upon the top roof, the full moon haloing its roaring head. The stars gleamed above, and the darkness of Eloria spread to the east, blanketing the hills, valleys, and river. In the west, the dusk glowed like a palisade of lanterns, the borderland dividing day and night. The orange light gleamed against the black bricks of the castle, and its windows forever gazed upon the gloaming, eyes to guard the lands of darkness.

"You died defending this border, Father." Koyee looked down at the grave. "Now a great castle bearing your name guards this land. Eloria will never fall again."

She closed her eyes, the memories like ice in her veins. It had been many years since her father had died, and Koyee herself was a parent now, but the pain never left her. She still felt very young, very alone, very afraid.

"I miss you, Father," she whispered.

She opened her eyes.

But no, I am no longer a youth, she thought. *I am thirty-six years old, and I have a child of my own, and I will forever defend this home so many died for.*

She raised her chin, clutched the hilt of her katana—the blade her father had once wielded—and climbed the twisting path up the hill. The wind billowed her silken black cloak, making its embroidered blue dragons dance. Her hair streamed across her eyes, a white curtain, and she tucked it behind her ears. Her shirt of scales chinked, the armor she always wore here, the armor she would not remove even so long after the war.

Once you've seen war, you're always a soldier.

She reached the gates of Salai Castle. Two dragon statues flanked its gates, large as mules, roaring silently. Embers crackled within their mouths. The doors stood closed before Koyee, forged of bronze that reflected the dusk behind her. When she craned her head back, the castle seemed to soar forever, reaching the stars. Once this had been a simple steeple, a place called the Nighttower. Once she had stood here alone, gazing into the light of Timandra. For ten years, workers had labored here, turning a tower into a great castle. Koyee placed her hands against the doors. She paused for a moment, savoring the cold feel of them, letting that iciness flow along her arms. Then, with a nod, she shoved the doors with all her strength. They swung open upon oiled hinges.

She stepped into a tiled hall, columns holding its ceiling. Braziers shaped as fish, wolves, and birds stood in rows, their embers casting orange light. A table of polished granite stood in the center of the room, its surface engraved with a map of Mythimna, showing two continents like the wings of a moth—one continent painted white, the other black. Eternal day and endless night.

Three hundred men and women stood in the hall, clad in scale armor, silvery helmets upon their heads. As Koyee entered, they drew their katanas as one and raised the blades in salute. Their large Elorian eyes gleamed blue and lavender as they stared at her.

Koyee raised her own katana—the sword Sheytusung, a blade of legend, the blade she had fought with in the great war many years ago.

"Under this moon, we dedicate Salai Castle!" she announced, her voice echoing in the hall. "A fortress rises. Eloria will never more fall. We are the night!"

Three hundred voices called out together. "We are the night!"

Here were the greatest soldiers in Qaelin, this empire of the night. Koyee had chosen every one herself, the brightest stars of the darkness. They stood strong, brave, clad in steel, and they would defend their homeland.

Koyee lifted a goblet from the table. She raised it high. "Nearly twenty years ago, an enemy sailed down the river and rode upon the plains, and only a single tower stood here, its only guardian fallen. We have forged peace since then. And I pray to Xen Qae, our wise master in the stars, that this peace lasts ten thousand years. But if ever the fire burns again, if ever the light falls upon Eloria . . . we will be ready. Drink, children of darkness. May wine warm your bellies. The night is eternal; so is our strength. Our watch begins."

They drank. The wine poured down Koyee's throat, warming her belly.

Wine fermented from grapes grown across our border, she thought. *A drink of sunlight for soldiers of the night.*

They feasted then, the meats, mushrooms, and fish filling the chamber with their savory aroma. Soldiers talked and laughed as they ate, and one began to sing a song. A fireplace crackled at the back. Koyee ate little, spoke less, and did not sing, for too many worries lay upon her.

I built this castle to defend the darkness, she thought, *and yet I sent my daughter into the very heart of sunlight.*

Koyee had traveled across the sunlit lands of Timandra, and she had seen the looks people gave her and Madori—two women with eyes as large as chicken eggs, one an Elorian with pale skin and white hair, the other with dark hair and tanned skin, marking her mixed blood. The sunlit lands shunned them, yet what could Koyee have done?

"I'm shunned in Eloria too!" Madori had shouted at her, eyes damp. "I'm just as monstrous in the night—a girl with black hair and tanned skin—as I am in Timandra. So at least let me be monstrous at the university where I can learn magic."

Koyee had tried to embrace the girl, to tell Madori, "You are blessed, pure, and beautiful."

But Madori would not listen. She would shout, stamp her feet, and bring tears to Koyee's eyes. And finally Madori had left. And now she was gone. And even now, sitting here in this fortress across the border, Koyee missed her daughter and wished she could embrace her one more time.

"Wherever you are, Madori," she whispered as soldiers laughed and sang around her, "I love you, and I pray that you're safe."

After the meal ended, Koyee climbed the castle's coiling staircase. Still holding her goblet of wine, she stepped out onto the roof, climbed the tiled slope, and stood beneath the bronze dragon and the moon above. A soft smile touched her lips. She thought back to her youth, an urchin living barefoot and wild on the streets of Pahmey. She had often climbed roofs then.

"I was not much older than Madori," she whispered, "when I sat upon some shop's roof in that distant city, watching the floating lanterns and fireworks during the Moon of Xen Qae." She sighed. "May you have a better youth than mine, Madori. May you never know fear, hunger, and cold like I did."

She gazed downhill. South of the castle nestled the village of Oshy, its clay huts embracing the Inaro River, its boats swaying at the docks. When Koyee turned her head westward, she saw the dusk. The scar stretched across the land, gleaming orange, yellow, and gold. From up here, Koyee could just glimpse the green forests beyond—Timandra, the land of daylight.

You're there, Madori, she thought. *Somewhere in that light. Be safe.*

She whispered into the wind, speaking to her invisible friend, the shoulder spirit Eelani. "I built this castle and brought these soldiers here, praying their watch is silent, praying this castle forever remains only a thing of beauty, never of warfare." She gestured down at the river where boats were sailing in and out of dusk. "Look at them, Eelani. Merchants. They deliver our silk, mushrooms, and fireworks into the lands of daylight. They return with wine, fruits, vegetables, the fare we cannot grow in the darkness. Perhaps that is how we will prevent war. Trade. Merchants will defend us more than any fortress or wall. Where ships of trade sail, ships of war are less likely to fire their cannons."

She felt warmth caress her cheek, a hint of her invisible friend upon her shoulder. *If you truly believed these words,* a voice seemed to speak inside her, *you would be sailing upon one of those ships, not standing here above an army.*

Koyee raised her sword in one hand, her goblet of wine in another. "This will be Eloria—lifting the bounties of trade and peace in one hand, a sword in the other. Thus perhaps we will survive."

She left the castle.

She walked along the river, heading toward the light.

Rocky, lifeless hills rolled before her, but soon moss grew upon them, slippery under her boots. As she approached the light, thin grass rustled, then bushes, and finally trees. The sun emerged above the horizon, and Koyee pulled her hood over her head. She walked into the light. Trees grew taller with every step, their leaves dark and thin at first, then lush and sweetly-scented.

The shadows vanished behind her, and she emerged into the eternal daylight of Timandra.

The village of Fairwool-by-Night awaited her. Thirty-odd cottages rose around a pebbly square, their roofs made of straw, their walls formed of wattle-and-daub. An ancient maple tree grew from the square, and a stone library rose behind it, the place Madori would spend so many hours lost in. Past the buildings swayed fields of wheat and rye, and beyond them rolled green pastures dotted with sheep.

"Fairwool-by-Night," she said into the warm breeze. "My second home."

As Madori was torn between day and night, perhaps Koyee was too, spending half her time in the darkness, haunted by dreams of the war, and half her time here in daylight, being a wife, being a mother, seeking solace in the sun.

She walked into the village and approached her home. A garden bloomed outside the cottage, its sunflowers rising nearly as tall as the thatch roof, its peonies filling Koyee's nostrils with their sweet scent. She allowed herself a soft smile. This home would feel empty without Madori, but soon Torin would return to her. And in a few years, Madori would too, and perhaps someday— even if it's many years down the line—Koyee herself would feel at home here, would forget the memories, would find the peace she sought.

A scroll stuck out from Koyee's new mailbox, a little hollowed-out log perched upon a post. Soon after her accession to the throne, Queen Linee had founded the Sern Postal Company—two cogs that sailed along the Sern River every month, delivering mail between the capital and the riverside settlements. Koyee walked across the clover and pulled the parchment free. It was probably another letter from Linee; the queen enjoyed sending her letters full of poems, drawings, and tales from the capital. Holding the scroll and still smiling, Koyee stepped toward her front door.

She gasped.

The scroll fell from her hand.

Shock, then fear, then finally rage filled her.

With red paint—no, it was blood, its scent coppery—somebody had drawn a symbol onto the door. It looked like the sun eclipsing the moon. Below it appeared the words: "Elorian pigs go home."

A pig's head, a paintbrush still stuck inside it, lay upon the doorstep.

A slow whisper—more of a hiss—fled Koyee's lips. "Who did this?"

She spun around, her fist crushing the scroll. She stared across the village, seeking somebody who might be laughing, pointing, hiding. She saw nobody.

"Who did this?" she shouted.

Birds fled the old maple tree and a dog barked. Nobody answered. The villagers were all working in the fields, shepherding their sheep, or hiding in their homes.

The scroll crinkled in her fist, and she stared at it. The seal was blank; this letter had not come from Queen Linee. Fingers trembling, Koyee unrolled the scroll and instantly recognized her husband's handwriting; he had written in Qaelish, the language of the night which few in daylight could read. She read and reread the letter.

"Koyee, my love,

Billygoat has passed the Teel Trials and enrolled at the university. She is well but the world is not. A new movement—the Radians—are preaching hatred across the lands of sunlight. Sailith has died and they are its reincarnation. Tam Shepherd has enrolled at Teel too, and he'll look after

Billygoat. She is safe. I've met Cam here and am returning with him to Kingswall; he needs my help fighting this new threat. Koyee, be careful. Stay in Oshy until this blows over. Stay in your new fortress, surround yourself with soldiers, and be safe. I'll come for you when I can.

I miss you and love you always.
Your husband,
Torin"

Koyee closed her eyes, the old war pounding back into her. Cruel leaders preaching hatred. Soldiers pouring into the night with torches, lanterns, swords, and arrows. Blood and death across the night.

Her daughter was halfway across the world. Her husband was traveling into danger.

"And you leave me here?" she whispered.

She turned back toward her door, stared at the symbol drawn in blood, and again she saw the blood of the war—it washed over her in a wave of memory.

She grabbed a rag. She dipped it in water. She began to clean the door, her eyes dry but her heart trembling.

CHAPTER TEN
THE PEWTER DRAGON

Madori sat at a table with her quartet, ready to learn magic.

Many other tables filled the room, each seating four students. Scrolls, vials full of bubbling potions, monkey skulls, and mummified reptile claws crowded the tabletops, the shelves lining the walls, and the great desk at the back of the room. Before that desk stood little Professor Fen, bald of head, white of mustache—one of the professors who had quizzed Madori at the trials. He rolled up his flowing sleeves and cleared his throat.

"Class!" he said. "Welcome to Basic Magical Principles. This turn I shall teach you, well . . . basic magical principles."

Madori opened her notebook and dipped her quill in ink. It was an ancient notebook, probably even older than Fen—the parchment pages had been used several times, scratched clean of ink after every use. When she squinted, she could still glimpse bits of the old layers of writing and even a few dirty drawings. Her father had bought her several notebooks before leaving, and even the used ones had cost a full silver coin each—a small fortune.

When she glanced aside, she saw that Jitomi had unrolled a parchment of rich Elorian vellum, its edges tasseled; Madori's mother would hang similar scrolls in their home, each illustrated with birds, dragons, and Qaelish runes. Neekeya, still wearing her necklace of crocodile teeth, had a notebook that looked even shabbier than Madori's; the pages were tattered, burnt at the edges, and already covered with Daenorian letters, leaving only the margins available. Only Tam had a shiny new notebook, its cover blue leather engraved with landscape scenes, its parchment pages fresh.

"You can share my notebook if you like," the undercover prince said to Neekeya, moving the book closer to her.

The swamp dweller smiled. "It's all right. My notebook is magical. Like my sword." She patted the pages. "You see the writing that's already here? I just need to tap my quill against the letters, and they'll reorganize themselves into whatever words I like."

Tam seemed unconvinced and Madori sighed. Neekeya had spent the past turn claiming that everything she owned was imbued with ancient magic: that her sword glowed around goblins, her necklace of crocodile teeth could bite dragons, her shoes could walk on lava, and even her meals—dried frog legs—gave her magical health and longevity. So far, Madori hadn't seen anything magical about the girl.

Beside them, Lari and her quartet sat at another table.

"Look at those creatures," Lari said to her friends, pointing at Madori's Motley. The girl snorted. "Their books must be made from rat hides."

Lari's friends laughed—the twin girls and the tall, golden-haired boy. The four had named themselves Sunlit Purity, and all four wore Radian brooches pinned to their pricey green robes. Madori's robes were shabby and second-hand, the hems worn and the elbows patched, but the Sunlit Purity quartet wore fitted robes of lush, embroidered cotton with golden hems, tailored to look as fine as gowns.

"Rat hide?" Madori asked, waving her notebook at Lari. "Do you recognize a relative?"

A few students snickered. Lari's face reddened, but before a fight could break out, Professor Fen raised his voice again.

"Students! Please. Pay attention. You can chat with your friends after class. Right now listen to your old professor."

Giving Madori a sneer, her eyes promising retaliation, Lari turned toward the professor.

"Is your book really made out of rats?" Neekeya whispered to Madori.

Madori shushed her. "Of course not. Now let's listen."

Professor Fen, barely taller than Madori's own humble height, paced before his desk.

"The Basic Principles of Magic!" he announced. "Three simple principles form the basis of every spell you will ever cast. The chasm of puzzles you walked through. The magic of mending broken bones . . . or shattering them. Magic to see to the stars and under the ocean. All come from a remarkably simple foundation woven in incredibly complex ways. Once you learn the foundation, you will have the building blocks to create structures to dazzle the world. The principles are . . ." He paused dramatically, then raised three fingers. He tapped each in turn. "Choosing, Claiming, and Changing."

Students wrote furiously into their notebooks. When Madori glanced aside, she saw Neekeya tapping the existing words in her "magical notebook," then grunting as they refused to change shape. With a groan, the swamp girl scribbled her notes into a margin.

Professor Fen continued speaking. "These are the three steps to any magic. First you *choose* your material. Then you must *claim* your material. Finally, you will *change* your material. Choose, claim, change." He coughed into his sleeve. "Allow me to demonstrate. Say I wish to lift this vial off my table." He pointed as a glass vessel full of bubbling purple liquid. "How would I apply the three steps? Anyone?"

Lari's hand shot up. The young noblewoman smiled prettily, the proper and prim student.

"Yes, young Lady Serin," said Professor Fen.

Lari spoke as if reciting. "First you would choose your material—the air around the vial. Then you would claim the material—seizing control of the air. Finally you would change the material—changing the air pressure to levitate the vial." She shot a smug glance at Madori, then back at the professor. "My father taught me. I've been lifting objects at home since I was a toddler."

Professor Fen slapped his hands together. "Very nice, Lari! And very correct. Would you like to demonstrate for the class?"

"I'd love to." She looked again at Madori and spoke with just the hint of scorn. "Obviously, not all students are as knowledgeable."

Lari rose to her feet, smoothed her fine robes, and strutted toward the head of the class. She held her hands out toward the vial.

"First I choose the air as my material," Lari said. "The air will compress around the vial, eventually lifting it. Now I must claim that air. That is the hard part . . . hard for some, at least." Another look at Madori. "But I've been practicing claiming materials for many years. I will imagine the air—its little particles, the different gases floating within it, and claim control of it."

"The only gas here is the hot air leaving her mouth," Madori muttered to Tam.

Lari continued as if she hadn't heard. "I've now claimed the air and can change it." She raised her hand slowly. Two feet away, the vial began to levitate. "I am not magicking the vial itself; I am manipulating the air beneath and around it." She lowered her hand and the vial descended back onto the table. "Choose, claim, change."

She gave a little curtsy, then returned to her seat.

"Fantastic!" said Professor Fen, clapping enthusiastically. Several other students clapped too. "It's wonderful to see such a bright student. I'd have also accepted changing the glass itself to become lighter than air, but that would have been far less elegant, and would often cause the glass to shatter. Well done, Lady Serin."

Lari beamed and shot Madori a triumphant look.

Madori raised two fingers, knuckles facing Lari, a gesture so rude her mother—were she here to see—would have beaten Madori with a belt. Lari—raised in a palace where the rudest gesture was probably lifting the wrong dessert spoon—blanched and looked away, lips scrunching together.

"Don't goad her," Tam said.

Madori grumbled. "Just me being at Teel goads her. I might as well have some fun with it."

"Now!" said Professor Fen from across the room. "You will each find an assortment of items on your table. Choose one and levitate it. I will be moving between the desks to guide you."

Across the classroom, students began to mumble, squint, and thrust out their tongues, concentrating at lifting items off the tables. Conchs, animal skulls, chalices, and bubbling vials rattled across tables. Only Lari was successfully levitating an item: her Radian pin.

Madori stared at a pewter dragon statuette that stood on her table. She sucked in her breath, trying to claim the air. How did one claim air? When she glanced aside, she saw that Neekeya was staring at a wooden toy knight, her tongue thrust out in concentration; the figure was rattling. Jitomi was having some success levitating a Venus flytrap, but the pot kept falling back down after rising only an inch. Tam seemed as lost as Madori; the mouse skull he was staring at simply stared back.

Madori returned her eyes to the dragon statuette. It stood still upon the table, clutching a crystal.

Go on, Madori thought, *rise!*

"Having trouble, mongrel?" Lari came to stand beside her. She leaned against Madori's desk and smiled. "You don't seem to be doing too well."

"Get back to your desk, dear cousin, or I'm going to slam this dragon against your pretty face."

Lari pouted. "Oh, *tsk tsk*, such a temper on the little half-breed. Must be your savage nightcrawler blood." She crossed her arms. "Go on, let's see your magic."

Madori growled and returned her eyes to the figurine. She sucked in air through her nose, trying to detect its texture, the icy coolness, the smells of the bubbling potions.

Feel the air, she told herself. *Claim it. Make it yours.*

She let the air flow through her, moving down her throat to her lungs, then spreading throughout the rest of her, tingling her toes and fingertips. With every breath, she let that air flow through every part of her, tingling the hair on her head and wrapping around her bones.

Now change that air. Wrap it around the dragon and lift.

Upon the tabletop, the figurine began to rise.

Madori gasped.

"You're doing it, Madori!" Neekeya said.

Focus. Focus!

Madori tried to ignore everyone else, to direct all her attention toward the figurine. She raised it another inch, then another, until it hovered at eye level. A smile stretched across her lips.

With a *whoosh*, the dragon figurine shot forward and slammed into Madori's face.

She cried out and blood spurted from her nose.

The statuette clattered to the floor.

"Stupid mongrel," Lari said, smiling crookedly. "You didn't think it was you lifting it, did you?" She clucked her tongue. "Looks like the one with a face full of dragon is you."

Madori leaped to her feet and lunged toward Lari, fists swinging. Arms wrapped around her, tugging her back.

"No, Billygoat!" Tam said, pinning her arms to her sides. "You're only giving her what she wants."

Lari's eyes widened and she laughed. "Billygoat? Does the mongrel have a nickname?" She sighed. "She does smell like a goat."

Professor Fen rushed toward them, mustache bristling. "What is the meaning of this?" His eyes widened to see Madori's bashed nose. "What happened here?"

Suddenly Lari's face changed from cruel to distressed, and tears budded in her eyes. Her voice rose an octave, taking on a childlike quality. "Oh, Professor Fen! I was just trying to help her. She accidentally magicked the figurine onto her face, and when I went to check on her, she suddenly attacked me."

"I did not!" Madori shouted. "I— I mean— She hit me and—"

Lari covered her eyes. "Oh, Professor Fen! She frightens me. Can you punish her?"

"But—" Madori began.

"Enough!" Professor Fen's bald head flushed red. "Madori, go to the infirmary. Get your nose taken care of. Then report to the stables and spend the rest of the turn helping the horse master. You may return to your classes next turn—*if* you've learned how to behave."

As Madori stormed out of the class, her eyes burning, she heard Lari's voice rise behind her.

"I say, some girls simply can't curb their temper . . ."

When she was outside the room, Madori allowed her tears to flow. They streamed down her cheeks and dampened her robes, mingling with her blood. She heard the other students laughing inside the classroom, and Madori imagined them all mocking her. She leaned against the corridor's wall, her tears streaming, her chest shaking.

I never imagined it like this, she thought. *I miss you, Father and Mother. I miss you so much. I miss home.*

A lump filled her throat. She didn't want to go to the infirmary. She wanted to run outside the university, to hitch a ride with a peddler, to travel all the way home to Fairwool-by-Night. Why had she ever fought with her mother? Now Madori only wanted her mother to hug her, to smooth her hair, to tell her it would be all right.

"I'm sorry, Mama," she whispered, voice hoarse. "I miss you. I love you."

She walked outside, her sleeve held to her bleeding nose, and stood in the courtyard. Rainclouds were gathering and a drizzle fell. The columns and towers of Teel rose around her, marvels of architecture, and the domed library rose behind them, the world's greatest center of knowledge. Beauty and wonder surrounded Madori, but as rain and tears fell, she only wanted to return to her village.

"I can leave," she whispered. "I can sell my books and uniform in the town, and I'll have money for food, and I can travel home."

She let memories of Fairwool-by-Night fill her: her cottage with the garden of sunflowers and peonies, her horse Hayseed, her old bed and books, her rag dolls, her parents.

But even standing here, she knew that something was missing from that image.

There were no friends waiting for her at home. There was no future, no *dream*, not for her. Her parents had fought in the war; they had achieved greatness, and they had found peace in a quiet village and with each other. But she, Madori—what great things had she done?

She took a slow breath. Her father's words returned to her.

To survive, you only have to breathe the next breath. Breath by breath.

She took another trembling breath.

She was still here. She was still surviving, still at Teel.

"When you went to war, Mother and Father, you suffered too. And you could have gone back home, but you kept fighting." She laughed weakly. "You fought armies. I can handle Lari."

She nodded and wiped the blood off her face. A smile trembling on her lips, she decided to skip the infirmary. She headed straight to the stables, and when she stepped into their shadows, her smile widened.

For several hours, she tended to the horses—and she hugged them, and she whispered her fears to them, and they were her friends.

And I have human friends here too, she whispered. *I have Tam and Neekeya and Jitomi. My motley crew.*

When she left the stables, she felt better than she had in turns. She would stay, she vowed, no matter what. She would not let Lari drive her away.

"I swear to you, stars of Eloria," she whispered to the cloudy sky, imagining those stars hiding beyond rain, cloud, and light. "I will become a mage."

CHAPTER ELEVEN
SUNLIGHT AND MOTLEY

The bells of Teel University, high in the northeastern tower, rang the end of the turn. Madori's parents claimed that thousands of years ago, the world would turn, that night would follow day in an endless dance. The bells of Teel—like the hourglass her parents kept at home—tracked the old days and nights. With Moth frozen, Timandra now basked in endless daylight, and Eloria hid in eternal shadow, but still the bells rang, forcing the old cycle upon the university. Madori supposed she was the only student here used to such a routine; each turn was the same twenty-four hours her parents used back home.

Rubbing her sore shoulders—she had worked her arms down to the bone in the stables—she stepped into the eastern arcade, the dormitory for first year students. For a moment she stood in shadows, staring ahead. Here was the long, covered walkway that formed one of the cloister's four facades. A colonnade of many columns rose to Madori's left, affording a view of the cobbled courtyard and General Woodworth, the old elm tree. A long succession of archways rose above her, engraved with ancient runes. A brick wall, lined with doorways, rose to her right. First year students were moving back and forth, stepping in and out of chambers. Sounds of laughter, gossip, and even crying wafted down the arcade.

Madori bit her lip. *My new home.*

With a deep breath, she took a step forward, emerging from shadows.

At once, all the sounds of conversation and laughter died. Everyone turned to stare at Madori.

She raised her chin, squared her shoulders, and walked down the arcade.

Let them stare, she thought. *People have been staring at me all my life.*

She kept walking as eyes followed her. She was a half-breed. She was a freak on show for them. But she would walk with pride, as she always had—the girl with crazy hair, with the bronze skin of a Timandrian and the large, lavender eyes of an Elorian, with the famous parents adored or vilified across the world, with the fire inside her to learn magic—a fire none could tame. She walked by them all as they stared—Timandrians who whispered and gasped, Elorians who stood in shadowy corners. They were day and night, and she—she was the dusk.

Halfway down the gallery, she passed by Sunlit Purity, Lari's quartet. The four were leaning against the wall, the door to their chamber ajar. They had hung a Radian banner upon the door, and as Madori walked by, they shot her dirty glances. Derin, the tall blond boy, muttered something about mongrels under his breath. The twins—Fae and Kae—snickered.

"You stink of horse," Lari said as Madori walked by her.

Madori paused and turned to give Lari a cold stare. "I had a doll that looked like you at home—all golden tresses and freckled cheeks." Madori smiled thinly. "I ripped off her head and used it as a ball. Do you think your head would roll too?"

As Lari paled and covered her mouth, Madori gave her a wink and walked on.

Farther down the colonnade, Madori reached an open door and saw her friends inside the chamber. She stepped in and closed the door behind her.

"I'm telling you!" Neekeya was saying, standing with her hands on her hips. Her sword and helmet, shaped like crocodiles, hung on the wall behind her. "My pillow is magical! I brought it especially from home, and it always gives you good dreams."

Jitomi was sitting on a bed, painting a dragon onto a vellum scroll; it looked like the dragon tattoo that coiled up his neck. "I have never heard of such magic." The Elorian's eyes gleamed in the shadows of his hood.

Rummaging through his backpack, Tam groaned. "That's because no such magic exists. Her mother probably only told her that to get her to go to sleep."

Neekeya stomped her feet. "My mother is a great warrior! She wrestled crocodiles every day before breakfast. She wrestled a *magic* crocodile once, and—"

"Oh Idar's beard, here we go again!" Tam said, raising his hands in indignation.

Standing at the door, Madori cleared her throat. The others turned toward her, noticing her for the first time. Neekeya reacted first. She raced forward, her necklace of crocodile teeth jangling, and pulled her into a crushing embrace. Madori—almost a foot shorter—nearly suffocated in the swamp girl's arms.

"Air!" Madori gasped.

Neekeya only squeezed her tighter. "I'm glad you're here! I was worried. So much blood . . ." She stepped back, holding Madori at arm's length, and narrowed her eyes. "Are you all right?"

Madori nodded. "Bit peckish."

"I have some frog legs. And toffy!" The Daenorian reached into her pockets and produced both items of food. "Would you like some?"

"I was hoping maybe for some Ardish fare. Or maybe Qaelish food. Bread?"

Ignoring the request, Neekeya touched Madori's cheek. "Madori, you listen to me. I'm a warrior. A real warrior. I used to wrestle crocodiles with my parents. If Lari attacks you again, you step back and let me fight her." She snarled, revealing very white, very sharp-looking teeth. "I'll wrestle her good! I'm not scared of her. She and her friends . . . they think they're so mighty, what with their beautiful golden hair and blue eyes, proud Magerians in their homeland. They don't like us outsiders, do they?" Suddenly tears filled Neekeya's eyes. "But we're just as good as they are. We passed the same trials."

Suddenly Madori felt guilt pound through her. She had spent the past few turns focusing on her own misfortune—pitying herself, the girl torn between day and night. For the first time, Madori realized that Teel University was probably just as difficult for Neekeya. The swamp dweller—with her dark brown skin, heavy accent, and foreign ways—probably felt just as alienated here, just as threatened by the Radians.

Madori patted the taller girl's arm. "Thank you, Neekeya. You're right. We all passed the same trials. Every one in this room is just as smart, strong, and worthy as the Radians. We're all outsiders here, all far from home. And we'll face Lari and her gang together."

When she left Neekeya's embrace, Madori took a closer look at the chamber. It was small, no larger than her old bedchamber back at Fairwool-by-Night. Four beds took up most of the floor space, each carved of pine and topped with a mattress and woolen blankets. A large desk held scrolls, books, ink pots, and quills. A vellum scroll bearing an Elorian prayer hung upon a wall—presumably Jitomi had hung it up. A golden crocodile statuette, its emeralds eyes gleaming, stood upon the window sill—a Daenorian artifact, no doubt belonging to Neekeya. Meanwhile Tam was busy hanging up a painting from home; it showed the towers of Arden's royal palace.

Madori had no charms to add to this room, no mementos from her own home, nothing to make this chamber a new home. There was the dagger she kept in her boot, the one with the antler hilt, but she decided to keep this weapon hidden; she might yet need it, roaming a university rife with Radians. She reached into her pocket and fished out a copper coin, change from the meal she'd shared with her father at The Dancing Wolf tavern. It was a coin from Arden, showing Queen Linee—Tam's mother—on one side, and a raven—the sigil of Arden—on the other.

This is my memento, she thought. *A meal with my father, a last memory of my old life.* She placed the coin upon the shelf beside Neekeya's crocodile figurine.

Three of the beds already seemed claimed; her friends' packs, cloaks, and other belongings lay upon them. Madori made her way to the fourth bed, which lay under the window, and sat down. The straw mattress crinkled but seemed comfortable enough. Tam's bed lay to her one side, Jitomi's to the other.

Again, she thought, *I'm between night and day.*

She was about to kick off her boots and change into her sleepwear when chants rose from outside.

Madori froze. Her fingers tingled and her pulse increased.

The chants echoed outside in the corridor, dispersed and unorganized, and Madori could not recognize the words. But soon the voices, one by one, solidified into a single mantra. Madori sneered and leaped to her feet.

"Radian rises!" the voices chanted. "Radian rises!"

Boots stomped and the voices echoed across the hall. The floor shook beneath Madori. Above the chant rose a high, pretty voice—Lari's voice.

"Fellow students, do you wish to preserve the purity of sunlight? Do you wish to cast out the filth staining our fine university? Join the Teel Radian Society! Join us, receive your pin, and help banish the darkness."

Madori raced toward the door.

"Billygoat, wait!" Tam cried and tried to grab her. She slipped out from his grasp, yanked the door open, and raced outside.

Lari was marching up and down the columned gallery, chin raised. Her cronies marched around her. Many students had stepped out of their chambers; some gaped in silence, but others were marching with Lari and her group, chanting the cry.

"Radian rises! Radian rises!"

Lari raised her fist. "Join the Teel Radian Society! We will bring purity to magic. We will drive out the dark-skinned heathens, the nightcrawlers of darkness, and the mongrels of impure blood. Radian is purity! Radian is light!"

While Lari spoke, her friends were handing out Radian pins and papyrus pamphlets. One scroll fell and fluttered toward Madori's feet. On it appeared a drawing of an Elorian—the fingers clawed, the eyes cruel—feasting upon a Timandrian baby, ripping out its entrails with fangs. Below the drawing appeared the words: "Cast out nightcrawlers, mongrels, and heathens. Radian rises!"

Lari pinned one of the pamphlets to the wall. "Join us!" she cried. "Join me, Lari Serin, at the Teel Radian Society."

Madori had heard enough. With a growl, she made to leap forward, intending to throttle Lari. She felt ready to kill the girl, then flee into the wilderness.

Hands grabbed her.

"Madori, please!" Tam said, tugging her back. She thrashed in his grip, but Jitomi and Neekeya soon joined him. The three grabbed her arms and legs, holding her back. They stood in the doorway of their chamber.

Hearing the commotion, Lari turned toward them. A bright, toothy grin split her face.

"Look, friends!" she called out to the hall. "A swamp dweller, her skin like coal, a heathen and barbarian. A nightcrawler boy, a demon of darkness. A Timandrian boy, a traitor to his own blood. And finally, a feral little mongrel dog." She laughed. "The Radian Society will clean our university from their filth."

Madori screamed and tried to leap forward again, but her friends tugged her back into their room and slammed the door shut.

"Let me go!" Madori cried. "I'll knock her teeth in. I'll rip out her throat. Neekeya, you're with me, right? We'll attack her together."

"And if you do," Tam said sternly, "you'll only give her words credence." The prince released Madori and walked over to block the door. He glared at her. "If you hit her, you know what she'll do. She'll act the victim, cry fake tears, and trumpet the news across Moth that you're a menace. And all of Moth would hear that news. You don't know the power her father has."

"She doesn't know the power my fist has," Madori said, but she hated to admit it—though she fumed, kicked, and growled, she knew Tam was speaking truth.

If I attack Lari now, I turn her into a martyr.

"So what do we do?" Neekeya said, her voice hesitant. She let go of Madori and looked at the others, one by one. "Do we let her keep demonizing us?"

The chants still rose outside. More voices were joining them. Madori's heart sank to realize that, when she had stormed outside screaming, she had probably just made herself look like the wild animal Lari was painting her to be.

Jitomi spoke for the first time. The Elorian boy walked toward their table and slapped the pile of books. "What we do is study. The other students might call us barbarians. We will prove them wrong. We will prove that we can be smarter than them. We'll become more powerful than them. They want to banish us from their university? We'll beat them at their own game."

Madori heaved a sigh and leaned against the wall. "How? I can't even levitate a simple figurine."

"But I can," Jitomi said. "I know a little bit of magic. Neekeya does too. We'll work together. We'll learn to perform magic as well as Lari can—*better* than she can." He gestured at the door. "So let them chant. While they're outside parading like thugs, we'll open our books and study."

Demonstrating his point, Jitomi opened one codex and sat down to read.

Madori's body ached. She hadn't slept in over a turn, and she had spent hours working in the stables. She longed for a good half-turn of slumber, but Jitomi was right.

Next class, I won't let Lari humiliate me again, she vowed. She grabbed a book too. She sat beside Jitomi, opened the tome, and began to study.

CHAPTER TWELVE
CHAINS OF SMOKE

Her eyelids drooping, Madori began the next turn in a new class: Offensive Magic.

While Professor Fen taught Basic Magical Principles in a dusty chamber full of scrolls, vials, and sundry artifacts, this class took place in towering lecture hall with tiers of cold stone seats. There were no windows here; the light came from braziers that crackled upon the polished black walls. This looked less like a classroom, Madori thought, and more like the temple of a dark god.

She sat at the back of the hall with her quartet. The stage below was still empty, and students in the lower tiers rustled, leafed through books, and mumbled spells. Stifling a yawn, Madori tried to remember what she had studied last turn in her room, but the knowledge kept fleeing her mind.

"Who teaches this class?" she asked Tam.

Sitting beside her, the prince shrugged. "I don't know. Offensive Magic? Must be somebody angry."

Madori shuddered to remember her parents' war stories. They had fought the dark mages of Mageria during the great War of Day and Night. Mother still bore the scar along her arm, a coiling line like a serpent.

I saw Magerian magic tear flesh off bones, Koyee had told her, *flip ribs inside out, and crack skulls. I fought against siege towers topped with archers, cavalries of knights in armor, and great carracks firing cannons, but none frightened me like Mageria's black magic.*

Madori gulped.

"And now I learn this magic," she whispered to herself.

At her left side, Neekeya was whispering to Jitomi, "I have a ring of Offensive Magic. If I punch anyone while wearing the ring, it'll double my strength."

Jitomi tapped his chin. "Maybe the ring is just sharp."

Neekeya shook her head wildly, her black chin-length hair swaying. "No! It's magic. My father gave it to me, and he knows magic. I—"

"Hush!" Madori elbowed them. "Class is starting."

A door creaked open below and a shadow stirred. The students all fell silent, straightened in their seats, and stared down. A tall, balding man entered the room, wrapped in black robes.

Madori's heart seemed to sink down to her pelvis.

"Professor Atratus," she muttered.

The beak-nosed, hunched-over figure trudged across the stage toward the podium. The bald crest of his head shone, and what hair he did have—a ring around his back and sides like the feathers around a vulture's neck—shone with oil. He indeed reminded Madori of some great scavenger bird, here to sniff out rotten flesh. His black robes were so shabby they almost looked like a suit of feathers. The man's Radian pin shone in the light of the braziers, and Madori winced to remember their altercation at the trials.

He wasn't happy to see me pass the Trial of Wisdom, she thought. *And he won't be happy to see me here.*

"Class!" he barked when he reached his podium. He opened a few books and shuffled through them, then raised his eyes toward the tiers of seats. He cleared his throat—a horrible, gagging sound like a dying animal—and spoke in a voice that echoed through the hall. "You have come to study Offensive Magic. If any of you cannot tolerate pain, blood, or the gruesome damage our art can inflict upon the human body, I suggest you leave my university, return to your mother, and tell her you are a squeamish babe undeserving of true power."

A few scattered, nervous laughs rose from the crowd. Madori's heart sank even further; she swore she could feel it beating down in her foot.

Professor Atratus scanned the rows of seats, passing his eyes over each student in turn. "I see that this year, we have some students of excellent parentage." He let his eyes pause over Lari. "Indeed, the children of the purest pedigree are among us this turn." His gaze moved further along the seats, finally settling on Madori; that gaze changed into a withering glare. "And I see some among us are of . . . less distinguished heritage."

Madori clenched her fists in her lap. She wanted to leap down and challenge the professor, but Tam placed a hand on her thigh, holding her in place.

With a twitching sneer, Atratus tore his stare away from Madori and returned to his books and scrolls.

He spent the next hour rattling off magical theories, barking out fancy words like "material bindings" and "particle trajectory" and "physiological claims." Throughout the class, Madori could barely keep up; her wrist ached from scribbling down notes she didn't even understand. Lari, however, seemed the model student. Sitting at the head of the class, she kept raising her hand, answering every question properly, then turning toward the back tiers to give her fellow students smug smiles.

Throughout the class, as Madori kept furiously writing, Neekeya kept raising her hand. The tall Daenorian girl was practically bouncing in her seat, begging Atratus to answer his questions. Yet the balding professor wouldn't spare her a glance. His attention lay fully upon the Magerian students.

We in the back tier are the outcasts, Madori thought, glancing at her sides. Along with her quartet sat other foreigners, all ignored.

And no quartet is stranger than mine, she thought with a sigh, wondering how she'd ever pass this class. She could already see herself returning to Fairwool-by-Night a failure, flunked out of the university. Her mother would be furious, Madori thought. At first Koyee had not wanted to let her daughter—her only child—leave. Once Madori had insisted, shouting and kicking the walls, Koyee had agreed—on one condition.

"If you leave to the university," Koyee had said, jabbing Madori's chest, "you return to me a model mage. You will not loaf around at Teel like you do at home, sleeping entire turns, collecting stray animals, and wasting your time. If you go there, you will graduate at the top of your class, or by the stars of Eloria, do not return home at all."

As Atratus kept rattling out his lesson, Madori rubbed her sore wrist and heaved yet another sigh.

"Madori Greenmoat!"

The voice boomed across the hall and Madori started. Realizing she'd been lost in thought, she stared down at Professor Atratus.

"I asked you a question, girl," the professor said, brows pushed low over his beady eyes.

"I . . ." Madori's throat felt dry. "I'm sorry, Professor. May you repeat the question?"

Students muttered among themselves. Lari snickered.

Face turning red, Atratus grabbed a ruler and slapped his desk with a crack. "You will pay attention in class, girl, or this ruler will strike more than this desk. Do you understand?"

Madori ground her teeth and swallowed down her rage. She forced herself to nod silently.

With a disgusted grunt, Atratus left his podium and paced across the stage, tapping his ruler against his left palm.

"A volunteer!" he called out. "Step down. I normally wait a month before allowing magic in my classroom, but I believe that this year, with such bright minds, we may begin early. A volunteer! Raise your hand." Several hands rose in the class—none from the back tiers. Atratus didn't even turn to look. Still pacing, he cried out, "Lari! Lari Serin, step down please, darling child."

Lari rose to her feet, chin raised, a smug smile upon her face. She gave her fellow students a few nods, then strutted down the aisle and stepped onto the stage.

"I'm here, Professor Atratus," she said, voice sweet.

The stooped, balding man nodded and turned back toward the tiers of seats. He pointed his ruler at Madori.

"You! Greenmoat. Step down onto this stage. Since you've been daydreaming, you obviously know all about Offensive Magic already. Down!"

Madori glanced aside uneasily. Her friends winced, and Tam reached over to grab and squeeze her hand.

"You don't have to go down there," he whispered. "Just mumble an apology. You'll look a fool but it'll blow over."

Neekeya was struggling for breath. "Don't go," she whispered.

Madori stared down at the stage. Pretty and prim, Lari stared up from below, giving Madori her sweet little smile. And Madori felt it: the old rage rising inside her, the anger that always got her into trouble.

I once used this anger against you, Mother and Father, she thought. *I'm so sorry. I miss you so much now.*

She inhaled sharply through her nostrils and rose to her feet. She balled up her fists and walked down the aisle, moving between the rows of seats. As she passed by, hundreds of eyes followed her. Not a breath stirred. Her innards trembling, Madori stepped onto the stage.

You are the daughter of Torin Greenmoat, the great hero of the war, the man who united day and night, she told herself. *You are the daughter of Koyee of Qaelin, the great soldier who led armies, who slew the tyrant*

Ferius the Cruel. She took a deep breath and squared her shoulders. *You don't have to be afraid of a bitter professor and a pampered girl.*

"Lari," said Professor Atratus, "I do believe it's time for a little demonstration of Offensive Magic. My fellow professors tell me you've been demonstrating levitation, transformations, and bindings to your classmates. Will you now demonstrate some . . . real magic?"

Lari nodded and stared at Madori, her eyes full of cruel delight. She spoke to Atratus, but she never removed her eyes from Madori. "Gladly."

"Excellent!" said the stooped professor. "Of course, to demonstrate hurting another human, we need a human to hurt." He looked at Madori. "But I think in this case, a mongrel will suffice."

Madori sucked in breath with a hiss. How could he speak like that? She wanted to march out of the lecture hall, to find the headmistress, to demand she discipline this professor for his bile. Yet she simply stood frozen. What could Headmistress Egeria do, after all? Take the word of a village girl? Like it or not, Professor Atratus had power here at Teel, and he had power across Timandra; as a member of the Radians, proudly displaying their pin, he served Lari's father, perhaps the most powerful man in all of Moth.

Madori growled. *So I'll play your game, Atratus. And I'll defeat you at it.*

Swinging his ruler, Atratus nodded toward Lari. "Now, Lady Serin, please explain the principles of magically attacking a foe."

Chin raised, Lari recited as from a book. "The Three Principles of Magic still apply: choose, claim, change. Advanced mages often choose human flesh or bone as their material. Once claimed, they can change this material—bending or shattering bones, tearing flesh, twisting the body into death. However, in the heat of battle, war mages often choose a faster, simpler approach. They choose particles of matter floating in the air. The air is full of matter—gasses, dust, dirt, smoke, even invisible metal." Lari smiled wickedly. "A mage can form a storm in the air, striking her opponent with a might greater than any mace or hammer. Advanced mages can even animate the particles into astral, striking beasts with minds of their own."

Madori bared her teeth and raised her fists. All of Professor Atratus's words—and all the words she had read in her books last turn—cluttered inside her head. She had learned something about forming a shield of air; she could swear it. She mumbled to herself, trying to claim the air around her, to weave it into a dense, soupy force field. Sweat beaded on her brow. Nothing seemed to happen.

"Excellent, Lady Serin!" the professor said. "Now demonstrate."

Lari nodded, smiling primly. "Gladly."

The girl's face changed. Her smile turned into a snarl, and her eyes blazed with hatred. Her hands rose, collecting the air into a dark ball of smoke. With a growl, Lari tossed her missile.

The projectile hurtled across the stage toward Madori.

Shield yourself! cried a voice inside her. *Block it with air!*

But she could not.

The smoky ball, large as a melon, crashed into her chest.

Madori cried out in pain and slammed down onto her backside.

The ball shattered, breaking up into smoky serpents. The tendrils wrapped around Madori's chest, squeezing, constricting. She couldn't breathe, and tears budded in her eyes. She tried to grab the tentacles and rip them off, but her fingers passed through them. Her ribs tightened; she felt like they might snap.

"Madori!" somebody shouted somewhere above; she thought it was Tam.

Lying on the stage, she saw nothing but the smoke, and then through the unholy fog, she saw Lari's face—cruel, smiling, her hands raised like claws. As the girl curled her fingers inwards, the smoky tendrils tightened further around Madori, and she screamed.

Why wasn't Professor Atratus stopping this? Tears streamed down Madori's face. She wanted to die.

He'll let me die, she realized. *Lari is going to kill me and I'll die here upon the stage as they laugh.*

She gritted her teeth.

No.

She thought of the scars along her mother's arm. Her mother had fought this magic before and triumphed.

I am the daughter of a great heroine, a woman who fought the forces of daylight and defeated them. I can defeat Lari.

Through the fog of pain, the words from her books returned to her.

She chose her material.

She claimed the smoky tendrils that constricted her.

She screamed, lashing her hands, tugging the serpents off like a woman tearing off chains.

The tendrils left her body, and Madori sucked in air. She leaped to her feet, lashing the tentacles of smoke forward like whips.

The magic crashed into Lari, wrapped around her, and knocked her down onto the stage.

Madori rose to her feet, snarling. She tried to cling to the magic, to tighten the smoke around Lari, to crush the girl and snap her ribs. But the magic vanished from her grasp like dreams from wakefulness. The smoke dissipated.

Lari lay on her back, moaning. Silence filled the lecture hall. When Madori looked at the rows of seats, she saw her quartet companions on their feet; Tam stood halfway down the stairs, mouth opening and closing silently, as if he had been rushing down to protect her.

An angry wheeze sounded behind her. Madori spun around and gasped.

She had seen Professor Atratus mad before, but not like this. His face flushed red, and sweat beaded on his bald head. His nostrils opened and closed as he breathed raggedly, and his fingers curled like talons.

Madori took a step back. The man's rabid glare seemed almost as powerful as Lari's magic.

"I did not allow you to do magic, mongrel," he hissed, each word labored.

Madori found her rage. She met his gaze. "I had to defend myself."

With a howl, Professor Atratus raised his hands. The smoke, which had dispersed, coalesced into dark ropes. The bonds wrapped around Madori's ankles, pinning her feet to the ground. More smoky ropes wrapped around her wrists, pinning her left arm to her side and tugging her right arm toward Atratus. She struggled and tried to break these magical bindings, to claim them too, but she could sense this magic was stronger than Lari's. She could not free herself.

Sneering, Atratus took a step closer toward her. His lips curled back to show his yellow teeth. "You will not perform magic in my class without my permission, mongrel. You will be punished now. Three lashes of my ruler upon your hand."

She tried to pull back, but she might as well have broken through iron chains. His ruler whistled through the air and cracked against her outstretched palm.

Madori bit down on a yelp.

He struck her again, and two weals rose against her palm. Her hand was still sore from holding the iron wishbone, and this punishment was like tossing oil onto dying embers. Tears budded in her eyes.

He swung his ruler a third time, and Madori nearly passed out from the pain, but she would not scream. When he released his magic, and the magical chains left her, she placed her wounded hand under her armpit. It tingled and burned, reminding her of the pain of holding the iron wishbone.

"Now return to your seat, half-breed," Atratus said. "Be thankful I only struck you three times. Next offense it will be thirty. To your seat! And after your classes this turn, you will report to the kitchens, where you will spend half a turn scrubbing pots and dishes. Understood?"

Madori nodded silently, not trusting herself to speak; she felt that if she tried to answer, she would either shout or cry. Holding her throbbing hand under her armpit, she climbed the stairs and returned to her seat. She could feel everyone's eyes upon her, especially Lari's.

CHAPTER THIRTEEN
A WHISPER FROM HOME

Her palm was still throbbing, three welts upon it, as Madori made
her way down the corridor to her next class.

The rest of her quartet walked around her, forming a
protective ring. Tam especially was fuming, his face red, his fists
clenched at his sides.

"My father will hear of this," he said, barking out the words,
as they moved down the columned corridor. "Who does that
Atratus think he is? My parents donate to this university.
Hundreds of books in the library are their gifts." He growled. "I'll
get this Atratus sacked, I will, and I don't care what it takes."

"Tam, please," Madori whispered. "Lower your voice. It's all
right."

Many other students were walking to and fro around them,
not just first-years but older students too, clad in the lavender,
gray, and orange robes denoting their seniority. The last thing
Madori needed was for anyone to hear Tam's threats and report
to Atratus; that would goad the old dog to new heights of fervor.

Neekeya too fumed. Her eyes were wide with rage, her teeth
bared. "My father might not have donated to Teel, but he's a
mighty lord and warrior, and his magic is far more powerful than
Atratus's. He gave me a magical quill that can write curses to hurt
anyone. I'm going to write a curse to knock Atratus's damn hands
off!" She took the quill from her pocket and her expression
became woeful. "I only need to learn how to use it. I think I might
have broken it."

Madori doubted the "magical artifacts" Neekeya had received from her father—the quill, the ring, the sword, and dozens of others—had any magic at all. But at least Madori now knew: *I have magic within me.* Her hand still throbbed, and the humiliation still burned through her, but a hesitant smile tingled upon her lips.

I used magic. I defeated Lari.

As they walked down the hall, Madori raised her chin, letting that pride swell her chest. She knew she would face Lari again, and Madori vowed to study hard, to become stronger and stronger.

I came to Teel to learn healing, Madori thought, *but you, Lari, you will force me to become a warrior too. And you will rue your choice to make me an enemy.*

It took a while, but after exploring several corridors and chambers and making a few wrong turns, Madori's Motley finally found their next classroom—a sterile little chamber high up in Ostirina, the northwestern of Teel's four towers.

As Madori stepped inside with her friends, she breathed in deeply and her smile widened. It was finally time for the class she had awaited—Magical Healing.

A dozen other students were already here, seated at pale stone tables. Madori was relieved to see that Sunlit Purity was not attending this class. Of course Lari and her friends would have no use for healing magic; they seemed to care only for destruction. Madori sat down with her quartet at the last free table, opened her book, and caught a glimpse of her wounded hand. The welts were ugly and red and still hurt. Between them spread the faded scars from the iron wishbone.

"Students! Students, settle down."

The high, wavering voice drifted from the doorway. An instant later, Professor Yovan stepped into the chamber—the same professor who had supervised the battle with the wishbones, sending Torin a roast ham to atone for Madori's ruined hand. The elderly man's long, white beard rolled down to his feet, and his tufted eyebrows thrust out like the brims of hats. He seemed well into his eighties—even older than the bald, mustached Professor Fen, the teacher of Basic Principles. The greybeard reminded Madori of old Mayor Kerof, her great-grandfather, who had rocked her on his knee when she had been a girl. Dear old Grand Grand, as Madori called Kerof, had passed several years ago; old Professor Yovan, with his flowing beard and long, thin fingers, gave her the same sense of elder wisdom and grandfatherly love.

The students, already rather settled, turned their eyes toward the aged professor. Yovan made his way to his desk, slapped a hand against it, and announced, "Healing! Yes. Healing. Healing, healing healing . . . *Magical* healing, to be exact." He stroked his beard. "Magical Healing is about using magic to, well . . . heal." He cleared his throat. "And that is what I shall teach you!"

The students stared at him silently.

Seeming uncomfortable with the attention, Professor Yovan fumbled with the books, scrolls, and potions on his desk. "Who can tell me," he said, "how to heal the body using magic?"

It was nice, Madori thought, not to have Lari around to thrust up her hand at once. Hesitantly, glancing at her friends for encouragement, Madori raised her hand.

"Ah, yes!" said Professor Yovan. "You, little boy. What is your name?"

A few students giggled across the class.

Madori placed down her hand. "My name is Madori Greenmoat. And I'm a girl. Remember me from the Trial of Will?" She freed her two strands of long hair from behind her ears, letting them frame her face. With the rest of her hair cropped short and her body scrawny, she was often mistaken for a boy. "And . . . I'm not sure, but I'm guessing it has to do with the Three Basic Principles. Choosing your material—choosing the wound. Claiming your material—gaining control of the broken bone, injured flesh, or diseased tissue. And finally, changing the material—mending the wound."

Professor Yovan clapped his hands together, his face brightening. "Precisely, little boy!"

"Girl," she said.

He nodded emphatically. "You are most correct. However, reality of course is more complex. Any brute can magically shatter flesh. But to heal, ah! That requires the most innate, pure understanding of the body's structures. To injure is as easy as shattering a statue. To heal . . . that is to sculpt." He winked. "I use that metaphor every year. Rather proud of it."

The professor unrolled scrolls of human anatomy and launched into a lecture, describing the basic humors and energies that flowed throughout all living things. Madori found that, unlike with Professor Atratus, she could actually understand most of these words. Here was real magic, she thought—a force for goodness. Here was why she had come to Teel.

"Now," said Professor Yovan after an hour of speaking, "you will of course not be able to heal wounds for many months, maybe not for years. The effects of a mistake with such magic can be disastrous. When attempting to mend a bone, you could accidentally shatter every bone in the body. When attempting to withdraw poison from a wound, you could accidentally send the poison into the patient's heart. Many of you, throughout your studies at Teel, will learn to *harm*. Only the brightest among you will learn to *heal*. And so I demand from you, students: Do not attempt healing magic until your fourth year!"

But Madori was already summoning that power inside her—the power that had let her claim the smoky tendrils, let her change them to attack Lari.

"Madori, what are you doing?" Jitomi whispered at her side. He nudged her with his elbow. "You're not allowed to use magic."

But she ignored him. She closed her eyes and her lips whispered. Her nostrils flared as she claimed her material—not the welts upon her palm but the uninjured skin around them. Warmth filled her and tingled across her body as she changed her material—allowing her skin to push forward, erasing the wounds, pulling the injured flesh deep into her.

Gasps sounded around her.

Madori opened her eyes and stared at her hand.

The welts from Atratus's ruler were gone, leaving only pale scars.

Professor Yovan rushed over, eyes so wide Madori saw the white all around his irises.

"Little boy!" he said. "I told you! You may not practice healing magic. You— Oh my." He took her palm in his and examined the scars. "How old are these scars?"

"About ten seconds," she replied. "Professor Atratus struck me with his ruler only this morning. And I'm a girl."

Neekeya twisted in her seat, her necklace of crocodile teeth chinking. "It's true! Madori has magic—real magic!" She rummaged through her pocket and pulled out a lock of hair tied with a ribbon. "I have a magical lock of Healing Hair, and I tried to use it on Madori, but I think it only works on us Daenorians."

Professor Yovan clucked his tongue and patted Madori's hand. "Little boy—I mean, girl—you must obey me next time, and you must not heal without my permission—not even your own wounds. But . . ." His eyes watered and suddenly he was embracing her. "It's a delight to see such a naturally gifted healer. For sixty years I've been teaching here at Teel, and I've never seen a first year student heal a wound—let alone on her first day! You are a wonder."

Madori lowered her eyes.

"Thank you," she whispered. She could not speak any louder, and suddenly tears filled her eyes. For the first time in many turns, they were not tears of pain but of joy. Somebody appreciated her. Somebody thought she was a wonder. Perhaps Teel University was not the nightmare it had seemed but a place where she could learn, grow, become the woman she dreamed of being. Neekeya saw her tears and pulled Madori into an embrace, and Tam patted her healed hand.

After Magical Healing came Basic Principles again, followed by Magical History, then finally Magic and Sound—a class Madori had eagerly signed up for, teaching students to produce magical music. When the Teel Bells finally rang the end of the turn, Madori rubbed her shoulders, eager to return to her chamber for a solid sleep. Yet she sighed to remember Professor Atratus's punishment.

"I still have to report to the kitchens," she said to her friends. "Got to scrub some pots."

Tam sighed. "At least eat dinner with us first." He cringed. "We have to eat in the dining hall with hundreds of other students. Idar's beard, I'm not looking forward to that. Madori's Motley will stick out like monkeys at a banquet."

She smiled wanly. "I'm almost glad for my punishment. I think I prefer laboring in the kitchens than sitting in the dining hall. It's like polishing the armor instead of fighting in the battle." She bit her lip. "I'll grab some food to eat while I work, and I'll meet you back at our chamber."

Leaving her companions, she made her way south of the library and cloister, down a path, and toward the dining hall. The building rose from a grassy sward, its walls columned, stairs leading up to its gates; it seemed a building as fine as the library or towers, topped with statues of birds and beasts. Students were gathering in a courtyard, lining up to enter and eat. Madori spotted Lari standing at their lead, holding a Radian flag; others of her order gathered around her.

Feeling relief that she had an excuse to skip dinner—her punishment was probably kinder than the meal—Madori skirted the building, leaving the main gates and heading toward a back door. No students stood in this little corner, and only a few geese ambled between the birches.

A sudden memory flashed through Madori: her mother standing in the window of their cottage at home, calling Madori home for dinner. Madori would be playing outside with Fairwool-by-Night's animals—a few stray dogs, geese like the ones here, maybe a duckling or two—covered in mud, her elbows scraped. Animals had always been her only friends. At first Madori would ignore her mother, but then the smell of the woman's cooking would waft on the wind, filling her nostrils: stewed chanterelle mushrooms, fried lanternfish, and spicy matsutake mushroom cakes—Elorian food, the food Madori loved.

I miss you so much, Mother, she thought, heading toward the kitchens. *I wish I could be eating with you now at home.*

She opened the back door and stepped into the kitchens. She found a hallway lined with several doorways. Through one doorway she saw a chamber full of cooking fires, and the scents of meats, stews, breads, and pies filled her nostrils. Her mouth watered. Cooks dressed in white tended to the meals—mixing stews that bubbled in cauldrons, turning spits of roasting pigs, and pulling bread rolls from ovens. Reluctantly, Madori kept walking until she reached the dish washing room and stepped inside.

Three walls here were built of bricks. Instead of a fourth wall rose many shelves like oversized window shutters, each shelf topped high with dirty dishes. Between the shelves, Madori could peer into the dining hall where a thousand students were eating. Every moment another student, belly full, stepped forward to place a dirty plate and cutlery upon a shelf. A stone aqueduct ran through the chamber, flowing with water; it was about the size of a horse's trough. Several students stood around the canal, scrubbing dishes. All seemed dejected, and all bore welts upon their palms—other victims of Atratus's wrath.

"Another prisoner!" announced one of the workers, a tall boy with a thick Verilish accent. Madori had seen Verilish traders before—burly men from the northern pine forests, thick of beards, clad in fur pelts, warriors who prided themselves on strength. She guessed that for a son of Verilon, scrubbing dishes like a woman was the ultimate insult.

Madori nodded. "Let's get this over with. I'm tired and want to go back to my chamber."

Another washer—this one a petite girl with black hair—laughed. She spoke with the accent of Eseer, a desert kingdom far in the south. "There are hundreds of plates still to wash, and hundreds of students are still eating. We'll be lucky to leave before next turn."

Sighing, Madori turned to look at the shelves of plates. Indeed, students kept walking by, adding more dishes to the piles; it looks like many hours of work. When she returned her eyes to the aqueduct, she realized that all the scrubbers—punished students—were foreigners. It seemed Atratus was loath to punish his fellow Magerians.

Madori bit her lip and got to work.

She dunked dish after dish into the flowing water, scrubbing it with a rag and soap. But soon the shelves threatened to collapse; at first only the fastest eaters had left their plates to clean, but now hundreds of plates were rising in a sticky, dirty mess.

"If we break one, Atratus will know," said the tall boy. "He's got magical eyes all over the place. My brother broke a dish here last year; Atratus nearly tore off his hand, he beat him so hard with his ruler."

Madori winced, scanning the chamber for magical eyes, imagining eyeballs moving in the walls themselves. She saw nothing but she wouldn't put such magic past Atratus; she winced to remember how his smoky ropes had bound her. She scrubbed faster, rushing back and forth between the shelves and the water. Before long, with hundreds of students placing down their dishes, Madori no longer bothered scrubbing one at a time. She rushed back and forth, towers of dishes in her arms, placing the clean ones upon trays for another student to whisk outside.

"Got to go faster!" said the boy. "Shelves running out of space."

Madori glanced at the shelves to see a pile of plates tilt. She rushed forward and caught three plates just as they fell. Wincing, she ran with them to the aqueduct, then back again. When she hurried to the water with yet another pile of plates, she slipped in a puddle, wobbled for a second, thought she could steady the structure . . . then saw one plate fall toward the ground.

The Eseerian girl leaped forward and caught it before it could shatter.

"Be more careful!" the girl whispered, face pale and eyes wide. "He'll know. By the great god Amaran, he'll know. He is a demon."

Heart lashing, Madori kept working. Her eyes stung, and soap bubbles filled the air, and she kept moving faster and faster, and she knew she couldn't keep up. They were only several dish washers, and the mountain of plates kept growing.

She forced herself to sing as she scrubbed, her voice low, her lips tight, her eyes burning. She sang "Darkness Falls," the song from her trials, a song of home—a song to remember a better place, a place of peace, of love. It was a song her mother used to sing her—a mother Madori had always fought with, a mother Madori could not wait to hug and kiss again.

I'm so sorry, Mother. I'm so sorry I always yelled at you for making me wash dishes at home. She laughed through her tears. *What I wouldn't give to be washing dishes at home now!*

She turned back toward the shelves, intending to grab another batch, when she saw two pretty blue eyes staring from the dining hall beyond.

"Lari," she hissed.

Past the stacks of plates, Madori couldn't see more than her enemy's eyes, but those eyes were smiling.

With a clatter, mountains of plates—a hundred or more—tilted on the shelves. Madori glimpsed Lari's hands shoving them forward, and she heard a cold laugh, before the plates all came crashing down.

Madori winced and leaped back, knowing that Atratus would know, that he'd lash her in a fury.

She waited for the crash of a hundred breaking plates but heard no sound. She realized she had closed her eyes, and she peeked . . . and gasped.

The plates were hovering in midair.

"Leave this place, Lari Serin!" rose a voice from behind Madori. "Leave or these plates will drive into your face."

With the plates hovering off the shelf, Madori now had a full view of Lari, who stood with her friends in the dining hall. The girl sneered but spun on her heel and marched off.

Madori too spun around—toward the back of the kitchen. Jitomi stood at the doorway, holding his hands forward, sweat on his brow. He managed to give Madori a tight smile.

"I think," he said, "I finally figure out levitation."

If she weren't worried about the plates crashing down, she'd have leaped toward the Elorian boy and kissed him.

Two more students stepped into the room—Tam and Neekeya—both grinning.

"We came to help!" said Neekeya. She looked around at all the dishes and winced. "I wish I had my magical dish scrubber here. My parents had one back at home. It would wash all the dishes itself, floating in the air; you just had to very lightly hold the handle to guide it."

Tam rolled his eyes and stepped around the Daenorian girl. "Well, we don't have magical scrubbers, but we have a bunch of hands and about a million dishes to wash." He reached toward the floating ones which Jitomi still kept magically suspended. "Now let's help the little billy goat."

Madori had expected to spend at least half a turn here, nearly going mad, but with her quartet's help, they were able to finish scrubbing everything within a couple hours. When their work was finally done, Madori didn't even want to return to her chamber; she wanted to plop down right here in the kitchens and sleep for turns on end. After staying up studying last half-turn, she was wearier than she'd ever been. Her friends had to practically drag her out of the kitchens, across the cloister, and toward the first years' dormitory.

The arcade—a colonnade on one side, a wall of doors on the other—was empty. The bedroom doors were all closed. Madori shuffled her feet, barely able to keep her eyes open, walking among her quartet. When they reached their door, she yawned and stepped inside, ready to collapse.

Instead she froze and stared.

At her side, Neekeya yelped and dropped the books she held.

"What—" the swamp girl muttered. "What happened—?"

"Lari happened," Madori said.

Their books all lay torn on the floor, the pages scattered like autumn leaves. Their mementos from home—figurines, dolls, paintings—lay smashed. Somebody had drawn a large Radian symbol upon the wall in blood, and more blood stained Madori's bed; the coppery smell invaded her nostrils. The smell of rotten meat wafted too, and Madori nearly gagged.

A note lay upon her pillow. Moving carefully between the broken books and figurines, she approached her bed and lifted the note. Upon it appeared in neat handwriting the words: "Radian rises. Mongrels will be butchered like pigs."

Neekeya came to stand beside her. She grimaced and covered her mouth. "It stinks." She doubled over as if about to gag, then gasped and scampered backwards. Eyes wide, she yelped and pointed under the bed.

Madori lowered her gaze. When she knelt, she saw it too. She reached under the bed and pulled it out: a severed pig's head.

Tam made a queasy sound and turned green, and even Jitomi looked ill.

Madori placed down the head, turned around, and walked outside into the hallway.

"Madori, where are you going?" Tam said, hurrying after her. "The bells have rung. We're not allowed outside our chambers."

She kept walking, not turning to look back. "Stay behind. Stay safe and lock the door."

Neekeya raced up beside her, eyes wide. "You're not going to confront Lari, are you? Because if you are, I'm going with you. I'll fight at your side."

"No." Madori shook her head. "I will not fight Lari. That's what she wants. That's what she's waiting for—to lure us into a battle, maybe a trap. I'm going straight to Headmistress Egeria and putting an end to this." She turned around to face her friends; the hallway was empty around them, all the other students asleep in their chambers. "Go back. Clean up. Do not go outside into the hall; it's dangerous."

She left them there, heading between two columns into the courtyard.

Clouds hid the never-sinking sun of Timandra, and a drizzle fell. Madori's two strands of long, black hair stuck to her cheeks, while the cropped hair on her back and sides caught the raindrops like cobwebs catching dew. She made her way under the elm tree, across the grass, and toward the southeastern tower—the home of the headmistress. She found herself facing a brick archway, its keystone engraved with two scrolls, the sigil of Teel University. When she tried the towering oak doors, she found them unlocked; they slid open on oiled hinges.

I will find the headmistress, and I will tell her everything, Madori thought, stepping inside. She felt too hollow for emotion; no fear or rage filled her, unless these emotions lurked too deep for her to feel. She was hurt too badly, she had suffered too much; all she felt now was detached determination. *I will talk about my famous parents if I must, or I will talk about my friendship with King Camlin and Queen Linee. Lari isn't the only student here with lofty connections.* She walked down a hall, her clothes dripping, and tightened her lips. *I will end this.*

She rounded a corner, intending to stomp up the tower staircase, and found herself face-to-face with Professor Atratus.

Madori froze.

At once she raised her hands, sucking in breath, prepared to defend herself. Her heart leaped into a gallop.

He stared at her, looming like a vulture over prey, a foot taller than her. His eyes blazed and his nostrils flared, the hairs inside twitching. He bared his teeth.

"What," he spoke in a strained voice, "are you doing outside of your chamber after hours, mongrel?"

She refused to back down. She was half his size, a third his age, and as lowly as a worm compared to his power, but she faced him sternly.

"Move aside, Professor Atratus," she said. "I'm here to speak to the headmistress."

He raised his fist; it trembled, his knuckles white with strain. "Students are not to roam the university after hours. I thought that my punishments might have set on your the right path, but I see that you mongrels are truly rabid beasts."

His hand lashed out and struck her cheek. Before she could leap back, he slapped her again, a blow to the second cheek, rattling her jaw. She stood still, too shocked to react. She wanted to attack him. She wanted to cry, to scream, to run, to shout for the headmistress, but she could only stand frozen, and she cursed herself for her paralysis.

Atratus spat out spittle as he spoke, shaking with rage. "Since you obviously hate your chamber so much, you will sleep this half-turn outside in the rain." He grabbed her wrist and began tugging her down the hall. They burst outside into the cloister, the rain pattering against them. "You will remain standing outside until next turn, and if I ever catch you wandering again, I will show you no more mercy."

She tried to free herself from his grasp, but he was too strong. He dragged her across the cloister, down a gallery, past the library and dining hall, and finally toward a craggy wall. They stepped through an archway, emerging into a grove of elms and birches outside the university grounds. It was a cold, wet place in the shadows of the mountains, overrun with brush, a place forbidden to students. Atratus finally stopped walking behind a twisting oak with a trunk like a face. There he released her wrist.

She tried to run, to barrel past him. She knew that if she could only reach the headmistress, she'd have a sympathetic ear. But her legs would not budge. When she looked down, she found her feet sunken in the mud down to her ankles. Smoky tendrils wrapped around her legs, keeping her pinned in place.

"Atratus!" she began to scream when more smoke invaded her mouth, muffling her words.

"Spend a few hours outside the university," he said. "And think very carefully if you want to return. If I were you, when the spell is broken, I would wander deep into the forest, and I would live like the feral beast that you are. I cannot officially banish you, mongrel, not yet. But know this." He pointed a shaky finger at her. "If you do return, you will suffer. I will make you suffer greatly."

He glared at her and lightning flashed, sparking against his hunched form and hooked nose, gleaming in his eyes like white fire. He spat and turned to leave. He vanished back into the university, leaving her outside in the rain.

She could not move. She could not scream. She could only breathe through her nostrils, and lightning crashed again, hitting a nearby tree. Throughout the storm, she could hear the sounds of her friends calling for her, but she knew they wouldn't find her, not out there.

It was hours before the spell broke, freeing her legs and releasing the smoke in her mouth. She fell to her knees in the mud and took a ragged breath. She tilted over, lay on her back, and gazed up at the sky. The last clouds were dispersing, and a single beam of light fell upon her. A rainbow glimmered for just a few heartbeats before fading away.

Tears streamed down Madori's cheeks.

What do I do? Do I flee Teel? Do I try to make my way home?

She raised her head and looked at the university walls. The bells were ringing; a new turn of classes was beginning.

"I can't return," she whispered to herself, trembling in the mud, weary and weak and so afraid. "Lari would attack me, or Atratus would, and . . ." She covered her eyes. "I can't do this, Father. I can't, Mother. I'm not strong like you two are."

She closed her eyes.

She couldn't do this.

A faint hint of a caress, like a falling feather, tingled her hand.

Madori opened her eyes, and there she saw it, resting on her hand—a duskmoth.

She had seen duskmoths back home at Fairwool-by-Night; they were denizens of the borderlands, of the twilit strip that separated day from night. The animal was shaped like Mythimna, this world they called Moth, one wing white and the other black. A creature like the one tattooed onto her wrist. A creature like her, torn between day and night.

"What are you doing here?" she whispered. "So far from home . . ."

It twitched its feathery antennae. Perhaps, she thought, it was asking her the same question. Or perhaps it had come to comfort her, to remind her she wasn't alone. It seemed to meet her eyes, and she gently caressed its downy body.

It took flight, rising in spirals, and she watched as it ascended into the blue sky, and tears streamed down her cheeks. Lying in the mud, she reached up to it.

"Goodbye, friend. Be brave up there."

Trembling, her cheeks wet, she forced herself to take a deep breath.

Another.

Again.

Her father's words filled her, as warm and comforting as mulled wine: *To survive, you only have to breathe the next breath.*

"But how can I?" she whispered. "How can I even breathe when their magic can suffocate me?"

She saw her parents again in her mind. Her father's face was humble and kind, his eyes warm—one eye green, the other black, eyes torn between day and night like she was. She saw her mother too. Koyee's face was paler and sterner, but her eyes were just as loving, large Elorian eyes like Madori herself had. In her mind, they both embraced her, enveloping her with love.

"You fought a great war," she whispered to them. "Perhaps I don't face fleets of warships, armies of knights, or great battles like you did. But I'm fighting my own war here, a personal war, and one I'll need all your strength and wisdom for." She knuckled her eyes. "I promise you, my parents, I will fight. I will win."

She rose to her feet. Her knees shook but she took another deep breath, steeling herself.

"I'm like a duskmoth," she said. "I'm torn between day and night, and I'm far from home. But I will fly."

She walked back to the university, wet, muddy, afraid, and more determined than ever.

CHAPTER FOURTEEN
BLOOD AT HORNSFORD BRIDGE

They rode across the wilderness, two men in a horse-drawn cart, and beheld the might and terror of the Radian menace.

"By Idar's flea-bitten bottom," Torin cursed and tugged the reins, halting Hayseed. The nag snorted and pawed the earth.

Sitting beside him, Cam smiled bitterly. "I told you it was big."

Torin grimaced. "The Palace of Kingswall is big. The fortress my wife is building is big. This?" He gestured ahead. "This isn't a big fortress, my friend. This is more like a city."

Hayseed sidestepped and nickered, and the cart swayed. The slender king clutched his seat and nodded. "Aye, a city of nothing but soldiers bred for hatred."

Sunmotte Citadel rose upon a hill, surrounded by a circular moat, farmlands, and valleys. Behind the water soared the castle wall, topped with battlements, archers, and Radian banners. Towers rose at regular intervals along the wall, each a palace unto itself. Behind the battlements peered the tops of more towers and keeps—a complex so large Torin thought it could rival all of Kingswall. As if the soaring battlements didn't sufficiently unnerve him, he saw many troops mustering in the fields outside the citadel—ten thousand or more soldiers stood there, armed with spears and swords.

Hayseed whinnied. Torin stepped out of the cart and stroked the old nag, seeking to comfort himself as much as her.

"Serin isn't playing games here, my friend," he said to Cam. "This isn't just the fortress of a lord. This isn't just an army to guard his home. He's preparing for war."

The king nodded grimly. He too stepped out of the cart, shook his legs, and pointed northeast. "And our homeland lies just a couple miles away."

Torin followed his friend's gaze. Across grassy fields flowed the Red River, the rushing border between this kingdom of Mageria and their homeland of Arden. The ancient Hornsford Bridge spanned the water, half-a-mile long, built of ancient bricks. A fortified gatehouse rose at each side. The Magerian gatehouse was large as a castle, its two towers displaying the banners of Radianism—a sun eclipsing the moon—alongside the banners of Mageria—a buffalo upon a red field. Across the bridge, the Ardish gatehouse was smaller—a single, humble tower—its battlements displaying Arden's sigil, a black raven upon a golden field. Beyond the gatehouse rolled Arden's countryside, bereft of its own citadel or army. An empty land. A vulnerable land.

"Camlin, old boy," Torin said, "we're facing an armored knight with a bread knife."

Cam sighed. "A bread knife? I'd settle for a bread knife." He gestured toward the lonely guard tower on the Ardish side of the bridge. "That's more like a wooden spoon. Maybe even a napkin."

Torin grunted. "We move forces here. As soon as we reach Kingswall, we muster men. We send them west."

"What men?" Cam rubbed his temples. "Torin, my dear, it seems half the lords in my kingdom are loyal to Serin; they're raising his banners and receiving quite a bit of his gold. And those lords who *are* loyal to my throne? They wax poetic of an end to war, of peace on earth, of never more lifting arms and watching Moth bleed."

Torin grumbled. "Moth will bleed whether they want it or not. And they won't be there to staunch the wound." He narrowed his eyes. "Let's go home, Cam, but I'm not crossing that bridge. Not if you pay me with my own fortress. We ride south. We'll cross the river at Reedford; that's where Madori and I crossed over."

Cam raised an eyebrow. "Reedford? But my dear lad, Reedford is boring." He gestured ahead and grinned. "Here we get to inspect Serin's forces up close." He tugged at his rough, woolen cloak and scratched his stubbly cheeks. "We're no King Camlin and Sir Greenmoat here. We're simply two weary travelers seeking a way home." He climbed back into the cart. "Come on, Tor old boy, it'll be an adventure. Like in the old days."

Torin grumbled. "The old days weren't an adventure; they were a bloody nightmare." He rubbed his stiff neck. "And we were younger."

Yet he too climbed into the cart, and they began to move again.

The bridge still lay a couple miles away, and Hayseed was a slow old horse. Cam had wanted to buy two quick, sure-footed coursers at Teelshire; he had sold his own old horse at the town, as the beast had been too weary for a quick ride back. But Torin had refused. How could he sell Hayseed, his daughter's old friend? Madori was gone for years; the least Torin could do was keep her favorite horse—even if it meant the journey home would take twice as long.

He sighed. The journey home? No. He was perhaps returning to Arden, his kingdom, but not to his home. Not to Fairwool-by-Night, and not to his wife.

"The first time I traveled to Kingswall," he said softly, "I went there with Bailey to stop a war. Now we travel there to raise an army."

Cam nodded as the cart bumped down the pebbly road. "The two actions are not contradictory. We raise an army to stop a war. An army along your borders can bring peace more readily than the hearts of men. Hearts cannot be trusted; steel can be."

Torin raised an eyebrow. "Look at you, King Camlin. You almost sound like a military leader. Where is the young boy who fought for peace?"

"He grew up." Cam grunted and scratched his chin. "Idealism was fine when we were youths, just kids in a war the adults led. But we're the adults now. Idar's Warts, Torin. I actually have gray hairs now, do you believe it? I pluck them out, but they just grow back, and perhaps they bring me some wisdom. Let Tam and Madori be the new preachers for peace. Let us adults prepare for war."

Torin scratched his temple; he had been finding a few white hairs there himself. "I envy Koyee. She's always had white hair. Doesn't have to worry about plucking a thing."

Cam barked out a laugh. "The woman never ages anyway. You and I . . . we're halfway through our thirties already, and we're starting to show it." He reached over to pat Torin's hint of a paunch. "But that wife of yours; she still looks like a youth. People might think she's your daughter."

"I already have one daughter, and she causes enough trouble herself." He lowered his head, sudden pain overtaking him. "Damn it, Cam. Don't talk about our age. Not because I'm scared of growing old. But because—Idar damn it—I wish they could have grown old with us." He let out a sigh that sounded dangerously close to a sob. "That old loaf of bread and that braided madwoman. They should have been here with us now."

Cam nodded sadly, but suddenly a smile spread across his face. "Hem would probably be even larger at our age; he wouldn't fit on this cart, that's for sure."

Torin smiled to remember the old baker's boy. "He could *pull* the cart, that one. And Bailey, well . . . I bet you she'd insist that she's a true warrior and could run the whole way. Scratch that; she'd charge toward Sunmotte Citadel and take on Serin's army single-handed."

"You don't think she'd have mellowed with age?" Cam raised his eyebrows. "We've mellowed."

Torin shook his head. "She'd be as crazy as always. I miss her. I miss them both. It's funny, isn't it? They say time heals all wounds. What a contemptible lie."

As they drew closer to the bridge in the northeast, they were also drawing closer to the massive fort in the northwest. Serin's army stood only a mile away now, the sun glinting on thousands of spears. Every soldier, it seemed, wore a full suit of plate armor; back in Arden, only knights wore the expensive armor, while common soldiers wore the less efficient—but cheaper—chain mail or leather armor. The Radians not only had many horses but chariots too, their wheels scythed. Smaller than Torin's cart and much swifter, several of the vehicles raced around the field, their riders shooting at targets with bows. Behind these drilling forces, the walls of the fortress loomed taller than palaces, brimming with many troops.

Torin and Cam fell silent. The air felt too hot, too thick; Torin could barely breathe it. He cursed Cam for convincing him to take this route.

"They'll stop us," he whispered. The soldiers were still distant, but Torin couldn't speak any louder. "They'll send riders to the road. They'll think us spies."

"We *are* spies," Cam said. "Sort of. But no, they won't stop us. That bridge there—costs an entire silver coin to cross. How do you think Serin pays for all that fine armor, those chariots, those high walls?" He patted his purse. "Bridge tolls."

"Bridge trolls?"

Cam groaned. "You're either losing your hearing or developing a penchant for bad jokes. Both are worse signs of aging than white hairs or paunches."

Perhaps the Shepherd King was right; no soldiers appeared to stop their passage down the pebbly road toward the bridge, and if the armies saw them, they gave no sign of it. Before long the cart turned eastward, leaving Sunmotte Citadel behind. They trundled toward the river. An arched gateway led onto the bridge, framed by two guard towers, each large enough that, removed and placed upon a hill, it could have proudly housed a lord. Several soldiers stood upon the towers, holding crossbows, while several more stood beneath the archway.

Torin tugged his hood low over his head. Cam did the same. Hunched forward, clad in old wool, they hopefully looked like nothing more than two weary, common travelers. The guards at the gate stood sternly, clad in black plate armor, their faces hidden behind their visors. Their breastplates bore two sigils—the buffalo of Mageria on one side, Radian's eclipse on the other.

"Halt!" said one, voice echoing and metallic inside his helm, and held out his hand. "Stop for inspection."

Torin tugged the reins, and old Hayseed slowed to a halt, snorting. Several soldiers marched forward, their plate armor so well-fitting and well-oiled it barely made a sound. Moving with the urgency of starving men seeking food, they began to inspect the cart—lifting blankets, rummaging through packs, and sniffing at jugs of water.

"We're only two simple travelers returning home," Torin said, affecting a lowborn accent. "A friend of ours—we took him to a see a healer in Teelshire. Aye, they got real healers there, not like back home—*magical* healers, they got at Teelshire." He shook his head and tsked. "Still, all in vain. Our friend died on the road before we could even reach Teelshire; all we could do when we got there is bury him. He was a dear friend, but I told him, I did, if he kept drinking spirits every morning and night, he'd soon come down with—"

146

"Silence," spat out a soldier. "We have no patience for peasant tales. Why didn't we see you cross from Arden? I never forget a face."

Torin sighed inwardly. A couple decades ago, in the war, he'd have charged at these soldiers with sword and shield, his friends at his side. He wasn't sure if that meant he was wiser or less brave; perhaps a bit of both.

"We crossed down south at Reedford," Torin said. "They got a nice inn there, they do. The smoothest ale you could taste. Do you like ale, friend? We got three casks in the back; feel free to take the small one for your troubles."

One of the soldiers stepped toward Torin and lifted his visor, revealing a hard, frowning face. The man's eyes narrowed. "Look at me," he demanded.

Torin gave the soldier a quick glance from under his hood. He held out a silver coin. "Here we are, our bridge toll, and that's real Arish silver, it is. Bite it if you like." Torin reached for his riding crop. "Now we hate to take up your time, so we'll just—"

Before Torin could tap his horse, the soldier grabbed Torin's wrist, stopping the crop.

"Wait a moment." The soldier leaned in, and his eyes widened. "I know you. One green eye, one black! We met in battle in the war. Torin Greenmoat, you are! Lord Serin said you might be passing here. He commanded us to bring you to him. You'll have to come with us."

The other soldiers—there were four of them—heard and stepped closer. Cam winced but Torin forced himself to laugh.

"Aye, I get that all the time. I always curse my eyes. Everywhere I go it's Terin Greenboat, Terin Greenboat— whoever that is. It makes a man weary. I—" He jerked his hand free and swung his crop. "Hayseed, go!"

As the horse burst into a gallop, tugging the cart onto the bridge, Torin grabbed the katana he kept hidden behind his feet—

the same sword he would wield in the war. He drew the blade with a single, fluid movement and swung it across the cart's side. It clanged into a soldier's helmet, knocking the man back. Cam drew and swung his own hidden blade, knocking back another man, while a third soldier leaped away from Hayseed's hooves.

For two or three heartbeats, they raced unopposed upon the bridge.

Then that old sound Torin remembered and hated filled the air.

Whistling arrows.

He ducked and pulled Cam down too. Arrows whistled above them, and one slammed into the cart inches away from Torin. Hayseed whinnied and kept running, her fear driving her.

"Now this is more like the old days!" Cam shouted, then winced and ducked lower as an arrow grazed his head, slicing a lock of hair.

The cart bounced madly. The river flowed at their sides, and the distant bank seemed miles away. When the cart hit a crack in the bridge, it bolted into the air, and Torin winced when they slammed back down. A cask of ale fell from the cart, and Torin spun around to see it roll and shatter, spilling its contents. Several soldiers were running across the bridge, slow in their armor; one slipped in the ale and crashed down.

For an instant hope leaped in Torin; they would make it across the bridge! But when he heard the hooves beating and the horns blowing, his heart sank down to his belly. He watched, grimacing, as a dozen Radian riders galloped onto the bridge, pointing lances.

"Hayseed, go, girl!" Cam was shouting.

Torin, meanwhile, climbed from his seat into the back of the cart. An arrow whistled, and he winced as it slammed into another cask of ale. He shoved, sending the cask tumbling down. A rider tried to dodge the rolling barrel but was too slow; his horse slammed into the obstacle and fell. Torin ducked, hiding behind more supplies as arrows flew. He shoved again, knocking down bundles of firewood; a horse entangled in the rolling logs and crashed down.

When Torin glanced back eastward, he saw that they had only crossed half the bridge. The remaining riders were gaining on them. Visors hid the Radians' faces, and their lances rose, ready to thrust.

Torin raised his sword, prepared to fight as best he could. But rather than charge from behind, the horses raced around the cart and came to block its passage. Hayseed whinnied and bucked, and the cart halted so suddenly it almost tilted over.

A ring of riders surrounded the cart, lances pointed inward like the teeth of a lamprey. The sunlight blazed against the Radian emblems upon the soldiers' breastplates and shields.

"Torin Greenmoat," said one rider, the tallest among them. He raised his visor, revealing the stony brow, haughty blue eyes, and strong jaw of Lord Serin. "Hello again. And . . . I do believe this is Camlin of Arden, the Shepherd King."

Sword raised, Torin nodded at the lord. "Hello again, cousin." He turned to glance at Cam and spoke in Qaelish, a language of the night they both had learned in the war. "The rider to my left—the shorter one?"

Cam nodded and spoke in Qaelish too. "After you."

Torin didn't waste another instant. He leaped from the cart, katana swinging, and lunged toward the knight. Cam leaped behind them. The horse bucked. The knight's lance thrust, and Torin's katana knocked it aside. Cam lashed his own blade, driving the horse back.

The two friends raced around the rider, free from the encircling enemy, and ran toward the bridge's ledge.

"Stop them!" rose a voice behind.

A crossbow thrummed and the quarrel whizzed by Torin's ear. He ran with Cam, arms pumping.

They reached the bridge's ledge and kicked off. Torin's heart hammered and his legs still ran in the air. They plunged down toward the rushing water, crossbow quarrels flying above them.

"Yes, definitely like the old days!" Cam shouted at his side.

With a a great splash of icy water, they crashed into the river.

They sank, kicking and swimming underwater. Torin's eyes stung and he kicked off his boots, propelling himself eastward—at least he hoped it was eastward. Arrows pierced the water around him, and one grazed his calf. Blood rose like dancing red demons.

Yes, I don't miss the old days, he thought as they swam, arrows filling the water like raindrops cutting through mist.

CHAPTER FIFTEEN
SEEKING MAGIC

She walked through the library of Teel like a woman walking through a temple.

"Here is my temple," she whispered. "Here is my solitude, my peace, the wisdom I seek."

She took a deep breath and smiled. She stepped forward slowly, head tilted back, her fingers tingling at her sides.

Madori had spent many hours of her childhood in the library of Fairwool-by-Night, a hall cluttered with creaky shelves, dusty books, and piles of scrolls. That had been a place like a womb, warm, comfortable, worn in, the book spines smoothed by many fingers, the air rich with the scent of papyrus and parchment. But here . . . here in the great Teel Library she found a different world. This was no womb; it was a palace. Porphyry columns rose several stories tall, their capitols shaped as Mageria's buffaloes, the beasts supporting a vaulted ceiling painted with scenes of sunbursts, pink clouds, and birds of all kinds. Marble statues stood every few feet, depicting the ancient gods of Riyona, their nude bodies paragons of beauty. Oil paintings of landscapes and ancient battles—the canvases as large as sails—covered the walls. Giltwood tables and upholstered chairs, themselves masterpieces, supported silver counter-square boards with jeweled pieces.

But more than any painting or statue, the books filled Madori's heart with warmth like mulled wine.

Thousands of books stood upon the shelves—*tens* of thousands, maybe millions. Some books were great works of art, their spines jeweled, their leather covers engraved with landscapes. Some books had jeweled covers of silver and gold, others covers of olive wood engraved with animals. Other books were mere bundles of parchment tied together with string. Some were great codices, three feet tall; other books were so small Madori could have hid them in her pocket.

She walked around in wonder, her smile growing, her head tilted back to take it all in.

"Books," she whispered. Portals to other worlds. Keepers of secrets. Chests of wisdom. Madori had seen the stars of the night, the white towers of Kingswall, and the pagodas of Qaelin, but to her books were the greatest wonders in Moth. They were more than objects; they were magic. Simple pages, that was all—pages with ink—and yet each contained a life, an entire world, a wisdom from beyond the ages.

As she walked here between the shelves, suddenly her troubles outside—Lari's aggression, Atratus's hatred, her troubles with this or that spell—seemed trivial. Here she felt safe, a star floating in a sky of light.

She pulled down a great, heavy book as long as her arm; inside she found ancient drawings of healing herbs. She spent a while reading an ancient codex with a red leather cover—a bestiary detailing all the animals of the world, from the humble shrew to the mighty elephant. For an hour, she read stories of adventure, the old heroes of Riyona battling sea serpents, cyclops, and dragons. She read a small book of ancient poetry—words two thousand years old—and shed tears for a pair of lovers whose song echoed through the ages.

The others have a home, Madori thought. Neekeya had the swamps of Daenor, Tam was from a great city of white towers, and Jitomi was from an island in the night. Madori caressed a pile of books on the table before her. *This is my home—anywhere among books. My home is the world of words.*

When she finally stepped outside the library and stood under the sky, she inhaled deeply and smiled. A new strength filled her, a tranquility like the sea after a storm. Whenever troubled, she knew she could return to this place, to her anchor.

"Madori!" The voice rose ahead, and Neekeya came racing toward her, panting. "Madori, where have you been? I've been looking all over for you. Professor Yovan said we have a test tomorrow, and you're the only one who understands healing magic." She grabbed Madori's hand and tugged her. "Come on! Back to our chamber. Tam cut his finger *on purpose* and tried to heal himself, but he can't, and Jitomi is laughing so hard I think he'll die. Quickly!"

Madori allowed herself to be dragged away. She looked back once, saw the library dome gleaming in the sunlight, and smiled silently.

* * * * *

The bells had rung, the turn was over, and most students and professors slept in their chambers, but Neekeya would not leave the workshop, not until she found a hint of magic.

"What about this one?" she said, placing her pewter mug upon the table. "It's a magical mug. My father said that you can drink and drink from it forever, and it'll never be empty. I tried it, and it doesn't work for me, but I think we just need to remove a little hex clinging to it, and—"

"Neekeya, please," said Professor Rushavel, his brow creased with weariness. His orange mutton chops, normally bristly like the cheeks of an orangutan, drooped like empty wine skins. "The turn is over. Return to your chamber to sleep, child. You must be weary."

Neekeya shook her head vehemently, her hair swaying and her necklace of crocodile teeth chinking. "I'm not! I'm wide awake! What about this one?" She took out a smooth river stone and placed it on the table. "This one is definitely magic. My father says if you add it to a pot of boiling water, the water will magically turn into soup. It sort of works for me, but I have to always add potatoes and carrots and leeks, so I think if you can just test it maybe, you know, with a spell to detect magic, we can—" She blinked and nudged the old man. "Professor Rushavel, wake up!"

The professor's eyes had closed, and he almost slipped off his seat. He woke with a snort and blinked a few times. His red, bulbous nose twitched as he sucked in air. "Yes, yes." He cleared his throat. "Perhaps next turn, child. Perhaps?"

Neekeya groaned so loudly it blew back a lock of her hair. She looked around her at the workshop. So many magical artifacts! They covered the shelves, the tables, even many of the chairs: figurines of animals that moved at the corner of your eye; horns that played any tune you just thought of; seashells that sounded like the sea, complete with seagull cries and the songs of sailors; model ships in bottles whose sails billowed and oars stroked; and a thousand others. Professor Rushavel himself had made many of these items. How could it be that none of Neekeya's own artifacts—and she had brought dozens from Daenor—wouldn't work?

"But my father told me these artifacts are magic," Neekeya said. "You have to help me fix them. I— Professor Rushavel?" She nudged him again. "Professor!"

But the old man was sound asleep, his cheek resting against his fist. His mutton chops rose and fell with every breath. When Neekeya nudged him, he only slumped down onto the table, his lips fluttering as he snored.

She sighed.

After a few more attempts, she gave up on waking the old man, wishing she had brought her magical snuffbox from Daenor, the one that could rouse a man from any sleep of weariness or wounds. She stuffed her artifacts—the mug, the stone, the ring of power, and two dozen others—back into her pack. With a sigh, she left the workshop.

She wandered across the university grounds, moving down columned galleries, along grassy courtyards, and through gardens full of statues and fountains. The halls and towers of the university rose all around, their bricks golden in the sunlight, their steeples so high Neekeya felt dizzy to look upon them. The library loomed to her right, a great dome rising into the sky. The first autumn leaves were scuttling along the grass and porticoes of Teel. With the hour so late, most of Teel University was deserted, the professors and students sound asleep. Only birds, squirrels, and an occasional lizard kept Neekeya company as she walked through the sunlit grounds, for which she was thankful. Animals were her friends, better than most humans here at Teel.

She sighed. "I'm like an animal myself to most of them," she whispered, and tears stung her eyes. Nobody outside her quartet ever spoke to her. Whenever Neekeya moved through a busy crowd—at the dining hall, in the cloister, or even the library— students moved aside, pointing, whispering, even laughing.

Neekeya paused by a pool of clear water in a garden. She knelt beside a statue of a winged cat, gazing into the pool.

"Who am I?" she whispered, looking at her reflection. "Who am I to them?"

She saw the same girl she had always been, a girl she had been proud to be. Her skin rich brown, her eyes large and black, her lips prone to smile, her smooth hair just long enough to fall past her chin. She looked at her crocodile tooth necklace, at the scale armor she always wore beneath her school robes, and at her magical bracelets of bronzed coffee beans.

"You are the most beautiful, talented, magical girl in the world," her father would tell her, muss her hair, and kiss her cheek. "You make me proud, and you are a great warrior."

He was a great warrior too, a lord of Daenor, a man who commanded a great stone pyramid rising from the swamps, wisely ruling over many people. He loved her dearly, and once Neekeya had loved herself too, but now tears streamed down her cheeks.

The memories of home—of her last turn there—pounded through her. She had walked through the swamps, leaping from stone to stone, a feral thing, hunting frogs with her long, silver-tipped spear. She had spent hours in the wilderness, needing to hunt, to run, to sweat, to drain herself of her nervousness, of her fear of leaving home. It had been a turn of fear.

"But I will face my fear," she had whispered that turn in the swamps. "I will learn magic—real magic."

The swamp waters gurgled around her, the frogs trilled, and the mangroves swayed in the breeze. All her life, her father had spoken to her of magic, gifting her his many artifacts, telling her tales of magical shields to block the fists of giants, cricket choirs that could sing so beautifully grown men would weep, and islands that floated through the sky.

"I'm going to study magic too," she told her father that turn. "At the great school they call Teel. I'm seventeen now, Father, and I must go. I must become not only a warrior but a sorceress."

They stood in their great hall, the mossy stone pyramid that rose from the swamplands, so tall only the bravest bird could reach its peak. From the throne room, Neekeya could stare out the windows at an endless land, green and lush and fluttering with birds, that rolled into the misty horizons. When she returned her eyes to her father, she saw a kindly man, his head bald, his eyes warm. Necklaces of gilded cocoa beads hung across his bare chest, and a sword hung from his side, its silver hilt shaped as a crocodile's claw.

"My daughter," he said to her, eyes dampening. "The outside world is cruel and dangerous. I fought in the War of Day and Night years ago. I saw not only the horrors of the night but the horrors of the day. We are Daenorians. We are outcasts even among the sunlit kingdoms. They mock our ways. They call us the backwater of Timandra." He rose from his wooden throne, stepped toward her, and held her hands. "Please, child, stay with me here. Daenor is lush, warm, a place of family, of friendship, of righteousness. Do not step out into the cold, cruel world where greed and hatred fill the hearts of nations."

She squeezed his hands. "But I would learn of these things! How can I fight for righteousness without knowing of cruelty? How can I be a just ruler some day, a lady of this pyramid, if I haven't seen injustice? How can I surround myself with your gifts, your artifacts of magic, when I don't have the power to use them?"

He could say no more; his voice choked. The tall warrior, stronger than any man in Daenor, pulled her into his gentle embrace and kissed her head.

"Goodbye, my daughter. Goodbye. I will miss you."

Neekeya sniffed, her tears falling. That had been many turns ago, and here she knelt in Teel University, this land that was so strange to her. This land where people wore cotton robes, not beads and iron and leather. This land where people whispered cruel secrets, taunted one another, mocked anyone who was different. Neekeya had never feared the swamplands' crocodiles or warriors who drank and cursed too much; she had always been able to fight them, but how could she fight in a place like this? She could survive in the wilderness, but how could she survive within the walls of Teel?

"I miss home," she whispered to her reflection in the pool, and her lips shook. "I miss you, Father."

Laughter rolled behind her.

A voice rose in exaggerated falsetto. "I miss you, Father."

Neekeya leaped to her feet, spun around, and saw them there.

She growled.

Sunlit Purity—Lari's quartet.

"Well, look at what we have here," Lari said, hands on her hips. "The swamp monster."

Neekeya balled her hands into fists. The four were everything she was not—full-blooded Magerians, their hair blond, their skin pale, their eyes blue, their clothes woven of meticulous cotton, their accents perfect and highborn. Neekeya was the daughter of a great lord, but to them she was a barbarian, uncouth and no better than an animal.

She began to walk away from the pool, but they moved forward, blocking her passage. Lari stood before her, smiling crookedly. The twins—Fae and and Kae—blocked her left side, while tall Derin stood to her right.

"Get out of my way," Neekeya said.

Lari laughed. "Or what? Will you curse us with one of your 'magical amulets?'" She spoke those last two words in a mockery of a toddler's voice. "Will you hex us with a dead rat, attack us with an enchanted stick, or maybe kick us with a magical boot?" Lari's smile turned into a sneer. "You have no magic, Neekeya. You never did. You never will. You are nothing but a swamp monster and you need to go home."

Neekeya tried to shove Lari aside, but the girl stepped back, laughing, and slapped Neekeya's cheek.

"Oh, she's going to cry!" said one of the twins and laughed.

Lari too laughed. "Awful! I'm going to have to scrub my hand now. It already smells like the swamp."

Neekeya growled and tried to shove past them again, but they blocked her way. She tossed a punch but Lari dodged the blow, and one of the twins sneaked behind Neekeya and shoved her forward.

"I'm warning you, Lari," Neekeya said, raising her fists. "I used to wrestle crocodiles in my spare time, and if you don't step back now, I won't just slap you. I'm going to bash your skull against the cobblestones."

They only laughed harder.

"Crocodiles!" said Derin, his chest shaking with laughter. "I can just imagine her wrestling those creatures in a pit of mud."

"Just like in the story I drew," Lari said. She reached into her pack and pulled out a scroll. She unrolled it and held out the parchment.

Neekeya froze and her heart seemed to freeze too. Her eyes stung. Upon the scroll appeared a drawing of her—a cruel cartoon, displaying her not as a lord's daughter but as a savage barely better than an animal. Words appeared below the text: "The Story of Neekeya, the Half-Crocodile Swamp Monster." Below the title appeared a story; Neekeya only read enough to realize it portrayed her as a beast whose father was a crocodile.

Neekeya shouted hoarsely, tears in her eyes, and tried to snatch the parchment, but Lari pulled the scroll back.

"Calm down, savage!" Lari said. "We copied this scroll fifty times. It's all over the university already. Every first year quartet has a copy."

Neekeya didn't know if to weep or scream, and for a moment, she only froze.

Father was right, she thought. *Father warned me. I should have stayed home. I can't survive here. I can't face such cruelty.*

She closed her eyes. She wanted to run—across the gardens, outside the walls, all the way home to Daenor far on the western edge of the world. She was a joke here, nothing but a joke.

"Lari!" rose a voice from across the gardens. "Lari Serin! I heard you say you like magic?"

Neekeya's eyes snapped open and she gasped.

Tam stood under the stone archway that led into the gardens. Autumn leaves clung to his brown hair and green robes. He smiled, eyes bright, and thrust his hands forward.

With a chorus of shrieks, a dozen bats filled Lari's hair.

The young Magerian screamed.

"Get them off!" she cried. "Derin! Twins!"

But Tam pointed again, and suddenly bats were clinging to the others' hair too. They all shouted and ran, fleeing the gardens, tugging the bats off one by one.

Tam watched them leave and sadly shook his head. "They're only bats. I think they're cute." He pointed up at an oak. "They live in that tree. I only had to choose them as my material and move them a few feet downward."

Neekeya wanted to run to her friend, to thank him, to embrace him, but she only stood, still frozen like a damn fool. And her damn tears still flowed.

I'm acting like a baby, she thought. *I'm a warrior. I'm the daughter of a lord. I—*

She covered her eyes, her body shook, and her tears kept flowing.

Warm arms enveloped her, for for an instant Neekeya struggled, afraid, sure that it was Lari returned to torment her. But when fingers stroked her hair, she opened her eyes and saw that it was Tam who held her.

"It's all right," he said softly. "They're gone."

Her tears wet his shoulder, and her body pressed against him. "I can't do this, Tam. I don't belong here."

"None of us do." He touched her cheek, taking one of her tears onto his finger. "Not Jitomi, not Madori, not me. We're all outcasts at Teel but we have to stick together."

She looked away. "Jitomi? He has other Elorians here. Madori? She's half-Elorian herself; she often speaks to Jitomi of their home, a home they remember together. And you, Tam?" She looked at him. "You fit in here. You look like everyone else and you talk like everyone and—"

"And I'm not like everyone," he said, stiffening. "I'm from Arden. I'm the *Prince* of Arden. Maybe that's not a land of swamps and pyramids and crocodiles, and maybe like Mageria it's a fragment of the old Riyonan Empire, but it's still a different country . . . a country I miss." His voice softened and he sighed. "I'm sorry. You're right. Maybe I don't know how you feel. But I'm here for you. We all are."

She nodded. Her voice was choked; she could barely speak louder than a whisper. "I know." She smiled tremulously and held his hand. "Thank you, Tam. Our quartet means everything to me." She trembled and smiled through her tears. "Well, our quartet and those cute little bats."

He laughed softly, and she touched his cheek, and she didn't know how it happened, but somehow he was kissing her. Their laughter died, and as he held her close, it felt like she was melting into his kiss. His one hand stroked her hair, and the other held the small of her back. They kissed for what seemed like ages, desperate for each other, scared of letting go, wanting to forever stay like this in these gardens, together, one, whole, no longer afraid but warm and full of tingling joy. She had never kissed a boy before but it felt right, it felt natural, it felt like the best thing in the world.

They walked back to their chamber in silence, sneaking glances at each other, then lowering their eyes—a little afraid, a little embarrassed, a little joyous.

CHAPTER SIXTEEN
THE HOUNDS OF SUNMOTTE

Lord Tirus Serin—The Light of Radian, Duke of Sunmotte Citadel, Warden of Hornsford Bridge, and Lord Protector of Mageria—stood upon the bridge and watched the two Ardishmen breach for air.

At his side, Lord Imril—a wiry baron with a gaunt face and beaked nose—raised his crossbow, aiming it at Torin's head.

"Got him," he said, a hint of hunger and delight twisting his thin lips. He pulled the trigger.

Serin nudged the crossbow aside, and the quarrel skimmed over Torin's head, vanishing harmlessly into the water. Sir Imril turned toward him, and for an instant irritation filled the man's pale blue eyes. The show of defiance vanished quickly, however, replaced by the servility Serin demanded from all in his order.

"My lord?" Imril said.

"Let them be," Serin replied calmly. He waved down his other crossbowmen's weapons. "Let them swim."

His men lowered their crossbows as one, moving in perfect unison. Down in the water, Torin and Cam were still swimming to the Ardish riverbank, unaware that Serin had just spared their lives—for a while at least.

"But, my lord," said Imril and cleared his throat. The ratty nobleman was high ranking enough to speak while the others dared not. "The Shepherd King is a friend of the darkness. Sir Greenmoat is wed to one of the nightcrawlers. Why spare the lives of these scum?"

Serin turned slowly to stare at the shorter, gaunter man. Lord Imril's pencil mustache quivered just the slightest; to challenge Lord Serin himself, the Light of Radian, was an offense most men would be tortured for.

"You disagree with your lord?" Serin said softly, letting a hint of a smile tingle his lips. "Perhaps you think the Light of Radian is fallible?"

"No, my lord!" said Imril, that mustache twitching. He slammed his fist against his chest in salute. "I worship the Light of Radian. I only—"

"Tell me, Lord Imril." Serin placed a hand on the baron's shoulder. "Do you think I do not know who those two vermin are?"

"I only—" Sweat trickled down Imril's face.

"And tell me, Lord Imril, do you know the punishment for challenging the Lord of Light?"

Imril's throat bobbed as he gulped, and a glob of sweat ran down his cheek. "I— Yes, my lord."

"Describe it to me," Serin said, smiling, his voice pleasant. He leaned closer, his grip tightening on the man's shoulder. "In loving detail."

Lord Imril blinked and paled. He spoke hoarsely. "You whip them. You disembowel them. Then you tie them to four horses and send each running in another direction."

Serin nodded, his smile breaking into grin. "Excellent! And quite accurate." He laughed. "But of course, you are my loyal baron. You are far too high ranking for such lowly punishment. You feel free to speak your mind to me. I understand. I will show you mercy."

Imril laughed nervously and blinked sweat out of his eyes. "Thank you, my lord. I—"

He sputtered as Serin's dagger drove into his eye.

"This is my mercy," Serin said, twisting the blade inside the man's skull. "I give you a painless death. Your wife and children will enjoy the same mercy."

He pulled the blade free. Imril gave a last gasp, then collapsed upon the bridge.

"Remove his armor!" Serin barked at his soldiers. "Take his sword too. Then kick the body into the water; let the fish eat."

Upon the eastern bank, Greenmoat and the king were now climbing onto the Ardish bank, safely back in their homeland, that pathetic kingdom of magicless imbeciles.

Go back to your capital, Serin thought, watching them with a thin smile. *Tell your generals what you saw here. Tell them of the armies in my fields, of my mighty fortress, of the wrath that surely will descend upon you.* He licked his lips. *Tell them . . . and be afraid.*

The soldiers were unstrapping Imril's armor. Leaving them to their task, Serin mounted his horse and rode back west to the Magerian bank.

The world rose and fell as he galloped, and Serin smiled, still savoring the sweetness of the kill. It was not a good turn without at least one good kill. Ahead rose his fortress, large as a mountain, a city for an army, this army that would soon bring the light and truth of Radianism to the world.

He rode through the field, his banner raised high. Soldiers stood at attention at his sides, creating a path between them. Serin rode through this sea of steel. Men pounded their fists against their chests, chanting for their cause.

"Radian rises! Radian rises!"

When he reached his fortress, his guards pulled down the drawbridge, then saluted as Serin rode past them and through the gates. Past the walls, a vast courtyard awaited him, full of more soldiers. In great pits dug into the earth, collared slaves toiled, their backs lashed, their ankles chained. They were raising siege machines—catapults to hurl boulders, trebuchets to fire flaming barrels, and battering rams to swing on chains. In one pit, deeper than the rest, men stirred mixtures in great pots, creating the secret, flammable powder stolen from the night. The Elorians were weak, maggoty creatures, but they had invented cannons of fire, and Serin licked his lips hungrily to imagine turning their own weapon upon them.

"Greenmoat, you fool," he whispered as he rode between the pits. "Do you think I care a wit or jot for Arden, that cesspool you call a kingdom? Arden will be a wasteland when I'm done with it. Your only worth to me is the land to your east. You are a road to the night, nothing more, Greenmoat." He clenched his fist. "Your bones will pave that road."

Past the slave pits, he reached a second layer of walls, these ones even taller. A dozen towers rose along them like teeth from a stone jaw, topped with archers. The banners of Radianism draped the walls, displaying the triumph of the sun over the moon, the triumph of Timandrian blood—pure and hot and red—over the Elorian vermin, the subhuman creatures who spawned in the shadows. He rode through more gates here, across another courtyard, and toward his keep—the center of his domain. The building rose taller than any palace in Timandra, even taller than the palace of Serin's king in the south. Its towers scraped the sky, blades of stone. The King of Mageria perhaps wore the crown, but he—Lord Tirus Serin—ruled from the kingdom's greatest castle, commanding the greatest armies in all Mageria, perhaps all the world.

He dismounted his horse outside the gates of his hall, letting his stable boys lead the beast away. Servants bowed and guards stood at attention as he walked forth. He walked under an archway and entered his throne room—a vast hall lined with red columns, their gilded capitals shaped as sunbursts. A mosaic spread across the floor, depicting a battle of thousands, the soldiers of sunlight slaying the demons of the night. The mosaic was designed so that, as Serin walked toward his throne, his boots spared the Timandrian soldiers but stomped upon the faces of the twisted Elorians. He climbed the stairs onto his dais and sat down upon the throne, his banners hanging around him, framing him with their might. His soldiers stood across the hall, spears in hands, armor bright.

Serin clutched the armrests, leaned forward, and barked, "Bring them in!"

He had been waiting for this moment all turn, and he sucked in breath with delight and hunger as his guards stepped forward, dragging the chained prisoners.

Truly, these Elorians were pathetic beings, he thought, his nostrils flaring as he smelled their blood.

"Look at them!" Serin said, pointing at the chained wretches. "They are worms. They are subhuman."

The Elorians could barely stand; the guards had to hold them upright. Whips had torn into their flesh, and bruises surrounded their freakish, oversized eyes. They reminded Serin of naked moles. He had caught these creatures—seven in total—traveling into Mageria to peddle their silk.

"We will cleanse Timandra of their filth!" Serin cried, rising to his feet. "The lands of sunlight will be purified of shadows. We will allow no creatures of darkness to crawl upon our land."

The Elorians tried to beg in their language. One fell to his knees, bowing. Serin sneered.

Pathetic, he thought. *Groveling insects.*

Across the hall, the guards laughed. One soldier lashed a whip, knocking the bowing Elorian down, incurring more laughter.

Serin too laughed. "Bring in the dogs!" he shouted, voice echoing across the hall. "They are hungry. Let my pets feed!"

Growls sounded followed by mad barks. Guards stepped forth, leading chained dogs larger than men, creatures twisted and augmented with dark magic. The beasts howled, smelling the blood, hungry for meat. At a nod from Serin, the guards released the animals.

The Elorians yowled in fear. Some tried to escape only for the dogs to tear them down. Blood splattered the mosaic.

"Fantastic," Serin whispered, leaning forward in his seat, his eyes wide. "I wish you were here to see this, Lari."

As the dogs fed and guards cheered, Serin imagined bringing the mongrel—that little wretch Madori—here for a show. His pets would enjoy her young, supple, sweet flesh.

"Soon, Madori," Serin whispered. "Soon it will be your blood spilling across my hall."

The dogs fed and Serin grinned, inhaled deeply, and licked his lips.

CHAPTER SEVENTEEN
AUTUMN MOON

They sat in their chamber, sheets hanging over the windows, cloaking them in shadows.

"Are you ready?" Madori whispered.

The others nodded, huddling with her. They had pushed their beds back against the wall and sat upon the rug. Madori had prepared the scrolls, drawing Qaelish runes upon them—prayers to Xen Qae, father of her nation. The parchments now hung upon the walls. Jitomi had constructed the lanterns, stretching paper over thin wooden frames. They now floated, candles glowing within, tethered to the bedposts. Here in their little bedchamber, in the heart of a sunlit university, they had created a bit of home, an enclave of the night.

"It's beautiful," Neekeya whispered. She reached over and clutched Tam's hand. "Isn't it, Tam?"

He nodded. "It makes me want to visit Eloria."

"We *are* visiting Eloria now," Neekeya said and smiled.

Madori looked at the pair, and a strange chill filled her. She had seen the two hold hands, share hidden glances, and whisper many times these past few turns. The prince and the swamp dweller were growing close, and looking at them now, holding hands and smiling at each other, Madori felt something cold inside her. Was it jealousy? Did she herself want to hold hands with Tam, her childhood friend? Or did she feel outcast again— the half-Elorian, not good enough for the two children of sunlight?

Jitomi spoke at her side, interrupting her thoughts. "We're ready, Madori."

She turned toward him. He stared at her, his blue eyes solemn—large, luminous eyes, eyes like hers, eyes for seeing in the darkness of the night. Jitomi was from Ilar, a nation in the south of Eloria, far from Qaelin, the great empire of darkness where Madori's mother had been born. Their cultures were different— their two nations had fought many wars in the darkness—and yet here in the daylight, he was the closest thing she had to a kinsman, to somebody who understood the importance of darkness, the loneliness here deep in sunlit lands.

She nodded. "I've never done this magic before, but . . . I'll try." She took a deep breath and looked at her friends, one by one. "It's the Autumn Equinox. On this turn thousands of years ago, the great teacher Xen Qae arrived on the shore of the Elorian mainland, and there he met his wife, a young fisherman's daughter named Madori. I am named after her. Together they founded the Qaelish nation whose children spread across the night. This turn all Qaelish people celebrate their love."

She smiled softly, remembering the stories her mother would tell her of Xen Qae, the wise philosopher with the long beard, and his wife, a beautiful woman with hair like spilling streams of moonlight. As Madori sat here in the shadows, she felt almost like a full Elorian, a true daughter of darkness. When she spoke again, she found that even her voice changed, speaking with just a hint of a Qaelish accent—the accent her mother spoke with.

"On the Autumn Equinox, we pray to the moon, for we believe that its light blessed our great father and mother that turn. It is a time for moonlight."

At her side, Jitomi spoke softly. "I am from Ilar, an island nation south of the Elorian mainland, but we too celebrate the Autumn Equinox. We do not know the teachings of Xen Qae, but for thousands of years our people have danced under this moonlight. We call this autumn moon the *Domai Jatey*, the Half Light, a milestone between the turn of the seasons. It is blessed, a light of peace when our warriors may rest and pray."

Madori took a deep breath and closed her eyes. "Let us pray to the moon."

She looked at the soft light from the floating lanterns. It glowed a pale silver through the paper frames. A smile touched her lips as she chose the light, as she claimed it, and she changed it. She pulled wisps like glowing silk from the lanterns, weaving them together in the center of the room, a ball of twine woven from strands of candlelight. The others gasped but Madori only smiled silently, pulling the light more tightly together, raising the glowing ball to let it float above them. It pulsed softly under the ceiling, the size of an orange, a makeshift moon.

"It's beautiful," Neekeya whispered. "I've seen the moon from the daylight before. It's just a wisp from here like dust in a sunbeam. Is this how the moon looks in the night?"

Madori shook her head. "The true moon in the night is many times brighter, many times more beautiful. But this is the limit of my magic. Perhaps no magic can capture the true moonlight."

A low humming rose, and at first Madori thought it was the moonlight emitting the sound. Then she realized it was Jitomi singing, his voice low, a hum that soon morphed into words. Madori's eyes watered for she knew that tune. It was the song "The Journey Home," a song her mother used to sing, a song known across the lands of night.

Her tears fell and she clasped Jitomi's hand, and she joined her voice to his. She had never sung with anyone but her mother, and at first her cheeks burned with embarrassment, but then she closed her eyes and let the music claim her. In her mind, she was back in Oshy, the village in the night, the place where she had spent so many summers in her childhood. She was singing there again under the true moon. "The Journey Home" had always been the song of her childhood, but now she understood its true meaning. It was a song of being in distant lands, of dreaming of the moonlight, of taking a long path back into darkness.

My journey home will be long, she thought as she sang. *It will be years before I see the night again. And perhaps the night is not my true home, for I am half of daylight. And perhaps I have no true home. But here, now, holding Jitmoi's hand and singing our old songs, let the darkness be like a home to me. Let me sing to the moon and dream of the night.*

Their song ended, and she leaned against Jitomi, and he placed an arm around her and kissed her cheek.

Neekeya was blowing her nose into a handkerchief. "That does it, you two. That does it! When we graduate as mages, I'm visiting Eloria with you."

Madori laughed. "Only if you take me to visit Daenor too."

"Of course." Neekeya grinned. "But I'm not singing any Daenorian songs. My singing would make your ears fall off."

Madori wiped her tears away, the joke easing her mood of almost holy yearning. She smiled, hopped toward her drawer, and began pulling out Elorian foods she had taken from home and saved for this holiday: jars of chanterelle, matsutake, and milkcap mushrooms; salted bat wings; crunchy dried lanternfish; and sweet candies made from the honey of firebees, glowing little creatures that flew on the northern Qaelish coast. Soon the companions were laughing as they ate.

I miss my home in Fairwool-by-Night, Madori thought, listening to the others laugh about how Professor Yovan had stepped on his beard last turn. *And I miss my home in Oshy. My journey is still long, but maybe . . . maybe despite all the pain and fear, this is a home to me too, and this is my new family.*

Again her eyes dampened. Jitomi saw and gave her shoulder a squeeze, a small smile on his lips. She smiled back and reached for a handful of chanterelles.

"Eat," she said, handing him one. "A little taste of home."

* * * * *

They walked through the forest, hand in hand, an undercover prince and a swamp dweller, strangers in a strange land.

"Are you sure you want to do this?" Tam asked softly.

Neekeya turned to look at him. The forest canopy rustled above, casting mottles of light upon his sun-bronzed face and brown hair. His eyes gleamed in the light like amber. His face was kind, his voice soft. Neekeya couldn't help herself. She leaned toward him and kissed his lips.

"I'm sure," she whispered. "I have to do this. I have to let go. I have to become a new person."

She hefted her pack across her shoulders. Its contents jingled, a hundred artifacts her father had given her, claiming them to be magic—little figurines, rings, coins, seashells, and sundry other items. Neekeya had been collecting them since her childhood, sure that she owned a treasure, a magical horde worth more than a palace.

Now—a grown woman, a mage in training—she understood.

They're trinkets. Her eyes stung. *They're worth less than a single silver coin.*

"I've been a fool." Her eyes stung. "I believed my father's stories. I wanted to believe them. I wanted to think I'm powerful, magical, an owner of great artifacts." She wiped her eyes. "They were foolish stories told to a foolish girl. We'll find a place here, a peaceful place under a tree. We'll bury them." She nodded. "I've come to Teel to learn magic—and I will. Real magic. To do that, I must let go of the past."

He stroked her hair and kissed her cheek.

They kept walking, moving between elms, birches, and oaks. Neekeya wanted to walk farther; she could still see Teel's towers behind her. She needed a secret place, a place Lari and the other students would never reach. Chickadees and robins sang in the trees, crickets chirped, and pollen floated. The autumn air was cool, the leaves red and orange and golden. It was a beautiful forest, a forest for her secrets.

"This looks a lot like the wilderness of Arden," Tam said, looking around. "My brother and I used to spend many turns hunting in the woods. Just the two of us, a couple bows, and a couple hounds. We'd drive our mother crazy. She'd insist on sending guards, horses, knights in armor, a whole cavalcade to hunt with us, but where's the fun in that? So Omry and I would sneak out alone to a place like this, spend a turn or two away from the palace, and just be boys. Not princes. Not rulers. Just two regular people." He inhaled deeply, watching a cardinal flit from branch to branch. "We'd come home covered in scratches and bruises, our faces muddy, our hair a mess, our boots all torn up. Most times we wouldn't even catch any game. Mother would be furious, railing about how we ruined our priceless outfits, but Father always laughed. He was a commoner once, did you know?"

Neekeya smiled and slipped her hand into his. "I would go hunting too—just me alone. I'd hop from log to boulder in the jungle, a spear in my hand, hunting frogs. I'd collect whole baskets of them, bring them back home to our pyramid, and we'd feast on fried frog legs." She looked around her. "Daenor looks nothing like this. The trees there are thrice as high, and you can barely see the ground; it's mostly water. The birds there are larger and very colorful, and great crocodiles roam around everywhere." She touched her tooth necklace. "Each one of these teeth is from a beast I battled. We'd eat them too, you know."

He wrinkled his nose. "Crocodile meat? Frog legs? I'd rather eat chicken and deer."

She shrugged. "One's as good as the other." She mussed his hair. "You speak so fondly of your home. Why did you come here? To Teel University? You're a prince! A prince of a mighty kingdom. I know that all students at Teel are highborn, their parents wealthy enough to pay the tuition, but princes? That's unique even here."

He blew out his breath thoughtfully. "I told you that in the forest, my twin brother and I were only two boys. But whenever we returned to our palace, we were different." He kicked a pine cone. "Omry is ten minutes older than I am—that's it, only a moment, the length of a song or two. That means he's the heir to Arden. He was ten minutes earlier than me . . . and now worth ten times more." Tam passed a hand through his hair. "I love my twin dearly, more than anything. I always will. But I had to find my own path, my own power. I couldn't watch us grow older together, him a great heir, myself always worth less. When Madori told me she'd try out for Teel, I knew that was my path too. To become a mage. To find my own strength. To feel . . ." He looked at Neekeya, brow furrowed. ". . . to finally feel equal to my twin."

Neekeya grinned. "Oh, you silly boy!" She tugged him toward her and kissed him again—this kiss longer and deeper— and when it ended, she tapped his nose. "I'm trying to keep walking here, and you keep making me kiss you." She squeezed him closer to her. "Your brother might become a king, Tam, but you'll be a great mage." She looked around her and smiled. "I think this is a good place."

A rivulet gurgled between alders, full of smooth, parti-colored stones and orange fish. Twisting roots, fallen logs, and carpets of autumn leaves covered the forest floor. A hole in the canopy let in a ray of light, gleaming with pollen. Boulders rose ahead, moss nearly hiding the ancient runes of old Riyonans, a people who had faded from the world many years ago. It was a secret place, Neekeya thought, a beautiful place. A place for hiding her childhood.

She knelt by an oak and began to dig. Tam helped her, and they worked in silence. When the hole was a couple feet deep, Neekeya upended her pack. Her trinkets spilled into the hole— pewter figurines, seashells, rare coins, spoons, scrolls, and more.

Her eyes stung. "Thank you, Papa," she whispered. "Thank you for letting a little girl believe in something secret, something magical. I love you. But now I seek true magic. Now I leave my childhood here for safekeeping."

She wiped her eyes and began to shove soil onto the items.

"Neekeya . . ." Tam spoke softly. "Neekeya, wait."

She shook her head. "No. I have to do this. This is right. I—"

"Neekeya, look! The seashell. It's glowing."

She tilted her head and squinted down into the hole. Indeed, the little shell—no larger than a coin—was glowing a soft blue. When she lifted it, the glow faded.

"A trick of sunlight," she said, yet when she placed the shell back down in the hole, it glowed again.

Tam scrunched his lips, reached into the hole, and rummaged in the soil. He smiled and pulled out a truffle. "Well, I do think you have something here, Neekeya." He held the seashell in one hand, the truffle in the other. When he brought them near, the shell glowed brighter. When he separated them, the glow faded. "A magical artifact."

Neekeya gasped and snatched the shell from him. She tested it again and fresh tears budded in her eyes. "It's true! My father was speaking truth. It's magic. It's a real artifact. It's . . . not very useful, is it?" She laughed through her tears. "It's a truffle finder. Hardly a great artifact."

Tam grinned. "It's very important. It means your father was right, that you spent your childhood surrounded by magic. Or at least, that one of these items is magic. That means there's hope for the other items too." He lifted a few of the figurines and examined them. "Professor Rushavel never found anything magical about them, but this might just be swamp magic, a different sort." He looked at Neekeya and his face grew solemn. "I think you should keep these things."

She nodded. "We'll never lack for truffles again."

He rolled his eyes. "You'll never lack for *wonder* again. You'll never see your childhood as a lie." He began to place the items back in her pack. "Take these back, Neekeya. Keep them. They're important."

As they walked back through the forest, Neekeya grinned. "You know, some of these items might be *really* important, like . . . a magical shoelace un-knotter."

He nodded. "Or a magical nose hair plucker."

She grimaced. "Maybe something more pleasant—a magical cup that removes the skin off your milk."

"That's some powerful magic there. Maybe even some magical, wooden, Lari-biting teeth? A pair that would chase her around, biting her bottom?"

Neekeya laughed. "Now that would be a mightier artifact than even those Rushavel makes." She sighed and leaned against him as they walked. They stepped back into the university, carrying with them a little magic.

CHAPTER EIGHTEEN
WINTER SNOW

The bells rang and the seasons turned, and the first snow of winter fell upon Teel University, coating the gardens, walls, and roofs with white blankets. When Madori walked outside, the first to rise, she smiled for beneath her feet she saw a field of stars, a memory of the glistening sky of the night.

She smiled not only for the snow but because she was heading toward her favorite class, Magical History. As much as Madori enjoyed fostering her growing powers, she enjoyed learning about the wizards of old: how the wise mage Sheltan traveled to the distant isle of Orida and tamed the cyclops; how the Ten Rogue Mages holed up in the mountains for a hundred years before the Crystal Alliance hunted them down; and even tales of the war against Eloria where mages shattered the walls of Yintao but perished against the Eternal Palace.

It helped that Elina Maleen taught the class, the youngest professor at Teel; Madori had dearly loved the woman since Maleen had first quizzed her at the trials. The rest of Madori's Motley found Magical History to be a bore; Neekeya was taking Artifacts this morning while Tam and Jitomi were both at Magical Transformations. As much as she loved her friends, Madori savored this time away from them. It was a time to dream.

This turn we will learn the story of the ancient Elorian mages, she thought. She had been waiting for months for this lesson, for once the night had been full of magic now lost. Madori hoped that some turn she could return to Eloria with the lost art and teach magic again to the children of the night.

She walked to the back of the university, past the library and Agrotis Tower. She climbed a cobbled path, moving up a hillside dotted with snowy trees, their branches encased in ice. Cardinals and chickadees flitted between the birdhouses Professor Yovan had hung here, and a rabbit darted ahead, leaving prints in the snow. The old stone building rose between several maple trees, frost upon its bricks. Once a mill, the little building had become a classroom three hundred years ago when Teel expanded outside the cloister, its original complex. Now this was Madori's favorite classroom. Her smile widening, she opened the door and stepped inside . . . and her smile faded.

The other students were already in their seats—thankfully none of them Radians, but all of them Timandrians. But it was not Professor Maleen who stood at the podium as always, her wild brown hair falling in a great mane, her blind eyes staring up in wonder as if at living scenes of history. Instead, hunched over a book and wrapped in black robes, it was Professor Atratus.

The vulture-like man spun toward the door and hissed at Madori. She was so shocked she took a step back into the snow.

Atratus sneered and checked his pocket watch. "Late as usual. A lack of punctuality is typical of mongrels." He snorted. "Shocked to see me, half-breed? Your precious Maleen has taken ill, and you'll find I am less tolerant of tardiness. You will report to my office after class for three strikes from my ruler. Take your seat now lest I increase the count to thirty!"

Madori winced and rubbed her palm, already feeling the punishment; it seemed that a turn couldn't go by without him striking her. Ignoring the many eyes following her, she rushed to her seat and sat down.

Professor Atratus leaned over his podium, eyes blazing, and slammed his book shut with a shower of dust. "It says here," he said, a snarl twisting his voice, "that I am to teach you about ancient Elorian magic." He barked a laugh. "Elorians know only cheap tricks to fool their own feeble-minded kind. This class I will teach you something far more valuable about Elorians." He licked his lips. "I will teach you the history of their race and prove to you its inferiority."

Madori's heart sank. She wished she had fled the classroom the instant she had seen him. She wanted to bolt up now, to race to the door, but fear kept her frozen in her seat.

"Mongrel!" Atratus barked, pointing at her. "Stand. Come. To me, dog."

She could not move. She simply stared, mouth hanging open.

"Ten lashes from my ruler!" he shouted. "Stand! To me!"

Reluctantly, Madori rose to her feet. Before she could take a step, his magic shot out like grapples. The smoky ropes wrapped around her, tugging her toward him. More magic slammed against her mouth, stifling her scream. Across the classroom, students gasped, and one boy leaped to his feet, but glares from Atratus silenced them.

Madori struggled in the magic, trying to rip it off, to claim and change the bonds, but his magic was too strong. He pulled back his arms, moving her like a marionette, until he placed her beside him. She stood facing the class, trussed up like an animal awaiting slaughter. The students stared with wide eyes, faces pale.

"Behold!" said Professor Atratus. "Behold the menace of Eloria. Behold the wretched product of the nightcrawlers' invasion of our lands. Before you you see the corruption of our blood, the mingling of poison with purity. A mongrel! A creature of sunlight tainted with the blackness of night."

Madori tried to free herself, to scream, to talk back to him, even if it earned her a thousand lashes. But only a muffled whimper passed through the smoky gag.

He tapped her head with his ruler. Tap. Tap. Tap. Every blow rang through her skull.

"Observe the smaller cranium," he said to the class. "It is barely larger than a dog's skull—the result of the Elorian infestation." He smacked her chest. "Behold the frail frame. This specimen stands barely five feet tall, weighing less than a child. The Elorian blood weakens her." He placed his fingers around her left eye, tugging and stretching as if he'd let her eyeball pop out. "Observe the freakish orbs. Imagine how much space they take up in the skull, leaving less room for the brain. Those, my friends, are eyes for seeing in the dark—for sneaking up, scuttling, and snatching Timandrian children for their feasts of human flesh."

One student, a young girl of only fifteen years, raised her hand. "But Professor Atratus! This one is only half-Elorian. Does her Timandrian half not make her worthy?"

Atratus sighed and shook his head. "Sadly, my dear child, the presence of her Timandrian blood only increases her obscenity. A pure-blooded Elorian is like a maggot, a foul creature that crawls in the muck. But a mongrel . . ." His voice trembled with rage. "A mongrel is like a maggot found inside the body of a beloved pet—more foul by far, for it has ruined something pure." He stared at Madori and covered his mouth as if about to gag. "She sickens me."

Another student raised his hand. "Professor Atratus, how can we protect ourselves from the Elorian menace?"

The professor nodded. "A good question, my boy." He tapped the pin he wore upon his lapel, showing a sun eclipsing a moon. "The Radian Order will protect us. Lari Serin leads the Teel Radian Society; I urge you all to join, receive your pins, swear allegiance to Lord Serin, and learn how to protect yourself from nightcrawlers and mongrels."

A third student, this one a skinny boy with pale cheeks, spoke next. His voice shook, but he managed to stare steadily at Atratus. "Professor, the headmistress has said that Radians are dangerous. She says . . ." He gulped. "She says that Elorians are welcome in the lands of sunlight, that—"

Professor Atratus shouted so loudly the boy started and fell back into his seat.

"Headmistress Egeria is a fool!" Spittle flew from the professor's mouth. His fists shook. "And you are a fool to believe her! Who is the headmistress? A frail old woman, coughing and trembling, her one foot in the grave. Tell me, boy, do you have any siblings?" He trudged forward, grabbed the student's collar, and twisted it. "Do you?"

The boy—his face wet with Atratus's flying saliva—nodded silently.

Atratus growled like a rabid animal. "Do you want Elorians to snatch them from their beds, to cut them open in their solstice festivals, to feed upon their organs? Or perhaps you want Elorians breeding with your siblings, producing foul, mixed-blood offspring that are lower than animals?"

The boy, pale and trembling, shook his head.

Now, Madori thought, straining. *Now, while his back is turned toward me.*

Atratus was busy chastising the boy, railing against all the evils Elorians could perform to his parents, siblings, and countrymen. With the man deep in his tirade, Madori sucked in air through her nose, focusing all her effort on claiming the magical bonds he'd placed around her. She forced herself to clear her mind from anything else—to ignore Atratus's words, to ignore her humiliation, to ignore the eyes of the other students.

Choose your material.

Claim it.

Change it.

She tried but could not, and her eyes burned. All she had learned here at Teel, all her months of practice and studying, could not save her from his shackles.

Choose. Claim. Change.

Yet she could not; his magic was too strong.

"—and the Elorians will bring their disease, the Night Plague, into our wells, our farms, our very beds!" Atratus's words were piercing Madori's consciousness, rising and fading from her awareness. "I have jars of the Night Plague in my office, and I have seen its evil, and . . ."

Madori inhaled slowly through her nostrils, letting the breath fill her throat and her lungs, letting it flow to every part of her.

Breath by breath.

Her eyes stung. It was her father's voice speaking in her mind. She saw his kind face again, his wise eyes, his proud smile.

Breath by breath, Billygoat. That's all you must do to survive.

She exhaled slowly, inhaled again, savored the calming energy, and this too was like magic, a magic that cleared her mind. Breath by breath. Healing. Soothing.

Choose.

Claim.

And she had it.

His magic snapped into place in her awareness. She understood every single particle that comprised his ropes, saw the links between them, saw the logic that bound the magic like countless rings in chain mail.

Change.

She tore the links free.

The smoke fled her mouth and she gasped.

The tendrils tore free from her wrists and arms.

"He lies!" Madori shouted, tears in her eyes. "He lies to you! He's nothing but a liar. Elorians are not monsters, but Professor Atratus might be. Reject the Radians! Don't listen to their poiso—"

She could not finish her sentence.

His magic slammed against her with the might of war hammers.

Vaguely, Madori was aware of herself flying through the air. Her back slammed against the wall with a thud, knocking the breath out of her. She slumped down, pain clutching her chest, squeezing her lungs. She could not breathe.

Something was constricting her. Not the black smoke this time. She winced and tears ran down her cheeks, and the skin on her arms tightened, and she realized what material Atratus had chosen this time—not particles in the air but her own flesh. He was squeezing her like an orange.

With a jerk, he raised his hands. She rose into the air, her very skin tugging her body upward. She gasped, sputtered, struggling for breath.

"You will pay for your insolence, mongrel," he sneered, holding her suspended in the air. "You have hereby failed Magical History. I banish you from this class, and at the end of this turn, you will report to my office for thirty lashes, then go work in the kitchens for two straight turns."

He tugged the door open from a distance, then swung his arms. She flew outside like a discarded bit of cloth and landed in the snow. The door slammed shut, sealing her outside, bruised and struggling for breath.

* * * * *

"You have to go to Headmistress Egeria." Tam stood before her, staring at Madori sternly. "He can't do this to you!"

Sitting on her bed, Madori looked down at her throbbing palm. Professor Atratus had forbade her to heal the welts from his latest lashing, vowing to inspect the wounds every turn. Scrubbing pots for half-a-turn hadn't helped her hand feel any better.

"What could Egeria do?" Madori said softly. "She has no important family, no wealth, no influence . . . only a title. Lord Serin is the most powerful man in Mageria, possibly in all Timandra, and Professor Atratus is his pet."

Neekeya sat at Madori's side, wringing her hands. "But there's got to be something Egeria can do! Madori, please. Let's all go speak to her together."

Jitomi nodded. "We all go." His pale cheeks flushed, and the dragon tattoo twitched on his neck as he clenched his jaw. "We will demand she do something about this Atratus."

Madori lowered her head, her two strands of hair drooping. "No. I will go alone. Students are forbidden from entering her tower, and if Atratus catches us—if *any* professor catches us—I will not have you punished for my sake."

Her friends glanced at one another. Before they could argue, and before Madori could lose her courage, she rose to her feet and left the chamber, closing the door behind her.

The sun was bright and the hour was late; Atratus would be sleeping in his chamber, and if he caught her outside after hours, well, he had already punished so much there wasn't much more Madori feared.

She thanked both Idar, the god of her father, and Xen Qae, the wise philosopher her mother worshiped, when she reached Cosmia Tower without encountering any professor. When she creaked open the door and stepped inside—the place where Atratus had once caught her—she breathed in relief. This hall too was empty.

She climbed the spiraling stairs, looking out every window she passed, seeing more and more of the land as she ascended: the university grounds, with their columned halls and domes and gardens; the town of Teelshire beyond, its roofs tiled, its streets cobbled; and the fields and plains of Mageria. The road she had taken here snaked across the land, and a lump filled Madori's

throat to remember the journey with her father. She had groaned
at Torin's jokes, called him the dullest man in Moth, and couldn't
wait to reach this university. Now she wanted nothing more than
to see her father again, run toward him, hug him tightly, and never
let go.

*If you were here, Father, you wouldn't let any of this happen. You'd
fight them all—like you fought the monk Ferius and his armies. I'm so sorry,
Father.* She stared at the road and the mist beyond. *I'm so sorry I
never told you how much I truly love you.*

She knuckled her eyes dry. A few more steps, and she
reached a door and knocked.

As if reacting to her touch, the door unlocked and slowly
swung open.

The tower's top chamber was large and round, its brick
walls covered with shelves. There were as many artifacts here as in
Professor Rushavel's workshop. Madori saw animal statuettes
with blinking crystal eyes; counter-square boards whose pieces—
soldiers, horses, and elephants—moved as if locked in true battle;
model ships whose sails billowed with air and whose oars stroked;
toy soldiers with ticking hearts; books whose voices filled her
head when she read their spines; little pewter dragons who blasted
out sparks of true fire; and many more. An oak desk rose in the
room's center, its top hidden under piles of codices, hourglasses,
and scrolls. Behind the desk, in a great armchair that nearly
swallowed her, sat the headmistress.

Madori expected Egeria to rail, to punish her, to shout that
Madori was insolent for bursting in here uninvited and after
hours. But the little old woman, barely larger than a child, simply
smiled kindly, her face creasing into a map of wrinkles.

"Hello, my dear," the headmistress said.

Madori flinched, for an instant—a single heartbeat—sure
that the headmistress was hurtling insults at her, was reaching for
a ruler to strike her like Atratus. When the kind tone sank in,

Madori realized that this kindness hurt her more than a ruler or insults could. Tears filled her eyes and streamed down her cheeks, but it was a good kind of pain, the pain of a scab peeling off.

"Child!" said Egeria, eyes softening.

The headmistress rose to her feet, rushed toward Madori, and embraced her. Madori was used to being the smallest person at Teel, but the headmistress was just the same size, her arms so warm.

"I'm sorry," Madori whispered. "I'm sorry I came here after hours, and I'm so sorry for everything. I had to see you. I had to tell you. I . . ."

She took a deep breath, and she told her.

She spoke of Lari and her quartet vandalizing her room, threatening her, attacking her. She spoke of Atratus binding her in front of the class, striking her palm almost every turn, and sending her to scrub pots after classes so that she could not study. She spoke of all her fear and pain, the nightmare that had been the past few months.

"I'm frightened," she finally said. "I'm frightened of the Radians and I don't know what to do."

She stared expectantly at the headmistress, waiting for soothing words, a promise of protection, some wise advice or at least another embrace.

Instead, the headmistress lowered her head and spoke in a soft voice. "I'm frightened too."

Madori gasped. "But . . . you're a great mage! You're powerful. You're—"

". . . the daughter of a shoemaker," the old woman said. "An old woman. A teacher who loves her students. That is all." She stepped toward the window and stared at the university grounds. "And I love Teel more than anything. For a thousand years the headmasters and mistresses have watched over our school from this tower. We defended Teel even through the great wars with Arden and the kingdoms of Eloria. We were a beacon of knowledge and light, and now . . . now I fear that a great light rises, a light to blind, to burn us all, a light that will sear Mythimna. The light of Radian." Her voice dropped. "They do more in Teel than write pamphlets, chant slogans, and spread hatred. Madori, I have sad news to share with you. Professor Maleen has died."

Madori gasped and covered her mouth. Her eyes stung anew. "Died?"

Egeria placed her hand upon a book of herbalism. "Poisoned. The Night Plague—a disease some claim comes from Eloria, a disease Professor Atratus has been studying. I myself have fallen ill with it; for ten turns I writhed in pain before finding the magic within me to vanquish the illness."

A growl fled Madori's throat, and she clenched her fists. "Atratus! He poisoned you! He— He murdered Maleen!" She clutched the headmistress's hands. "How can you let him still teach here? Can't you dismiss him or . . . or fight him? Or do *something*?"

Egeria seemed to age and wither before Madori's eyes. "I could do all these things, and then his master would come to avenge his wounded pet. You have met his master." Egeria's voice twisted in disgust. "You have met Lord Tirus Serin."

Madori nodded. "Lari's father."

She thought back to her encounter on the road. How she wished she could return to that turn! She would have stabbed the snake in the throat had she known the full extent of his evil.

The headmistress looked at a parchment map that hung upon the wall. She tapped a drawing of a northern fort. "In Sunmotte Citadel he musters an army, and many more of his forces spread across our kingdom. His pets bark in all centers of power: Professor Atratus here at Teel and other, even crueler men in our great cities. His servants whisper in the ears of our king, guiding all his actions. And his arm reaches beyond Mageria. In all kingdoms of the daylight his men work. Already Radian chapters rise in Arden to our east, Verilon to our north, and Naya to our south."

Madori spoke in a small voice. "So what do we do?"

The headmistress turned toward her and held her hands. "We must be brave. We must fight them at every turn. You will stay at Teel, Madori, and you will learn magic. I am old and I am fading; you and your friends must pick up this fight. We need mages like you—not warriors but healers."

Madori glanced down at her hand; welts still rose upon it. "Atratus said I'm not to heal my wounds anymore."

The headmistress winced, her eyes pained. She stepped around her desk, opened a drawer, and rummaged for a moment. When she returned to Madori, the headmistress held a ring in her hand; it was shaped as a dragon biting its tail, its eyes gleaming gemstones. When she placed it on Madori's finger, the pain of Atratus's lashes faded.

"A ring of healing," Madori whispered. "Neekeya will be delighted."

Egeria shook her head. "No, not a ring of healing, for Atratus would see your wounds healed and find other ways to punish you. It is a ring to soothe pain."

Madori caressed the silver dragon.

But it does not stop the pain inside me, she wanted to tell the headmistress. *It does not stop the pain of my mixed blood, my memories, the hatred of others and my humiliation.*

She spoke softly. "I don't want you to fade, headmistress. I don't want you to stop fighting, to tell me that I must fight without you. I'm only a child. My friends are only children." She blinked a little too much. "I've always depended on my parents, and on you, to guide my way. How can I face this enemy? I'm not wise. I'm not brave. I'm not strong."

Egeria smiled—a smile of kindness, warmth, and sadness all at the same time, a smile that lit her eyes and creased her face. "The greatest heroes are rarely unusually wise, brave, or strong. They are ordinary people who stand up and do what's right."

When Madori left the tower, she kept running her fingers over and over the dragon ring. When she returned to her chamber, her friends were already asleep, but even when Madori climbed into her bed, sleep would not find her. She lay awake, staring at the ceiling, caressing her ring.

CHAPTER NINETEEN
POISON AND STEEL

Torin stood on the city walls, staring down at the sprawling Ardish army.

"Thousands of our finest men and women," he said, the wind in his hair. "The might of Arden."

They mustered in the western fields outside the walls of Kingswall, the ancient capital of the kingdom. Thousands of horses stood in formations, bedecked in armor. Riders sat upon the beasts, all in steel, holding the banners of their kingdom: a black raven upon a golden field. Behind the horses stood the ground troops: pikemen clad in chain mail, their pole weapons hooked and glinting in the sun; swordsmen clad in breastplates, their shields and helms displaying the Ardish raven; and finally archers in leather armor, one-handed swords hanging from their belts, their longbows as tall as men. Finally, behind the warriors, gathered the support troops: engineers, cooks, washer-women, blacksmiths, arrowsmiths, fletchers, cobblers, jugglers and singers, and many other tradesmen.

"I don't know if it's enough," said Cam. "And it pains me to move these men away from the capital. But Hornsford Bridge is where Serin musters, and that is the border we must defend."

Torin looked at his friend. To him, Cam would always be the shepherd's boy from Fairwool-by-Night, his oldest and dearest friend—a scrawny boy with a ready smile, bright eyes, and an easy laugh. Yet now on the walls, Torin saw a leader burdened with worry. Cam had married Queen Linee of House Solira, and he'd been sitting upon the throne for seventeen years now, and those years of concern had left their mark upon him. The first hints of wrinkles spread out from Cam's eyes, and the first gray hairs had invaded his temples.

Torin placed a hand on his friend's shoulder. "Are you sure you should ride out with them?"

The wind billowed Cam's hair and cloak. Looking down at the army, he nodded. "Yes. I will ride out with them. Linee will stay here upon the throne, and you'll be here with her. Serin hungers for our kingdom; I don't doubt that. Mageria has been aching for revenge since our two kingdoms fought a few decades ago. They conquered this city once; it was King Ceranor who drove the mages out. They've never forgotten that humiliation, and Serin will want his revenge, even if he was only a babe during that war." Cam wrapped his fingers around the hilt of his sword. "I will ride to Hornsford. I will stare him in the eyes, and I will not let him cross that bridge."

Torin stood on the city walls for a long time, watching as Cam joined the forces, watching as the thousands rode and marched into the distance, their armor bright and their banners high.

When he closed his eyes, Torin saw the war years ago. In his memories, he sailed south along the Inaro River with Koyee, two youths in a little boat, witnessing the horror of Mageria's magic: villages burned to the ground; skeletons of children sprouting two skulls; the charred remains of men and women, their ribs flipped inside out; gruesome hills of bones and the scent of death; and everywhere the buffalo of Mageria painted with blood. He and Koyee had fled the mages in the night city of Sinyong, and Koyee's arm still bore the scars of dark magic.

The last raven banners were now flying over the horizon, and the sunlight glinted against the last troops' armor; it reminded Torin of the strip of dusk back home. He took out the scroll he kept in his pocket, unrolled it, and read Koyee's letter for the tenth time since he received it last turn. It was written in Qaelish, the delicate characters written from top to bottom in neat columns:

> *Dear Torin,*
>
> *I miss you and Billygoat and think about you every turn. I've been alone many times in my life, but now the loneliness fills me like icy water invading a cave.*
>
> *I am frightened. You wrote to me of a menace, of a great light to sear all in its way, of a sun eclipsing the moon. This menace has stretched its fingers across all Timandra; it has reached even our village of Fairwool-by-Night, and its sigils are drawn upon doors and raised as flags in our fields.*
>
> *I've been spending more time in Oshy across the dusk, and I cannot speak to you of our defenses lest this letter falls into the wrong hands. But I will say this: If we must fight, we are ready. We stand strong.*
>
> *I've written to Billygoat, but I've not heard back, and I worry our letters our being intercepted on the roads of Mageria. I'm so afraid for her but I know she's strong. I love you and her and pray to see you again soon.*
>
> *Your ever-loving wife,*
> *Koyee*

Torin rolled up the letter. He missed his wife, he missed his daughter, and he missed home. He wore the armor of a lord now—a breastplate sporting a raven sigil, greaves and vambraces, and a helmet—and a rich cloak hung across his shoulders. Here in Kingswall he was a knight, a hero, a warden of the throne. Yet all he wanted to do was wear his old clothes again, return to his village, and be a gardener and husband and father.

He climbed off the wall, mounted his new horse—not Hayseed but a swift courser from the queen's stables—and rode through his capital city. He looked around him at the city: the narrow brick homes, their roofs tiled red; the workshops of potters, smiths, tanners, gem-cutters, barbers, and other tradesmen, their signs swinging in the wind; towering barracks, most of their soldiers gone to war; and finally the palace, a white castle rising upon a green hill.

As he looked at the gardens and towers, he remembered coming here with Bailey years ago, and the pain of missing her stabbed him.

"Twenty years ago, you and I first came to this palace, Bailey," he whispered, his eyes stinging. "We fought against this kingdom, but now I must defend it. Now I'm here, fighting for Arden lest evil once more corrupts the lands of light. I wish you were here, Bailey, still fighting with me."

Almost two decades, he thought, *and I still miss her so badly it hurts. Time heals all wounds; never was a greater lie spoken.*

He let the stable boys take his horse, and he spent a long time walking through the gardens, thinking of those old days and old friends.

* * * * *

As flowers bloomed and spring's leaves rustled outside the window, Madori sat in the classroom, prepared for her final exam.

The exam paper sat upside down on her table—printed on real papyrus, a rarity here in the north. All around the classroom, other students sat before their own exams, waiting to flip them over. Madori nibbled her lip, trying to bring to memory all she had learned about Magical Principles—not only the three basic axioms but the hundreds of theorems structured atop them. When she glanced to the head of the class, she cursed the sight of Professor Atratus there. The stooped, hook-nosed man was pacing, staring at a draining hourglass, and waiting to announce the exam's beginning.

The vulture will unnerve me through the exam, Madori thought. *He's going to do something to ruin this for me, I know it.*

"Good luck, mongrel," rose a sweet voice to her side.

Madori glanced to her left, and her belly tightened further. As if it weren't enough that Atratus was overseeing this exam, his favorite student—Lari Serin—was sitting here beside Madori. The girl smiled sweetly, her golden locks tied in blue ribbons. She sat straight, her hands in her lap, her quills and inkpot organized like soldiers upon her desk.

Wishing she had been assigned a different seat, Madori forced herself to stare down at her desk, trying to banish Atratus and Lari from her thoughts. She stared at her silver ring which the headmistress had given her, a dragon chewing its tail.

Bring me luck, Shenlai, she thought; it was the name she had given the ring, the name of the legendary Qaelish dragon her mother had once ridden in battle.

Finally Atratus flipped over the hourglass.

"Begin!" he barked.

Hundreds of papers rustled as the students flipped them over and began their exam.

Madori took a deep breath and quickly scanned the exam. She breathed a shaky breath of relief. Despite spending most of her time scrubbing dishes rather than studying, she knew this material. Professor Fen had prepared the exam, covering all those topics Madori had mastered: application of the three principles to different states of matter, weaving Herafon's Law into the Fourth Principle, claiming multiple materials simultaneously, and other topics Madori had been practicing in lieu of sleep.

I already failed Magical History thanks to Atratus, she thought. *But I can pass this class.*

She began to write furiously, answering question by question. Thanks to Shenlai, the ring that dulled feeling in her hand, her wrist didn't even hurt.

". . . through application of Sheritel's Fifth Principle, we can prove that the links between particles grow denser in direct proportion to the length of the claiming . . ." She wiped her brow and kept scribbling. ". . . thus, as steam does not rise from water heating under a claim, we demonstrate Karn's Law that changing states of matter requires a new cycle of principles . . . " She blew out her breath, blasting back her two strands of hair. " . . .stacking multiple materials in a forked chain allows us to skip from one to another, stacking claims simultaneously . . ."

Soon her arm itself was aching from so much writing, and she wished she had a magical dragon armlet too.

The hourglass spilled its sand.

An hour went by. Two hours. Three.

A few students finished their exams and placed them on Atratus's desk. Madori shook her arm and got back to writing, putting down the final words.

Perfect, she thought with a satisfied breath. *This is one class I don't have to worry about fai—*

Something hard hit her leg under the table, interrupting her thoughts.

She grunted.

The blow struck her again, and when she looked down, she saw a pulsing funnel of air—magic flowing from Lari's direction.

Madori growled and snapped her head toward Lari.

The young Magerian gave her a wink, then gasped and raised her hand. "Professor Atratus! Madori is looking at me! She's cheating!"

Madori leaped to her feet, knocking over her inkpot. "I was not!" She spun toward Lari, growling. "You're a liar. You're a filthy liar!"

She couldn't stop herself; rage flooded over Madori, blinding her. She leaped at Lari, knocking her off her seat. The cousins crashed onto the floor.

"The mongrel is rabid!" Lari screamed.

Madori grabbed the girl's hair, tugging and tearing those perfect golden locks. "I *am* rabid, and I'm going to destroy you, Lari. I'm done with your—"

Her words turned into a scream as fingers grabbed and twisted her ear.

Professor Atratus dragged her to her feet; Madori thought he could rip her ear straight off. When she struggled against him, he grabbed her wrist and twisted her arm behind her back.

"Professor Atratus, she's crazy!" Lari said, lying on her back in a puddle of ink. "I only tried to be a good student, and she just attacked me, and . . . and . . ." She covered her eyes, giving a rather convincing show of weeping.

Madori struggled to release herself as Atratus dragged her to the head of the class.

"Professor, she wasn't cheating!" Neekeya shouted, leaping to her feet at the back of the class.

Tam too leaped up. "Professor Atratus, Lari is lying, she—"

"Silence!" the professor boomed. "Whoever says the next word fails this class." He glared at the students. "Everyone, back into your seats. I will not tolerate impudence." He gave Madori's arm a painful twist, nearly dislocating it; she yelped. "And I will not tolerate filthy mongrel scum copying their answers from pure-blooded Magerians. The half-breed will be punished for this."

Her friends still stood at their desks, cheeks flushed and eyes wide. Jitomi had his hands raised as if prepared to cast a spell against the professor.

Standing by Atratus's desk, Madori looked at them and spoke softly. "It's all right. Sit down, friends. Don't fail your test because of me."

Reluctantly, glancing at one another, they sat down. She had told her friends about her magical ring; they knew Atratus's punishment wouldn't hurt her. Dozens of other students filled the classroom, staring at Madori. A few—foreigners from Arden—

stared with pity. Many of the Magerian students, Radian pins upon their lapels, stared with smug delight.

"Hold out your hand, mongrel," Atratus said, raising his ruler.

Madori gulped and stretched out her palm. His ruler would raise more welts, but she knew the ring would protect her from pain.

"Lari, sweetness," said the professor. "Please, step to the front of the class. You've suffered the bane of this mongrel; I feel it most fair that you administer the punishment."

Smoothing her robes, Lari nodded. "Gladly." She stepped toward the front of the class, chin raised, and took the ruler from Atratus. She turned toward Madori and a cruel smile spread across her face. "I will make you pay for what you've done, mongrel."

Madori's heart sank. Her ring would protect her from pain, but not this humiliation. To have Lari strike her? She pulled her hand back.

"No," Madori said with a snarl. "You are no professor here, Lari. You are nothing but a rich, pampered little—"

Lari swung the ruler. It sliced the air with a whistle and slammed against Madori's cheek. Blood splattered.

Madori gasped. Pain bolted through her, so powerful she nearly collapsed, and she raised her hand to her cheek. Her heart seemed to stop and she couldn't breathe.

Before Madori could react, Lari swung the ruler a second time, lashing it like a whip, striking Madori's other cheek.

Madori stood, shocked, in too much pain to react. She could barely see. She could just make out Lari standing before her, smiling in delight, raising her ruler for a third strike.

Madori blinked.

Thoughts raced through her mind as Lari licked her lips hungrily, preparing to strike again.

I have to stop this now. I have to end this. Even if I fail this class. Even if I'm tossed out of Teel. She growled and raised her fists, prepared to attack. *This ends now—*

The classroom door burst open.

Professor Yovan raced into the room, stepping on his long white beard and nearly crashing to the floor. He panted, his hair in disarray, his cheeks flushed.

"The king is dead!" he cried out, arms raised, tears on his cheeks. "The king of Mageria is dead!"

Everyone turned toward the elderly wizard. Lari froze with her ruler in the air, Madori with her fists raised. Her friends had run halfway across the classroom to join the fray; they too stood frozen as if somebody had cast a spell, turning everyone to stone.

Professor Yovan panted, his lips trembling. "They say he was poisoned; his sons too. Lord Serin has ridden to the capital. Until a new king can be chosen, Serin sits upon Mageria's throne." A sob fled Yovan's lips, but he managed to square his shoulders and raise his chin. "May Idar bless the king's soul! May Idar bless our new Lord Protector!"

Madori stared at the old man, and her horror was too great, too horrible, too impossible to exist, to feel, to shake her. Everything seemed like a dream. She felt numb, surprisingly calm, as if her terror had risen so high it formed a circle with calmness like her ring, a dragon biting its tail.

Yet no other king will be chosen, she realized as the blood dripped down her cheeks. *And even Idar cannot save us now.*

She turned to look at Lari, and Madori saw something new in the girl's eyes—no longer hatred, anger, or even mockery. Looking into those blue eyes, Madori saw victory.

CHAPTER TWENTY
SUNS AND SERPENTS

They huddled in their chamber, the door bolted shut with magic, a chair propped up under the knob for extra protection. More magic shielded the window, gluing the shutters shut, but still the chants pounded into the room, and the walls shook.

"Radian rises! Radian rises! Hail Lord Serin!"

Jitomi stood guarding the window, hands raised as if prepared to cast magic. In the shadows of the room, he had doffed the thick cloak and hood he normally wore, revealing a lean body clad in black silk and leather. The dragon tattoo that ran up his neck and face seemed almost a living thing.

"They are growing in numbers," the Elorian said grimly. His large, oval eyes gleamed a dangerous blue. "Hundreds now march outside, chanting for this tyrant."

Guarding the door, Tam sighed. "If only Serin *were* a tyrant, we could hope to rebel against him. But it seems he's more of a beloved leader, at least judging by the reception he's getting here at Teel."

While Jitomi stood ready to cast magic, the young prince had opted for his dagger. Weapons were allowed at Teel only for ceremonial reasons—family heirlooms, religious blades, or magical artifacts—to be kept sheathed at all times. Yet this was no normal turn, and Tam's blade gleamed. The prince's eyes were dark, his lips tight, his muscles stiff.

Neekeya too stood with a drawn blade. Her sword was long and thick, its silver hilt shaped like a reptilian claw. The swamp dweller—normally bright-eyed, ready to smile, a naive girl lost in a foreign land—became a fierce tigress here, a beast ready to pounce. Her lip peeled back, revealing her teeth, and her eyes blazed.

"I say we fight them!" she said. "I'm a warrior. I'm not afraid. We'll slay Atratus and take Lari hostage and not release her until Serin steps off the throne."

Tam raised an eyebrow. "That's not a bad idea."

They all turned to look at Madori—Neekeya growling, Tam somber, Jitomi staring silently.

Madori sat upon her bed, caressing the copper coin that was her last memento from her father.

Simple change from our meal in the tavern, she thought, looking at the coin. *I was so scared then, but now I miss that turn. Things were so much simpler then.*

Her cheeks still stung from Lari's assault. Madori had healed the wounds with her magic, but the scars remained, pale and prickling. As her mother bore the scars of nightwolf claws upon her face, Madori's countenance now too was marred, perhaps forever, mementos from a different sort of beast.

"Well, Madori?" Tam said. "What do you think? What do we do?"

She raised her eyes back toward her friends, and a lump filled her throat.

"Why do you ask me?" she said, not without anger, and closed her fist around the coin. "What makes you think I know what to do? Why listen to my words?"

Neekeya tilted her head, her crocodile tooth necklace chinking. "Because . . . we're Madori's Motley. This is our quartet and you're our leader."

Sudden rage filled Madori, and she leaped from her bed. The chants still rose outside, and the walls shook as hundreds of feet pounded down the hall outside their door.

"Your leader?" Madori's voice rose so loudly she was almost shouting. "I never asked to be your leader. I don't want to lead anyone. Who am I to choose for you?" She looked at them one by one. "Neekeya, your father is a mighty lord, ruler of a pyramid. Tam, you're a prince for Idar's sake. Jitomi, you're the son of a noble warrior of Ilar, heir to a great pagoda overlooking the moonlit sea. Me?" She gestured at herself. "I'm the daughter of a gardener. I'm a half-breed. I'm from a backwater village. I'm . . . I'm . . ."

Her words failed her, and her eyes stung.

"You are the strongest, wisest student in this school," Jitomi said, finishing her sentence. Leaving the window, he stepped toward her and held her hand. His grip was warm and firm, his eyes soft. "I will follow your guidance. If you ask me, I will fight for you."

Fight? Madori walked to the window and peered through the crack between two shutters. A hundred students or more were marching outside, trampling grass and raising torches.

"Radian rises!" they chanted over and over.

Lari led the march, shouting out her hatred. "The Light of Radian now rules Mageria! Our light will purify our kingdom, driving out the mongrels, the nightcrawlers, the swamp barbarians, and all the cockroaches that infest our fatherland." The crowd roared their approval and Lari cried out louder. "Undesirables will burn in our fire!"

Madori turned away, facing her friends again.

Neekeya was shaking with rage. "That spoiled daughter of a snake! I'm going to wring her neck. Who does she think she is to speak like that?"

Madori sighed. "She knows exactly who she is. Mageria's new princess."

"And I'm Arden's prince," Tam said. "We can go to Arden—all of us. We'll sneak out of the school. We'll take refuge in Kingswall at least until this blows over." He sighed and his shoulders stooped. "Maybe this is a fight we cannot win. Maybe all we can do now is flee."

Again they looked at her for guidance. Again they awaited her words.

And I? I just wish my parents were here. They're war heroes. They would know. She lowered her head. *But perhaps that is my greatest lesson at Teel University—that I must become my own woman now, no longer a girl in the shadow of heroes but a heroine myself.*

She spoke carefully. "We cannot flee. Serin's fortress guards Hornsford Bridge, the nearest crossing into Arden. Magerian castles watch all major roads and smaller crossings; with the king dead, those castles now belong to Serin too. If we flee this university, Lari will have her father hunt us. Nor can we fight Lari here; she's too powerful, and too many follow her."

Neekeya wrung her hands. "If we can't flee or fight, what do we do? Just cower?"

Madori thought back to Headmistress Egeria's words in her tower. *We must be brave. We must fight them at every turn. You will stay at Teel, Madori, and you will learn magic . . . you and your friends must pick up this fight.*

"We *survive*," Madori said. "Lari might march outside, and Atratus might be spewing his bile in his classrooms, but Headmistress Egeria still leads this university. This is still an oasis of reason, even with a few mad dogs within our walls. The Radian Society of Teel wants us to either fight or flee; one way they can crush us, the other be rid of us." Madori squeezed her coin. "So I say we do exactly what they hate, exactly what they're railing about outside our window. We stay. We study. We show them that we will not be intimidated, we will not be drawn into a war, and we will not run." She nodded, gaining confidence with every word. "The year's classes are ending. Next year we will take all our classes together, and none of those Atratus teaches. Madori's

Quartet will remain together always. We will take turns watching even as we sleep. We are in danger, but we will withstand this."

Figurines shook on the shelves, and a picture frame fell, as the boots stomped in the hallway and the cries pealed.

"Radian rises! Hail Lord Serin!"

* * * * *

A strange silence blanketed Teel University next turn. As Madori's Motley walked along a columned gallery, heading toward their next exam, they heard none of the usual laughter, conversation, and songs that filled the university. The chants from last turn had died too. The ash of torches swirled upon the floor, the only remnant of the Radians' rally. The quartet passed by only one other student, a jittery girl who rushed down the corridor, her head lowered. Even the birds seemed subdued; only a single crow cawed as it circled above.

The quartet was near the northwestern Ostirina Tower, about to enter and climb to their classroom, when they heard the horns blare.

"The Horns of Teel," Madori whispered, a chill gripping her. "The headmistress calls."

She shuddered. Madori had spent many hours reading history books in Teel's library; according to them, the Horns of Teel blew only in the most dire circumstances, calling all students into the cloister to hear the headmaster or mistress speak.

The horns blared again—a high, ethereal sound like the cry of some unearthly being. Madori had never seen the fabled dragons of Eloria—it was said that only one still lived—but she had always imagined their cry sounding like this.

Students began to emerge from classrooms like ants from a disturbed hive. Eyes darted and hands were wrung. Madori's

Quartet was caught in the stream as hundreds of students headed toward the cloister.

When the horns finally fell silent, every student at Teel stood in the courtyard, first to fourth years. An eerie silence covered the university. Then, with the shuffle of robes, the crowd parted to let Headmistress Egeria walk toward the stage at the back, the place where she had first addressed Madori and her fellow applicants many months ago. For the first time since Madori had met her, the old headmistress walked with a cane, stooped over, and it seemed that she had aged many years since the last turn. Egeria had always seemed old but also vigorous and vivacious; now she reminded Madori of how her great-grandpapa had looked in his final days.

"Headmistress," Madori whispered as the elderly woman hobbled by her.

Egeria raised her head to look at Madori. Tears filled the headmistress's eyes. She whispered, her voice so low Madori barely heard.

"You must look after them, Madori. You must look after the others." The headmistress glanced behind her and paled. Furtively, she placed a folded piece of paper in Madori's hand.

Glancing behind her again, the headmistress kept moving toward the stage. When Madori too looked behind, she saw Professor Atratus standing between the columns of the eastern gallery, his arms crossed, his eyes blazing as he stared at the headmistress. He seemed like a master watching an errant pup.

The headmistress reached the stage. Leaning on her cane, she hobbled up the stairs and turned toward the crowd. Even standing at a distance, Madori saw that fresh tears filled Egeria's eyes. Murmurs of conversation swept across the crowd.

The headmistress raised a trembling hand, and the crowd fell silent. Egeria spoke for them all to hear, her voice soft at first but gaining strength with every word.

"Dearest students, you have heard many stories, rumors, and whispers over the past turn. The tidings from the south have been confirmed. The old king of Mageria is dead. The cause of death reported is . . ." Egeria glanced to the shadows where Atratus was watching her. She swallowed and a tremble filled her voice. ". . . the Night Plague, a disease spread from Eloria. Lord Tirus Serin, Warden of Sunmotte, has been crowned our new king."

A new murmur swept across the crowd. Several cheers rose, along with chants for the Radians. Madori forced herself to keep staring ahead, her jaw tight, refusing to look at Lari who stood across the field; she had a feeling that Lari was staring right at her.

The headmistress gestured to two fourth year students. Both stepped onto the stage, carrying a chest between them. Both sported Radian pins upon their lapels. The students opened the chest and tilted it forward, revealing hundreds of pins.

Egeria kept speaking, her voice trembling. "Henceforth, on orders from our new king, all Timandrian students at Teel University shall wear Radian pins, showing the sun eclipsing the moon." Her voice cracked. "All Elorian and half-Elorian students will wear a different pin, this one shaped as a snake. You will now step forth, one by one as your names are called, to receive your pins."

Madori glanced aside at Jitomi. He met her gaze, his eyes dark.

Professor Atratus stepped onto the stage next, unrolled a scroll, and spent the next hour barking out names. Students approached, one by one, to receive their pins. The Timandrians accepted their Radian pins with pride, some adding a chant for Lord Serin and Radianism. Whenever an Elorian student stepped onto the stage, Atratus sneered and held out the serpent pin in disgust.

Finally Madori's name was called. She trembled with rage when she stepped onto the stage and faced Atratus.

"A serpent for a worm," Atratus said, glee in his eyes, his lips curled back in a mockery of a grin. He slapped the brooch against her chest. "All will now know that Elorians and mongrels are beasts that crawl in the dust."

When all the students had received their pins, Egeria addressed the crowd again. She stood upon the stage and let her cane drop; it clattered onto the stage. Madori thought the old woman would fall, but Egeria spoke in a loud voice, tears streaming down her cheeks.

"Students of Teel University! Be strong. I promise you—no Elorians will be hurt on my watch. You are safe, my students, regardless of what pin you wear. Be strong and know that I protect you."

Madori's Motley spent the rest of the half-turn in their chamber, guarding the door and windows. All classes and exams had been postponed; instead, the Teel Radian Society rallied in the cloister. The sound echoed across the university, shaking the chamber walls. Standing at the window, Madori heard Professor Atratus shout of sunlit domination, heard Lari—head of the Radian Society and now Princess of Mageria—demand to drive out the undesirables. After every slogan, the crowds cheered and the walls shook anew.

"Perhaps Tam was right," Jitomi said. The Elorian stood guarding the door, his snake pin fastened to his cloak. "We can still flee. While they rally."

Madori bit her lip.

Perhaps they're right, she thought. *Perhaps we should leave.*

She tried to imagine returning home—to her parents, to old Hayseed, to her old bed, to her books and dolls and the silver flute her mother always tried to force her to play. Back in Fairwool-by-Night, she was nothing but a lonely girl, a misfit, powerless and aimless. Here at Teel she had found a purpose, but what hope did this place now have for her?

"I understand, Jitomi," she said softly. She lowered her head, her throat tight. "When the bells next chime, and everyone is sleeping, you should leave." She had to blink rapidly. "This place is no longer safe for you. But I must stay."

Tam stepped toward her and clutched her arms. "Billygoat, your life is at risk here. Leave Teel too. I'll go with you. I'll shelter you and Jitomi in Kingswall—all other Elorian students here too, if they'll join us."

"And I'll go with you." Neekeya nodded emphatically, placing a hand on Madori's shoulder. "This place is too dangerous. We all leave together."

Madori laughed mirthlessly. "You are both Timandrians. You wear the Radian pins upon your lapels. Jitomi and I wear the serpent pins; we're in danger, but you're safe."

It was Tam's turn to laugh. He tugged off his Radian pin, tossed it onto the ground, and stomped on it. "What Radian pin?"

Neekeya tossed down her own pin and shattered it beneath her foot. "I don't see any Radian pins."

"Atratus won't be happy." Madori bit her lip. "Those pins might be the only thing that keeps you safe now."

"Then I'd rather be in danger," Tam said. Holding her, he stared into Madori's eyes. "Billygoat, we've been friends all our lives. I'm not going to toss you to the wolves. If you and Jitomi have to leave this university, Neekeya and I are going with you, and we'll keep you safe on the road."

He pulled her into his arms, and Neekeya joined the embrace. Madori—almost a foot shorter than them—disappeared into their warmth, and she could not curb her tears, for despite the pain and fear she felt beloved, and she felt safe.

And yet . . . Egeria's old words returned to her.

You will stay at Teel, Madori, and you will learn magic.

Her eyes stung.

She thought back to the war stories her parents had told her. Torin and Koyee, the great heroes of the war, had many chances to return home. They had kept going—traveling into the heart of darkness, the flames of war, determined to fight for what was right, willing even to die for truth.

I am Madori Billy Greenmoat, she thought. *Billy after Bailey, the great heroine who fought with my parents.* Bailey had died in that war, fighting against the evil sweeping across Moth. She had given her life and saved this world. *How can I, the daughter of heroes, flee an enemy?*

"No," she whispered, still wrapped in the embrace. "No, my friends. I will not flee. When you escape danger rather than face it, it will forever hunt you. Here within the walls of Teel will I make my stand. Evil rises; I will face it. Like my parents did. Like Bailey did. I will become a mage."

Her friends stepped away, looking at her strangely, as if she had changed before them like a creature in Transformations class. And perhaps she had changed.

Hardship changes us. It turns us into heroes or cowards. When disaster strikes, we metamorphose into the person who's been sleeping inside us.

She was about to say more when the door shook madly.

The Motley spun toward the door. Madori sucked in breath and raised her hands, already readying herself for magic. The door rattled again and chips of wood flew.

"Death to Elorians!" rose cries outside. "Drag out the nightcrawlers and show them Timandrian pride."

Tam and Neekeya raced forward and pressed themselves against the door. It shook again and more wooden fragments flew. A hinge came loose.

"Drag them out and make them pay for their sins!" somebody cried outside.

Madori was already whispering under her breath, repeating the theorems she had learned in her classes. She quickly claimed the floor, rattling the tiles to send the hinge into the air. She switched to claiming the air, shoving the hinge back against the door, then switched again, claiming the hinge and bolting it back into the door and wall. At her side, Jitomi was busy casting magic too. A funnel of air left his hands, drove toward the door between Tam and Neekeya, and flattened against it, providing extra weight.

The door held. The window shutters smashed open behind them.

Madori spun around at once, claimed the flying shards of shutters, and tossed them back at the window. A student outside—a fourth year—cried out in pain, the wooden chips driving into his face.

"The snakes are attacking!" he cried.

"Jitomi!" Madori cried. She was already tossing a cone of air at the window, sealing the entrance with an opaque, swirling blob. Jitomi added his own shield. The air in the room thinned, most of it shoving against the window and door, leaving Madori lightheaded.

Behind her the door shook again; a crack tore open across it. Hands reached inside. Tam and Neekeya were still pushing their weight against the door when magic coalesced outside, forming a smoky battering ram, and drove forward.

The door shattered into countless pieces. Wooden shards flew. Tam and Neekeya fell and sprawled against the floor.

The empty doorway revealed a columned arcade swarming with Radian students, all proudly displaying their pins. Some were raising Radian banners.

Lari stood among them, hands on her hips. She pointed into the chamber and screamed, "Grab the nightcrawlers! Punish the creatures who poisoned our old king!"

Not waiting another breath, Madori thrust both her arms forward, palms facing outward. Collecting particles of dust and wooden chips, she wove a ball and tossed it forward. The missile flew toward Lari, but the princess was too swift. She swept her arm, diverting the projectile with a blast of air.

Radians spilled into the room, eyes blazing, teeth bared, feral animals on the hunt.

"Call them back or you'll pay for this, Lari!" Madori shouted. "Your father's arse might be warming the throne, but Egeria still rules Teel."

Lari smirked. "Such a mouth on those creatures. I will enjoy smashing that mouth."

Violence filled the room with shouts, thuds, and splatters of blood. Neekeya swung her sword, keeping the blade sheathed, slamming the wooden scabbard against an assailant's head. Tam thrust his dagger in one hand, a chair in the other. Jitomi was muttering spells and Madori made an attempt to claim a Radian's boots and tug him onto the floor.

A student—Derin, the tall boy from Lari's quartet—leaped toward her. Madori jumped back but was too slow; Derin's fist slammed into her cheek, knocking her down. She blinked, seeing stars, and kicked wildly. Her foot hit Derin's shin and he fell, muttering curses. Three other Radians replaced him, leaping onto Madori, and she screamed and punched one's face. Her ring cut through his cheek and he fell back.

Elorian curses filled the air, and Madori kicked off another student to see Radians mobbing Jitomi. The Elorian boy was swinging his fists, shouting battle cries in Ilari, the tongue of his southern empire.

But the Radians were too many; a dozen filled the room and a hundred others filled the arcade outside. Boots pressed down on Madori, pinning her to the floor. Fists slammed into Neekeya and

Tam, knocking them down. Hands grabbed Jitomi, tugging him outside.

"Jitomi!" Madori cried out, and another fist drove into her head, and for a moment she saw only shadows and lights, heard only ringing.

She thought that she would die here. Blood filled her mouth and dripped into her eyes. She had no time for magic; it was all she could do to keep breathing. She had to keep breathing. Breath by breath, like her father had taught her. Yet Torin had meant that breathing was easy, a rhythm always with her, an anchor to cling too. Right now breathing felt like the most difficult thing in the world, and boots drove into her stomach, and she doubled over.

No. I won't die here.

Lying on the floor, blows raining onto her, she balled her hands into fists.

Her parents had fought in the great Battle of Pahmey. They had sailed down the Inaro and slain mages in the port of Sinyong. They had faced the demon Ferius in Yintao, the greatest battle in the history of Moth, and finally slew him upon the Mountain of Time.

I am the daughter of heroes. I will not die in a school scuffle.

She pushed herself to her feet, and her magic blasted out of her.

Air slammed into her assailants. Furniture flew, crashing against them. Radians thudded against the walls, banged their heads, then slumped down, unconscious.

Neekeya lay on the floor, a gash bleeding on her forehead. Tam lay above her, shielding her with his body. Both were still breathing. Madori stood in the center of the room, feeling as if she held the air, the walls, the entire university in her arms. She had claimed objects before; now Madori felt as if she had claimed the world, held everything around her in her awareness.

Silent, her palms held outward as if carrying the weight of the air, she walked outside.

She stood in the cloister's eastern arcade—a portico of columns ahead of her, arches above her, the wall of chamber doors behind her. A mob of Radians had pinned Jitomi to one column. The Elorian was unconscious, his chin slumped to his chest, but the other students were holding him up. Fists and kicks thumped against the boy's thin frame. Blood ran down Jitomi's chin.

Madori thrust her arms out, palms facing toward the mob of Radians. Air blasted them, knocking them down. Standing a dozen feet away from him, Madori stretched out one finger, supporting Jitomi with a funnel of air. She gently lowered him to the ground.

A gurgling gasp sounded behind her.

Her strands of hair rising like seaweed in the water, crackling with energy, Madori turned around to see Lari.

The new Princess of Mageria stared, her own hair wild, her fingers curled up at her sides.

Madori smiled crookedly and took a step toward her.

With a strangled yelp, Lari spun on her heel and fled.

Madori wanted to chase the girl, to hurt her, maybe even to kill her, but her friends needed her. With the Radians all unconscious or fled, Madori released her magic, letting go of the awareness that connected her with all materials around her. She raced toward Jitomi and knelt above him.

Cuts covered him and blood dripped from his mouth. He was still breathing but that breath was shallow. Madori closed her eyes, trying to summon more magic, to heal his wounds, but she was too weary. Her body shook, and she found herself slumped next to him.

Footsteps thudded down the hall.

With a flutter of robes, Professor Fen burst into the hallway. The bald, mustached man gasped and sputtered.

"What— What—"

More feet shuffled, and old Professor Yovan raced from between two columns, nearly tripping over his beard. Madori tried to explain. She tried to tell them it wasn't her fault, but only slurred words left her mouth, barely words at all, merely sounds.

She tilted and Fen caught her head before it could slam against the floor. The last thing she saw was his concerned face, and then his eyes became blue oceans that she drowned in.

CHAPTER TWENTY-ONE
CAGED

Madori stood above his bed, her head lowered.

"I'm sorry, Jitomi." She tasted tears on her lips. "I'm so sorry."

He slept in the infirmary bed, breathing softly. Several other beds were occupied: some with other Elorian students, pulled from their rooms and beaten in the cloister, and other beds with Radians, many of whom Madori's magic had battered. Only by miracle had nobody died that turn.

But you came close to dying, Jitomi, she thought.

He seemed so peaceful, sleeping there. The dragon tattoo seemed to be sleeping too, its tail coiling along his neck, its head resting above his eye. Madori stroked the boy's hair. It was soft, smooth, and white as purest silk, the same hair her mother had, that all Elorians had. She leaned down and kissed his forehead.

"I'm sorry, Jitomi." Her tears splashed against him, and on a whim, not even realizing what she was doing, she kissed his lips.

He stirred and moaned. Madori pulled back, shocked at herself, raising her fingers to her mouth. She had kissed him! He was lying here sleeping, and . . . and . . .

She had never kissed a boy. One time back at her village, not long before leaving to Teel University, the brewer's boy had kissed her cheek and almost her mouth, a quick peck which had made her cheeks flush. But this—this had felt real, a kiss of compassion and excitement.

His eyes opened and he blinked a few times, struggling to bring her into focus.

"Madori," he whispered. "Why? Why are you sorry?"

She lowered her head and clasped his hand. "I'm sorry for Timandra, for the pain you experienced here. I'm half Timandrian. This is half my home. And . . . you came here, to our lands, seeking knowledge and magic. And this happened."

He smiled. "If you kiss me again, I will think it worth it."

She felt her cheeks flush and cursed herself. But she kissed him again. And it felt just as right.

Yet suddenly her eyes were damp, and a lump filled her throat, and she thought of the song she had sung—"The Journey Home." For a long time, Madori had thought that song meaningless to her, thought that her home lay hidden, a place she still had to find. But perhaps her home had always lain behind her old village, beyond the dusk, in the shadows of Eloria. Perhaps she had had to travel into sunlight to realize her home lay in moonlight.

"Someday, when we're mages, we'll return home," she whispered. "Our home lies in shadows . . . to the darkness we return."

She sat on his bed, then lay down beside him, placing her head against his shoulder. She laid her hand on his chest, and he stroked her hair—the stubble on the back and sides and the long, silky strands that framed her face.

"Do you remember just lying on a hill, watching the moon?" he said. "Did you ever imagine faces on it, dream of mountains and valleys?"

She nodded, smiling to herself, remembering her summers in Oshy. "Always. And do you remember the stars? I had a book of constellations, and I'd try to see them all in the sky. I used to imagine that the stars were distant worlds, millions of them, so far away I could never reach them. I imagined that I had a ship that could sail through the sky, and I visited every world, meeting dragons and clockwork soldiers and wise elders with long white beards."

"In Ilar we believe that the stars are great, distant flames, each borne by a great warrior." Jitomi smiled wryly. "In Ilar, most of our tales are of warriors, assassins, swordsmen, spies. Imagine me there—a thin boy who prefers to read books over swinging blades. My father thought me weak—no better than a girl, he said. You can imagine why I wanted to explore the lands of sunlight."

Madori thought back to her own kingdom of the night, the great land named Qaelin, a sprawling empire of crystal towers, pagodas as large as all of Teel University, and a little village by a starlit river. She nestled against Jitomi. "So when we graduate, come with me to Qaelin. Forget about Ilar if your people don't respect you. Forget about this land of sunlight. We'll both go to Qaelin, two mages. We can live by the river, imagine faces on the moon, and seek the constellations."

Robes fluttered and Professor Yovan shuffled toward them, clucking his tongue.

"Now now, little boy," said the professor, pointing at Madori. "You must let young Master Jitomi get his rest." The old man tossed his beard across his shoulder and rolled up his sleeves. "I've healed most of his wounds, but he's still weak, and he still needs more healing." He touched the scars on her cheeks, the ones Lari had given her. "Did you heal these wounds yourself, little one?"

Madori nodded. "I did."

The old healer beamed. "Excellent work! Since the first lesson I taught you, I knew you were a great healer, little boy."

"Girl," she said.

He snorted, fluttering his lips. "Same difference. Now get off that bed and let me do my magic."

Professor Yovan was rolling his sleeves back down, and Jitomi had fallen back asleep, when the Horns of Teel blew again.

* * * * *

When Madori stepped back into the cloister, answering the bells' call, she found the place transformed into a nightmare.

General Woodworth, the great elm tree, had been cut down. Where it had grown now rose an iron statue, twenty feet tall, depicting Lord Serin clad in armor. The tyrant was facing east toward the distant lands of night, his fist against his heart, his second hand holding his sword. From the galleries—four rows of columns that surrounded the courtyard, leading toward the dormitories—hung great banners of Radianism, depicting the sun eclipsing the Elorian moon. The old wooden stage was draped with more banners, and a podium rose upon it, displaying the sigil in gold and silver. Worst of all, soldiers surrounded the expanse, clad in black steel, holding pikes and shields.

For a moment Madori thought she had entered the wrong place. This seemed less like a university and more like a military camp.

When all the students stood in rows, the horns fell silent and Professor Atratus stepped onto the pulpit. He no longer wore his ratty old robes, the ones with the fraying hems. His new robes were darker than the night, hemmed in gold. Lari rose to stand at his side, wearing a golden tiara and holding a scepter, its head shaped as the eclipse of Radianism.

Across the cloister, everyone stared—other professors, Timandrian students with Radian brooches, and Elorian students with their snake pins. After a long moment, Atratus spoke, his voice so loud—magically amplified—that Madori started.

"Students of Teel. Fellow professors. I have some news that may upset—or delight—you. Headmistress Egeria has been accused of a terrible crime." Atratus sneered. "We all witnessed it at this very place only last turn. She stood upon this stage, vowing to defend Elorians—our enemy, the enemy of every pure-blooded Timandrian. Treason!" He pounded his fist into his palm, and students jeered across the cloister. "For her treachery, the illustrious Lord Serin, God of Sunlight, has sent forth his troops to protect us. Egeria has been sent to the capital in chains to stand trial for her crime." Some students gasped at this; others cheered. Grinning like a wolf over its prey, Atratus continued. "My great lord has named me, his humble servant, new Headmaster of Teel."

Madori could barely remain standing. Her head spun and Tam had to grab her lest she fell.

It's over, she realized. *My dream to become a mage, my hope of surviving here—gone.*

A drum beat and the sound of hooves rose from behind. Madori spun around to see two burly black horses—each twice the size of Hayseed—pull a wagon into the courtyard. The driver seemed almost as beefy as the horses, his frayed robe stretching tightly across his board shoulders, his hood revealing only a stubbly chin and thin lips. Upon the wagon rose an iron cage roughly the size of the Motley's bedchamber.

Atratus spoke again, restrained glee twisting his voice. "All subhuman undesirables, those wearing the serpent pin of shame, are henceforth banished from Teel University. You will step onto this wagon, which will transport you to the border of Mageria. There you may go where you will, so long as you never more set foot upon the lands of glorious Radianism."

The cloister burst into chaos.

Students gasped. Some cheered. At once the soldiers stepped forth, marching among the rows of students, shouting out the names of Elorians.

"Shen Quelon!"

"Heetan Doromi!"

"Danong Fan!"

A few of the Elorian students glanced around nervously, then followed the soldiers toward the wagon. Other Elorians were too slow to budge; the soldiers grabbed their arms, manhandling them toward the cage. The names kept ringing across the university.

"Keshuan Hatan!"

"Maen Hao!"

"Jitomi Hashido!"

Standing beside Madori, the tattooed Elorian boy glanced at her.

"Don't go," Madori whispered to him.

Jitomi touched her cheek. Fear filled his large blue eyes—but courage too. "It will be all right. I—"

Soldiers grabbed him, tugging him away from her. Madori shouted. She tried to tug him back. She leaped onto one soldier, only for the brute to shove her down. She landed hard on the cobblestones.

"Jitomi!" she shouted, a soldier's boot on her chest, pinning her down.

Jitomi looked at her, a sad smile on his lips, as the soldiers tugged him toward the wagon. Already they were shoving Elorians into the cage. One girl moved too slowly; a soldier backhanded her, spraying blood, and shoved her into the cage, slamming her against the bars. Jitomi climbed in solemnly, refusing to be shoved, holding his head high. He stood tall, staring at Madori between the bars, his face expressionless.

Finally twenty-five Elorians filled the cage, pressing against one another—the entire Elorian population of Teel. Madori still lay on the cobblestones, the soldier pinning her down, his boot nearly cracking her ribs.

It was Atratus himself who called her name, shouting it out like a curse. "Madori Greenmoat!"

The soldier lifted his foot off her chest and leaned down to grab her.

With a snarl, Madori hurtled a ball of air against him. With a clank of armor, the man fell.

"No!" Madori shouted.

Several more soldiers advanced toward her. She hissed and chose their armor, claimed the metal, and heated it. The metal turned red hot, and the soldiers screamed, pawing at the straps, trying to tear off the plates.

"I will not leave!" Madori shouted. She chose the air beneath her and shoved herself several feet above ground. She hovered, gazing at the crowd. "I am the daughter of Torin Greenmoat, a hero of Timandra, a warrior of sunlight. This sunlight flows through my veins. I will stay at Teel. I will become a great mage." She stared at Atratus across the crowd. "You cannot deny my Timandrian blood. I stay."

Atratus grinned—a horrible grin that seemed to split his face in two, stretching from ear to ear, revealing all his crooked teeth. He thrust out his palm, driving a ball of smoke and dust her way. The projectile took the form of a snake, hissing, fanged, its eyes blazing white. Madori tried to block the attack, but the snake tore through her defenses and wrapped around her.

She crashed down, writhing, the smoky serpent crushing her. Its fangs drove into her leg, and she cried out in pain.

"Chain her!" Atratus shouted, voice rising like steam, his amusement and hatred coiling together. "Chain her and toss her in with the others."

The soldiers tugged her to her feet. A fist drove into her cheek, and she saw nothing but darkness. Her chin tilted forward, and the magical serpent still wrapped around her torso, hissing, licking her with an icy tongue. She tried to struggle. She screamed, kicked, blasted out magic. But she was only one girl; she could not resist them all.

Chains clamped around her wrists, binding her arms behind her back. More chains hobbled her ankles. The guards dragged her toward the wagon.

"Look at me, Timandra!" Madori shouted as the guards lifted her. "Look at me and behold your shame! I curse you in the name of darkness."

Smirking, the soldiers shoved her into the cage. She thudded against the other Elorians, and the cage door swung shut. The lock was bolted, sealing her within. Blood dripped down her forehead, and she tugged at the door and bars, but they wouldn't budge. The cage was so crowded she had no room to sit; the Elorians pressed against one another like matches in a box.

The driver cracked his whip, and the horses began to move, tugging the wagon out of the cloister. The Radian students began to cheer, tossing mud and refuse onto the wagon. An egg flew through the bars and cracked against Madori's face. A rotten potato followed, spilling its liquid onto her. Every student they passed shouted in mockery, and one tossed a stone; it slammed into Madori's shoulder.

"Goodbye nightcrawlers!" the students chanted. "Radian rises!"

As the wagon trundled across the courtyard, Madori— covered in trash and blood—stared between the bars, and all her rage drained away. Chained, beaten, broken, she could only stare in stunned silence. Her eyes fell upon Tam and Neekeya; her friends were standing among the crowd of Timandrians, hugging each other, their faces pale and their eyes wide. Neekeya was weeping and Tam was shouting something toward Madori, but she couldn't make out his words.

She raised her eyes. Upon the stage, rising from the crowd, stood Lari Serin. The princess pouted mockingly at Madori, drew a fake tear down her cheek, and waved.

The wagon passed under the archway, and the doors of Teel University slammed shut behind Madori, forever sealing its secrets, knowledge, and magic.

CHAPTER TWENTY-TWO
GLASS AND STRAW

Cam stood in the rocky field, military tents surrounding him, and stared dubiously at the contraption.

"Are you sure this will work?" he asked, hearing the doubt in his voice. "It looks a little . . . wilted."

The camp bustled around him: troops marching between tents, smoke rising from a hundred cooking fires, swordsmen drilling in the dust, archers shooting at straw targets, and squires polishing the armor of knights. They had been camped here at Hornsford for several turns now, guarding the bridge from Mageria. Even from here, a couple miles away, Cam could see the tip of Sunmotte Citadel upon the western horizon.

You muster there, Serin, he thought, grimacing. *Twenty thousand of your troops drill for war. Soon you will try to cross Hornsford Bridge . . . and I'll be waiting.*

He returned his eyes to the contraption that swayed in the fields before him. The two dojai—assassins and spies from the darkness of Eloria—called it a hot air balloon. To Cam it looked more like a giant, half-inflated sack of wine.

He turned toward the two dojai who stood beside him. One was small, no larger than a child, clad in tight black silk. Many daggers hung on belts across her chest, throwing stars were strapped to her legs, and her large Elorian eyes gleamed in the sunlight. The second stood seven feet tall, his chest broad as a barrel, his long white hair flowing in the wind. His eyes, though also large, were narrowed to mere slits, mimicking the line of his mouth. A massive katana, large as a spear, hung across his back.

"Oh, you silly king!" said Nitomi, the smaller of the pair. "Of course it's looking a little wilted. It's not inflated yet! Once inflated it'll be the size of ten elephants! If you skinned them, that is, and sewed their skin together into a balloon." She tapped her chin. "Do you think it would float though? You know, because elephant skin is really thick and wrinkly, and besides, I like elephants and wouldn't want to skin them. Do you have elephants in this army of yours? I want to ride one! I rode a panther here—you know, we have lots of those in Eloria—but an elephant! With the trunk and all. Do you think their trunks can hold a sword? I can try to train one, maybe a whole army of swordsman elephants—I mean, swordselephant elephants. I mean—"

Beside her, the giant dojai groaned and covered his ears. "Qato hurts."

Nitomi looked at her companion, then slapped her palm over her mouth. She spoke between her fingers. "I've gone and done it again, speaking too much. My mother always told me: Nitomi, your mouth will fall right off. I've never seen a mouth fall off before, but once I think I saw a lizard's tail fall off, and—"

"Nitomi!" Cam said, interrupting her. The only way to have a conversation with the little dojai was to interrupt a lot. "Focus. The hot air balloon. Are you sure you know how to fly it?"

Her face brightened. "Of course I do! I've seen loads of hot air balloons! I—"

"*Seen?*" Cam asked, grimacing.

She nodded, grinning, and hopped around. "Oh yes, I've seen many paintings of them!"

Cam groaned. "Paintings?"

Nitomi nodded again. "Oh, they're so beautiful. I used to look at them all the time as a little girl. I can't wait to be in one myself! Hey, Cam, do you know how to fly hot air balloons?"

He gripped his head. "Nitomi! Idar's beard! You're the dojai here. You're the Elorian. You're the one who brought the hot air balloon here all the way from Eloria. How would I know how to fly it?"

She placed her hands on her hips, raised her chin, and glared at him. "Well, you're a king. You should really know these *spying* things, Camlin, especially since you intend to use this *spy* balloon to *spy* on the enemy. I mean, who do you think I am?"

"A spy!" he shouted. "Isn't that what dojai are? Spies and assassins?"

She looked down at her black silks, many daggers, throwing stars, and grapple, then back up at him. Her eyes widened. "A *spy*! That's what I am! Oh my, I did wonder why you brought me here. You know, I always thought dojai were just sort of sneaky and quick, but spying! That explains a lot." She turned toward Qato. "We're spies, Qato!"

The giant Elorian groaned. "Qato knows."

During the conversation, the hot air balloon had continued to inflate. The fire burned inside the basket, filling the balloon with more and more hot air. Soon the basket began to float, ropes tethering it to the ground.

Quick as a gazelle, Nitomi bounded into the basket and grinned. Qato followed, silent and grim; the basket dipped several inches, brushing the ground.

"Come on, silly!" Nitomi said, gesturing for Cam. "Step inside. We can't do all the spying for you."

Cam groaned. "That's the whole idea of me hiring spies."

Nitomi nodded vigorously. "And see? We brought you a hot air balloon. We've earned our keep. And I'm not flying without you! My mother always told me: Nitomi, if you ever meet a king, you can't fly off in a hot air balloon without him! Well, at least, I think she said that. She might have been talking about how I'm full of hot air, and how I'm not supposed to talk so much around a king, but I reckon I've already done a lot of that around you, so it's too late, and now you have to fly with me."

Cam couldn't argue with that logic. Sighing and rolling his eyes, he stepped into the basket and untethered the ropes.

The hot air balloon began to rise.

Cam leaned over the edge of the basket. Every foot ascended revealed more of their camp. The tents stretched out in rows. Between them, troops were drilling, sharpening swords, cooking meals, standing guard, and all awaiting the bloodshed. The balloon rose higher, revealing the edges of the camp: horses in corrals, palisades of sharpened logs, women washing clothes and pots in the river, engineers arguing over the construction of trebuchets, and dozens of supply wagons traveling along the road through the plains of Arden, bringing in supplies. Beyond the men rolled the vastness of the world: fields of swaying grass, hills speckled with boulders, copses of elms and birches, and the Red River flowing across the land.

The warriors of Arden, the bravest and strongest of their realm, are only ants from up here, Cam thought, the realization spinning his mind. *That's all we are, insects bustling across the world. Viewed from far enough above, the wars of men are no more significant than those of ants.*

"We're flying!" Nitomi's eyes widened. "Everything looks like toys from up here, as if I can just reach down and pick them up."

The little dojai leaned over the basket, reaching into the air, then yelped as she tilted over. Cam had to grab the seat of her pants and tug her back into the basket.

Qato groaned and clutched his belly. "Qato queasy."

Nitomi bustled about the basket, tugging ropes and pulleys. Vents opened in the balloon, releasing streams of hot air, propelling the vessel westward toward the riverbank. Cam himself felt queasy as the basket tilted, the balloon dragging it through the air, and he clutched the rim. Qato turned green.

Only Nitomi remained high-spirited. "It's like flying on a dragon!" She grinned. "Did you know that Koyee and Torin flew on a dragon once? Really, I saw it! Do you think they have hidden dragons in Timandra? Do you think we'll see one? Do you think they have elephants here?" She hopped about, rocking the basket. "Maybe it'll let us ride it—the dragon, that is, if they have one—though I hope it's not scared of this balloon, because when I was a little one, I saw a floating lantern once, and I thought it was a ghost, and then—"

"Nitomi!" Cam grabbed her. "We're sinking. Fly this thing!"

She gulped and nodded, tugging more ropes and twisting knobs. Vents closed and more heat blasted upward. The balloon began to ascend again, then veered westward. They left the riverbank behind, floated above the Red River, and were soon flying over the plains of Mageria. Hornsford Bridge seemed smaller than a toy from up here, its towers no larger than wooden counter-squares pieces. Further west, however, Sunmotte Citadel still seemed forbidding, even from this high above. Its mote, double walls, and guard towers shielded its inner core of many towers and banners. It seemed to Cam almost as large as Kingswall.

But Kingswall is a city of tradesmen, artists, thinkers, families, he thought. *This citadel houses nothing but soldiers dedicated to destruction.*

Myriads of those soldiers stood outside the citadel, drilling in the fields: swordsmen clad in black armor, riders upon horses, and mages in black robes. Lines and lines of the troops stretched across the fields, Radian banners rising among them. Most of the troops remained still, maintaining their orderly rows. Only a handful bustled about, pointing up at the balloon.

"Nitomi, take us a little higher," Cam said.

She nodded, tugging more ropes to seal the vents, then twisting knobs to release more heat. The balloon ascended higher, hovering over the army below. A few Magerian archers tugged back bowstrings, and arrows flew into the air. Cam winced and caught his breath, but they were high enough; the arrows reached their zenith below the basket and fell back downward.

Cam leaned over the basket, frowning. "Only a handful of archers are firing. Only a few soldiers are moving—mostly the ones on the perimeters." He tilted his head. "Something is wrong here. Nitomi, take us a little further west—over those lines of troops."

She nodded and the balloon moved across the sky. They hovered over the lines of horses and swordsmen. And yet the troops below stood frozen.

Nitomi opened a cylindrical case which hung from her belt and pulled out a long instrument. It looked like a leather scroll, but glass lenses sealed each of its ends. The little dojai brought one lens to her eye, leaned over the basket, and stared down. She gasped.

"Oh dear! They . . . Cam, they're just frozen. Frozen like freezing ice frozen by freezing spells!" She gulped, straightened, and handed him her instrument. "Look."

Cam frowned at the cylinder. "What is this tool?"

"A scope!" Nitomi grinned. "We build them in the Dojai School in the mountains. Nobody else in all of Moth knows about them, only us spies. Well, I guess you know about them now too. But don't tell anyone!" She growled and raised her fist. "It's supposed to be a secret, but I've gone and talked too much again, and now you know too, so you *have* to *promise* to be quiet, because if you tell anyone about scopes, I'd probably have to kill you—the Dojai School demands it!—but I don't really want to kill you, because I like you, almost as much as I like elephants, so—"

He patted her shoulder; the little woman seemed so agitated her eyes were dampening and her cheeks flushing. "I won't tell," he said. "I'll just look and return the scope to you."

Gently, he took the scope from her hands, placed the lens against his eye, and looked downward. His breath caught. He lowered the scope, raised it to his eye again, and shook his head in amazement. This piece of Elorian ingenuity amazed him as much as the hot air balloon. Staring through the scope, the soldiers below seemed several times larger, so large he could make out the Radian sigils upon their breastplates.

He frowned. "Something's wrong."

Nitomi nodded. "I'd say a massive army mustering right on our border is something wrong. Almost as wrong as skinning elephants. I—"

"Not that." Cam stared through the scope again, looking at the rows of swordsmen, horses, and archers. "They're . . . dummies. Straw dummies. Thousands of them."

Nitomi tilted her head, grabbed the scope from him, and stared down. She gasped and covered her mouth. "Evil magic! Somebody turned them all to straw!"

Cam's heart sank, and a tremble seized his legs. "No magic," he whispered. "A ruse."

He tightened his jaw and balled his fists. He thought of his wife, beautiful Queen Linee; of his best friend, Torin; of hundreds of thousands of people back in Kingswall.

He turned to the two dojai. They were staring at him silently—Qato somber as ever, Nitomi gasping.

"Take us back to our camp," Cam said, forcing the words past stiff lips. "Kingswall is in danger . . . and a month's ride away. We head back at once."

CHAPTER TWENTY-THREE
INTO THE WOODS

The wagon trundled down the road, jostling the Elorians inside their cage. With every bump, Madori slammed against the bars, and her fellow outcasts swayed and pushed her harder against the iron. They were only a few miles away from Teel University now, but bruises already covered her body. The gloomy sky and clammy rain did little to alleviate her discomfort.

"Damn shackles!" For the hundredth time, she chose and claimed the shackles that bound her wrists and ankles. Try as she may, she couldn't change the metal, only rattle it, nor could she snap the iron—it was too hard. "I can't break them."

Jitomi stood with his arms wrapped around her, providing only partial protection from the iron bars and the elbows of their fellow students. Still, she was thankful for his embrace.

"We're too weary for magic now." He kissed her cheek and tucked one of her strands behind her ear. "And it's hard to change something as intricate as a lock when the wagon keeps bouncing. When we stop, we'll try again."

She sighed and leaned her head against his shoulder, only for the wagon to bounce again and toss them against the bars. She winced. She imagined that under her robes, her body was striped like a zebra. Shivering with cold, weary, and aching all over, healing magic was beyond her grasp too. She made a halfhearted attempt—the latest in many—to claim and bend the cage bars, only to slump in weariness again.

"If only we had stayed at Teel another year, we'd be powerful enough to break out of this place," Madori said. She sighed. "I didn't think our first year at Teel would end like—"

"Silence, nightcrawler!" shouted the wiry, one-eyed soldier Madori had secretly nicknamed Patchy. Walking beside the wagon, the brute lashed his club between the bars. Madori tilted back just fast enough to avoid the blow. "You talk again, I open this cage and bash in your teeth."

On the other side of the cage, the second guard—this one a beefy, older man with white stubble—burst out laughing. "We'll soon do some bashing. Lord Serin said we reach the forest first. There we—"

"You too shut your mouth!" snapped Patchy. "I'll bash your teeth in too."

The larger guard fell silent. The two kept trudging through the mud, the rain pattering against their helmets and armor. Ahead upon the wagon, the third of their captors—the dour coach rider—leaned forward in his seat. Madori had still not heard that one speak nor seen his face. From the cage, the driver seemed like a gargoyle, hunched over and stony, the rain streaming off his cloak.

We'll soon do some bashing . . .

Madori looked at Jitomi. She saw the same concern in his eyes.

He leaned against her, pretending to kiss her ear, and whispered in Qaelish, the language of her Elorian homeland. A child of Ilar, his accent was thick but his words confident. "Conserve your magic. You might need it yet."

She stroked his head and nestled against him, pretending to nuzzle his cheek. "Where are they taking us, Jitomi?"

He held her close, stroking the stubbly hair on the back of her head. "I don't know but I doubt they'll just set us free." He let his hood droop, curtaining their faces, hiding them from the guards. When he spoke, his lips brushed against hers. "Whatever happens, I'll look after you."

She nodded, her eyelids brushing his cheeks. "And I'll look after you. I'm a better mage than you are."

He sighed. "With me battered and bruised, there are lumps of coal that are better mages than me right now."

She stifled a laugh, glancing back at the guards. "I've seen you in Magical Healing. There were always lumps of coal better at magic than you, at least in that class."

"Well, Madori, you are the best healer Teel has had in—" He bit down on his words and glanced out the bars; Patchy was walking near again, grumbling under his breath about nightcrawlers and their stench.

Madori too feel silent, deciding to conserve her breath along with her magic. She stood still, holding Jitomi, wishing the cage left her room to sit down or even stretch. The other outcasts pressed against them, silent and dour, rain dripping off their robes and white hair.

The hours stretched on and the guards gave them no rest. Thunder rolled in the distance and lightning flashed, illuminating a distant fort upon a hill. Madori was nodding off—even as she still stood on her sore feet—when she saw the marching army.

She stiffened. Jitomi inhaled sharply and held her closer. Around them, the other students narrowed their eyes.

Countless Radian troops were marching toward them along the road, each man clad in steel and armed with a sword, dagger, and spear. When lightning flashed again, the Radian eclipses shone upon breastplates, shields, and helmets. The wagon was moving north while these troops marched south, moving in two lines, mud staining their boots.

"Elorian prisoners!" one soldier cried out, his eyes widening to see the cage. "Damn nightcrawlers."

Another soldier guffawed and slammed his blade against the bars. "Hang these bastards. Death to Eloria!"

The wagon kept trundling south, and the soldiers passed them by, one line of troops on each side, as if the wagon were rolling down some great, steel throat. Some soldiers stared with wide eyes, others sneered, and some guffawed. One man began to sing a song, its words lovingly detailing the plunder of Eloria and the slaughter of "nightcrawlers." Soon all the troops were singing as they walked by. One man tossed a rock into the cage, hitting Jitomi in the shoulder. Another soldier dropped his pants and wriggled his backside at the cage.

"Kind of looks like Lari," Madori remarked to Jitomi.

"Enjoy your bars, scum!" one troop said and spat onto Madori. "Once we invade the night, we won't just cage you. We'll drive our swords into your bellies." He waved his sword as if to demonstrate.

It seemed an hour that the troops kept walking by, two by two; there must have been thousands. Finally the last stragglers passed them by, leaving the wagon to trundle alone along the cold, empty road.

"They're all riled up and look ready for war." Jitomi whispered. "Where do you imagine they're going?"

Madori chewed her lip. "Not to attack Arden; an army that size would have to cross at Hornsford, and they're moving the wrong way. Might be a battle on the southern border with Naya. Or maybe Serin just wants to bolster his troops in the capital, and—"

"Silence!" Patchy's club swung through the bars again, hitting Madori on the arm. "One more word and teeth spill."

She fell silent but her mind still worked feverishly. With Serin on the throne and his troops moving across the land, war was near. She had heard enough of her parents' war stories to smell it in the air. She thanked Xen Qae, Idar, and the constellations of Eloria that at least Mageria shared no border with the night. If Serin had access to Eloria, she had a feeling all those troops would be streaming into the shadows right now, plundering and butchering and burning.

Arden still separates Serin from the night, she thought, feeling some relief. *King Camlin and Queen Linee defend that land. Serin cannot cross.* She took a shuddering breath. *Eloria is safe.*

Trying not to remember the stories her parents had told her of the last invasion of Eloria, she leaned her head against Jitomi's shoulder. He held her close and stroked her hair, running his hand again and again between the stubbly back and the long, silky strands that drooped from over her brow.

They must have been traveling for at least a turn now, maybe two. Madori's belly ached with hunger, and her eyelids drooped with weariness. At some point she nodded off, pinned between the bars and Jitomi, sleeping fitfully even as the wagon bounced and her feet ached beneath her. When she opened her eyes again, the rain had stopped, though thick clouds still covered the sky; it seemed almost as dark as Eloria, and she was thankful for her oversized eyes. Jitomi was still awake, his own large eyes gleaming as they moved back and forth, scanning the landscape.

While she had slept, they had entered a forest. Oaks twisted around them, their trunks forming the shapes of beasts and cruel faces in her imagination. Pines coiled, sending branches like lecherous fingers to slap against the bars. With the canopy shielding the overcast sky, the light dimmed further. The leaves turned dark gray, the shadows dark like demons lurking between the trunks. Madori was reminded of the dusk, that twilit strip that lay many miles away, a land neither day or night. When lightning flashed, the trees—white, looming, twisted—seemed like goblins about to strike, their faces long and cruel.

Finally the wagon rolled to a halt.

The prisoners—Madori had come to think of them as prisoners rather than outcasts—jostled against one another. After moving for so long, even in stillness Madori's head spun and her legs swayed. Patchy—she still did not know his true name—spat into the dirt, unlocked the cage, and tugged its door open.

"Everybody out!" He banged his club against the bars. "Out, vermin! Out or I'll burn the lot of you."

Madori stood closest to the door. She had spent the ride wanting nothing more than to leave the cage. Looking around at the dark forest, she suddenly preferred staying behind the bars. Yet when Patchy raised his club again, she winced and began to climb out. Her ankles were still hobbled, her wrists chained behind her back, and she could only move slowly. Once past the cage door, she slipped off the wagon's edge, tilted over, and thumped facedown into the mud. The foul paste filled her mouth, and Patchy stood above her, his boot inches from her face.

"Up, maggot." He grabbed her by the collar and yanked her to her feet. Madori growled, spat out mud, and lunged toward him, intending to knock him down. He stepped back and Madori, weak and dizzy, fell back into the mud.

It was Jitomi who helped her rise, as gentle as Patchy was rough. The other Elorians emerged from the cage too. They stood together on the roadside, twenty-five banished students.

"Where are we?" Madori said. "You can't just leave us here. We're in the middle of nowhere. We'd never find our way home from here."

The trees creaked and a rider emerged onto the road, still cloaked in shadows. A voice rose, smooth and cruel as a blade.

"My darling Madori, that is exactly the idea."

The horse stepped closer, revealing the rider—a tall man in armor, his hair golden, his eyes cold and blue. The hard, handsome face twisted into a smile.

Madori sucked in her breath and took a step back.

"Lord Serin," she whispered.

CHAPTER TWENTY-FOUR
THE BATTLE OF MUDWATER

Torin walked through the palace gardens with his queen, missing his home so badly even the aromatic flowers, the bright birds, and his queen's company could not soothe his soul.

"I've never seen you so troubled." Linee's brow furrowed in concern, and she placed a hand upon his arm. "Torin, smile for me."

He looked at Linee—his queen and his very old friend. Her golden hair was raised in an elaborate construction of braids and curls, and her gown shone with jewels. Idar's sigil, a half-sun, gleamed upon her breast. Torin took her hands in his and squeezed them, thinking back to that turn—twenty years ago—when he had first come to these gardens and met his queen. Linee had been only twenty then, a silly young woman, flighty and careless as a butterfly. The years had filled her eyes with wisdom but had not dulled her beauty; her skin was still unlined, her hair untouched by white, the only sign of her age a lingering sadness that hung about her like a shadow over a summer garden.

"Queen Linee Solira," he said softly, her hands in his. "Few will know what we've been through, how we fought, how we suffered, what we saw all those years ago. We've lived in peace since then. We cannot let this peace burn."

"We will not!" she said. "Cam guards the bridge; it will not fall. Our walls here are strong; they will stand."

Torin watched a bumblebee fly from flower to flower. "Lord Serin sits upon Mageria's throne, and he will not sit idly, content to rule one land. He does not muster his forces for defense but for war. Eloria is the prize he craves . . . and we stand in his way."

Linee nodded. "And we will remain standing. We've sent word to the night; troops will arrive from Qaelin, swelling our numbers. Already our smiths work turn by turn, forging new swords and armor. Already our commanders train new men to fight upon our walls and in our fields." She touched Torin's arm. "We've faced enemies before and defeated them. Last war, we were not afraid."

He smiled thinly. "Last war we were young. Youths are too naive for fear, perhaps. But now we're older, and now, yes Linee, I'm afraid."

She smiled too, head lowered. "I lied. I was afraid last time too." She looked back up at him, and her eyes sparkled with tears. She pulled him into an embrace and laid her head upon his shoulder. "I'm glad you're here. I know how hard it is for you, being away from Koyee and Madori. Thank you."

He was still holding her when the alarm bells clanged across the city.

Linee gasped and stared at him with wide eyes. Torin grimaced and clenched his fists. The bells pealed across the gardens, not the high bells of festivals but the deep, harsh bells of war.

It's too soon, Torin thought. *Serin's forces are still at Hornsford. We're not ready.*

He tore apart from Linee. He ran.

He could barely remember leaving the palace gardens. Within what seemed like heartbeats, he was donning armor and riding his horse out the palace gates. A horseman met him there, riding up from the city streets, his face dripping sweat. Torin

recognized the youth: Prince Omry, the heir to Arden, a
seventeen-year-old boy several minutes older than his twin, Prince
Tam.

"Sir Greenmoat!" said the prince, his brown hair matted
across his brow.

Torin halted his horse. The bells still clanged across the city.
"What's the news, Omry?"

"An enemy in the south!" Omry panted. "They're emerging
from the forest across the river. They march onto Mudwater
Bridge."

Torin cursed and spurred his horse. The beast burst into a
gallop, and Omry rode at his side. They raced down the cobbled
streets of Kingswall, passing between tall buildings of white bricks
and red roof tiles, leaving the palace behind. Steeples, domed
temples, and squat workshops all blurred as he galloped, and
Torin's heart seemed to beat with the same intensity as his horse's
hooves. Other soldiers were bustling around him, heading to the
southwestern wall. City folk—merchants in dyed cotton,
tradesmen in leather and wool, and commoners in homespun—
rushed into their homes, climbed onto roofs to peer south, or
prayed in the streets.

Finally Torin reached Tigers' Gate, one of Kingswall's seven
gates. Two towers framed its archway, guarding the southwestern
wall. A thousand years old, Tigers' Gate had long been a
passageway for Nayan merchants. The fur-clad, fiery-haired
rainforest dwellers often entered this gate, bringing the bounty of
their realm: tiger pelts, ivory jewels, caged birds, cocoa and coffee
beans, exotic fruits, aromatic sandalwood, and spices not found
north of the Sern River. For a thousand years, Tigers' Gate had
been the valve connecting Arden with Naya.

The bells still clanging, Torin dismounted his horse and
entered the gatehouse. He climbed the spiraling staircase, finally

emerging onto the top of the western tower. Standing between the battlements, he stared south and felt himself pale.

A cobbled road ran out the gate, traveling across the plains to the Sern River, the border with Naya. The Sern was a mile wide, gushing and uncrossable, aside from a ford a mile southwest of the city. Here, where the river thinned, the road connected with Mudwater Bridge. The bridge was narrow, half the size of the great Hornsford in the north—a passageway for merchants, its bricks mossy, its foundations overrun with reeds. A single tower guarded the northern, Ardish side of the bridge; the southern side disappeared into the Nayan forest. Mudwater was usually empty, only seeing traffic every seven turns when Nayan merchants emerged from their forest, pushing carts full of supplies.

This turn, standing atop the tower, Torin beheld a host of hundreds emerging from the forest, bearing Radian banners.

"Magerians," he whispered, staring at their black steel plates, their longswords, and the dark robes of their mages. "Serin's men."

Omry emerged onto the tower battlements too, stared at the host, and drew the symbol of Idar—a semicircle—upon his chest. "Idar save us."

The forest rustled behind the enemy troops; it seemed to Torin that thousands of soldiers still hid among the trees. The chants rose, ringing across the land.

"Radian rises! Radian rises!"

Torin clutched the battlements, understanding at once. Of course. He gritted his teeth, and his heart banged against his ribs.

We were fooled. Of course Serin let us escape at Hornsford Bridge. Of course he let Cam and I come here with the news.

"Serin never intended to attack at Hornsford," he muttered. "The bastard drove through Naya, hidden in the rainforest, like a clot crawling hidden through a vein. And now he strikes at our heart."

Below in the courtyard, Ardish riders were gathering before
the gate, their horses armored. Spears glinted and shields
displayed the raven of Arden upon gold fields. Behind them,
along the streets of Kingswall, footmen were gathering, clad in
chain mail and bearing longswords.

"It's not enough," Omry said, echoing Torin's thoughts.
"With most of our troops in the west, this city is a ripe fruit for
the picking."

Torin grunted. "Yet we will fight the enemy nonetheless."

The two men raced down the tower, ran into the courtyard,
and mounted their horses, joining two hundred other riders.
Several hundred infantrymen stood behind them, swords drawn.
A squire blew a horn, and the doors of Tigers' Gate creaked open,
revealing the countryside, the river, and the distant bridge. Already
the enemy banners—the buffalo of Mageria and the eclipse of
Radianism—were crossing toward the northern bank.

At the head of the city forces, Torin raised his katana—the
sword Eloria had gifted him almost two decades ago, the sword
he had fought the last war with, the sword he would finally wield
again. "Men of Arden!" he shouted. "War! War is upon us. Fight
with me, with Torin Greenmoat. Fight for Arden!"

With a sound like thunder, the riders of Arden burst out of
the gates and galloped across the plains of their kingdom.

"Sons of Arden!" cried Prince Omry, rising at Torin's side.
"Raise the raven banners and send the enemy to the Abyss!"

The land rose and fell around Torin—a river to his left, the
plains to his right. They streamed forward, two hundred horses,
tearing up grass and dirt, as behind them surged hundreds of
footmen. Ahead, blood rose in a mist from the center of the
bridge; the Mudwater's defenders, a mere fifty Ardishmen, were
clashing swords with the enemy and falling fast. Before Torin
could even reach the bridge, the last defender fell.

Banners raised high, the riders of Mageria streamed across the bridge, heading onto the Ardish riverbank. Horsemen rode at their lead, all in steel, a vanguard of two hundred riders. Behind rode robed figures upon midnight stallions, their faces hidden inside their robes. Finally, behind these dark mages, marched the infantry of Mageria, emerging from the trees in two rows like serpents of many steel segments. Leading this host rode its captain, a figure taller than any Torin had ever seen. The man—if a man he was—rode upon a horse the size of an elephant, and four arms sprouted from his torso, each holding a blade. Upon his black breastplate, burning like red fire, appeared the eclipse of Radianism, shining with horrible light.

"Here rides Lord Gehena!" said Prince Omry, riding at Torin's side. "Books speak of him, a man magically enhanced, mixed with the blood of ancient giants."

The dark captain raised his head, and he seemed to stare across the plains directly at Torin. Two hundred yards still separated the hosts, and a black helmet like a barrel hid the giant's face, but Torin saw red eyes gleaming within, staring into him, searing like two embers pressed against his flesh.

He swallowed down the fear that choked him, tore his eyes away from the horrible half-man, and shouted to his troops. "For Arden! For our home! Send the enemy back and know no fear!"

Hoisting the raven standards, outnumbered many times, the forces of Arden galloped to meet their enemy.

The armies crashed on the northern riverbank with a shower of blood and shattered steel.

Spears flew Torin's way. One slammed into his horse, snapping against the animal's armor. Another shattered against Torin's shield, showering wooden shards. Torin's head spun. His heart leaped into his throat. His pulse thrummed in his ears. His hand shook around the hilt of his katana, and he was there again, back in the night, a youth fighting the hosts of sunlight, Koyee at his side.

He gritted his teeth.

Breathe.

He sucked in air.

Survive breath by breath.

He leaned forward in the saddle, driving into the enemy.

A rider charged toward him, swinging a sword. Torin blocked the blow with his shield, swung his own blade, and shattered the joints of armor at the man's elbow. The arm bent with a sickening *snap*, and Torin thrust his sword again, denting the steel. Blood seeped. A second rider attacked from his left, and Torin swung his shield, driving the wooden disk into the enemy's helmet. His fellow riders fought around him, thrusting lances and slashing swords.

"Omry, get back to the city!" Torin shouted. "Organize a defense on the walls."

The young prince shook his head, sweat dripping down his face. "I fight with you, Torin! I—"

Horses screamed.

The air thinned, streaming away from Torin, leaving him gasping.

He stared ahead, saw them, and felt the blood drain from his face.

Mages.

A dozen rode from the bridge, the soldiers of Mageria parting to let them through. The mages' hands were raised, collecting the air into swirling balls thick with dust, smoke, and pieces of shattered steel. As one, the mages tossed forward their missiles.

Torin tried to dodge the projectile hurtling his way. He tugged his horse left, only to crash into another animal. His horse reared, wind shrieked, and pain and darkness flowed over Torin.

Blood splashed. Armor cracked.

He fell.

He saw nothing.

Pain drove through him, and he realized he had fallen onto his back. Still he couldn't see. The smoke clung to him, covering his visor, tearing at his armor like a demon. He grunted, blinded, unable to breathe. He pulled off his helmet and tossed it aside, and the darkness cleared, revealing a shadowy beast that wrapped around the fallen helmet, crushing it into a steel ball. More smoke clung to Torin's armor, scratching, tearing, denting. Torin screamed as he tugged off the steel plates and tossed them aside, freeing himself from the translucent creature. His armor had shielded him from the magical attack, but Torin's heart sank to see that his horse had been less fortunate; the smoky tendrils were crushing the lifeless animal.

Torin barely had time to catch his breath. Through the smoke they came marching—the ground troops of Mageria, moving in columns, two by two, covered in steel, their swords held before them, their shields guarding their flanks. Their boots moved in unison, reminding Torin of a great, mechanical centipede.

He lifted his fallen katana. Fellow Ardishmen came to stand at his sides.

"We will send them into the river," Torin said. "Soldiers of Arden, you will defend your border. Turn the river red with their blood!"

His fellow Ardishmen pointed their swords forward, shouted, and ran with Torin to meet the enemy.

The forces crashed together with spraying blood and clanging steel.

Thousands of blades swung.

It seemed to Torin that they fought for hours upon the riverbank. Men fell every moment, both those of Arden and the enemy, and the river turned red. Everywhere the enemy surged: swordsmen, riders, mages tearing off armor and shattering flesh. Swords cut into men. Magic tugged bones out of living bodies. Soldiers lay in the grass, clutching wounds, screaming, weeping, calling for their mothers.

Torin limped along the bloodied grass, an arrow in his leg, and raised his head to behold a horror from the underworld.

The captain of the Magerian hosts, the creature Gehena, had joined the fight, no longer content to command the battle from the sidelines. His four arms swung, each wielding a blade the size of a plow. Men flew like scattered toys. The captain's horse, a towering black beast, drove down hooves larger than human heads, crushing bodies beneath them. Arrows, broken blades, and spears pierced the dark captain's torso, but the creature seemed unaffected. Still his red eyes blazed within his black helm, and still his blades swung, cutting down the men of Arden.

"The bridge is fallen!" Prince Omry shouted, clutching Torin's arm. The young man's armor was cracked, and blood coated him. "We must flee!"

Torin nodded grimly. Hundreds of Magerians now covered the Ardish riverbank, flowing into the plains. More kept emerging from the forest.

The bridge is lost.

A squire brought him a riderless horse. Torin climbed into the saddle and raised his banner.

"Men of Arden!" he shouted hoarsely. "Back to the city! To Kingswall!"

They rallied around him.

They fled across the plains.

And they died.

With the bridge abandoned to the enemy, the full wrath of Mageria flowed across the river, a great shadow spilling forth. Arrows flew into the fleeing men. Magic tore through them. The laughter of Gehena echoed in their ears, high-pitched, the shriek of demons. Every step it seemed that another man fell.

Bloodied, limping, their armor shattered, the last defenders of Kingswall entered their city.

The gates slammed shut behind them, sealing out the enemy.

When Torin climbed the tower again, he clutched the battlements, shaking, barely able to breathe.

The enemy covered the land in a carpet of black steel. A hundred thousand troops or more hid the plains, chanting, waving the Radian banners. Dark mages rode upon dark mounts. Siege towers rolled forth, topped with steel, as tall as the city walls. Catapults and trebuchets rolled into formation, their boulders ready to fire. A great wheeled cannon rolled among them, forged as an iron buffalo; Torin had seen these weapons in Eloria but never in the lands of sunlight. And still more enemies flowed across the bridge, a never-ending stream like gushing oil.

"Death," Prince Omry whispered, standing at Torin's side upon the gatehouse.

Torin closed his eyes for only a moment.

I love you, Koyee. I love you, Madori. I miss you and love you both so much. I wish I could tell you that one last time.

He forced himself to take a deep, shuddering breath.

Again.

Again.

He opened his eyes, looked at Prince Omry, and held the young man's arm.

"Death," he agreed. "But first war. We die here, but not without a fight. We go down firing our arrows, swinging our swords, and singing of our home."

The prince nodded, his eyes damp, and raised his sword upon the wall. Around them, a hundred archers emerged to nock arrows and tug back their bowstrings.

Ahead in the fields, the trebuchets and catapults swung. Boulders, arrows, and blasts of dark magic flew toward the city of Kingswall.

CHAPTER TWENTY-FIVE
GRAVES

Lord Serin stood among the trees, smiling thinly as he examined the Elorian prisoners.

"Men!" he said. "Step forth. Hand them their shovels."

Five Radian soldiers emerged from the forest. Three held loaded crossbows, pointing them at the outcast students. Two other soldiers tossed down long leather bundles; they thumped against the ground and unfolded, revealing many shovels.

"What are you doing here, Serin?" Madori spat out. Her ankles and wrists still chained, she hobbled closer to him. "Go back to your lair and leave us."

The tall lord burst into laughter. He looked over his shoulder and spoke to the shadows. "You were right about her, my daughter! She's a vicious little thing. I do admire the scars on her cheeks. Your work, no doubt?"

"But of course." A sweet smile on her lips, Lari stepped out from the forest, holding a crossbow. She aimed the weapon at Madori. "And I will hurt her worse if she tries to escape."

Madori sneered and made to leap at Lari, but the girl placed her finger against the trigger. The crossbow creaked and Madori froze, glaring at the girl and her father.

"Very good," Lari said, still smiling sweetly. "You will stand still. If you try to attack me, you will die. If you try to escape, you will die. You and your nightcrawler friends will do as we command." Her voice rose to a shout. "Dig!"

Madori growled, looking between daughter to father. "How about you two go suck on rotten eggs?"

Lord Serin sighed and nodded toward his daughter. Lari grinned, raised her crossbow, and fired.

An Elorian student—a studious boy named Shen—clutched his chest, a quarrel in his heart. He gasped, gazed at Madori, then fell.

Other Elorians screamed. Madori began to rush toward the fallen boy. Jitomi hissed and stepped toward Lari, hands crackling with magic. Soldiers laughed.

"Freeze!" Serin barked. "Any one of you nightcrawler scum moves an inch, unless it's to dig, your death will follow. Lari, if anyone else causes trouble, fire again. Fire at random." Serin's lips peeled back in a horrible grin. "Now, nightcrawlers, you will behave. Lift the shovels and begin to dig. Dig a trench here on the roadside. Go!"

Glancing around nervously, some weeping, the Elorians lifted their shovels. They approached the roadside and began to dig. Only Madori stood still, chin raised.

"I can't dig with these chains on me," she said, glaring at Serin.

He snapped his fingers, and her chains shattered and fell to the ground.

Madori brought her arms forward. After being chained for so long, her muscles screamed in protest, and blood covered her wrists. She was free! She could lunge at Lari and Serin. She could fight. She could—

Lari fired her crossbow. The quarrel whizzed by Madori's head.

"Dig!" the girl shouted, already loading another quarrel. "Dig or the next one hits your twisted mongrel heart."

Grumbling, her belly knotting with fear, Madori grabbed a shovel and joined the others. They dug along the roadside. Whenever Madori glanced over her shoulder, the soldiers raised their crossbows, and Lari shook her head while smiling her sweet smile. Madori returned her eyes to her work. The ditch was soon a foot deep, several feet wide.

Madori took a deep breath, summoning her magic. She was hurt, weary, and famished, and she doubted she had enough magic to fight with. But she could muster a little trick she had learned in her classrooms, a way to speak to her classmates without the professors hearing. Though her head blazed with pain, she chose and claimed the air between her and Jitomi. She formed an invisible barrier to block sound waves, then spoke softly.

"Jitomi!"

Digging beside her, he glanced at her. She saw in his eyes that he recognized her magic; they had often communicated like this in Professor Atratus's class. He whispered, allowing his words to reach her ear but not cross the magical barrier toward the Radians.

"Madori, I don't like this. We're digging our own graves."

She wouldn't look at him as she spoke. "I think so too. We have to attack them. Do you have enough magic in you to thicken this barrier of air? To block their crossbow quarrels?"

He nodded, an almost imperceptible movement. "Yes. Joined with your magic, yes. We'll create the barrier, then bolt into the trees."

"No." Madori tossed a shovel of dirt across her shoulder. "If we run, they'll track us. They'll catch us. We fight them."

Jitomi glanced over his shoulder, then back at her. "There are ten of them. Too many."

"Only two are mages—Lari and her father. The other eight are dumb soldiers. There are twenty-five of us and—"

A whip cracked. A soldier shouted behind them. "Get back to shoveling! Faster!"

Madori grunted and shoveled faster. She risked a glance at Jitomi and spoke before her shield of air could deteriorate, letting her voice through to the enemy.

"Pass the word on," Madori said. "On my signal, we raise barriers of air. The magic will block the first round of crossbow quarrels. Before the enemy can load again, we bang them with shovels."

Jitomi nodded and turned toward the Elorian beside him, conveying the information. The ditch was two feet deep by the time Jitomi glanced back toward her. He spoke two words, each one cold and hard as a blade.

"We're ready."

Madori took a deep breath, tossed a shovelful of dirt over her head, and spun toward the soldiers on the road.

"Now!" she shouted.

She claimed the air. She thickened her barrier. At her side, her fellow Elorians spun with her, and the air thrummed and solidified, forming an opaque shield.

The Radians fired their crossbows.

The air rippled like a pond under hail, wobbling as the quarrels slammed into the force field. The bolts shattered. Shards of metal and wood flew. Several shards passed the barrier and hit Madori's body, cutting her skin but not sinking deeper. The shield of air vanished, and the Radians began to load more quarrels.

Madori and the Elorians charged at them, shovels swinging.

A flash of fear filled Lari's eyes, bringing a smile to Madori's lips; she couldn't wait to slam her shovel into that pretty face. Lord Serin, however, smiled too—a smile lush with cruelty, amusement, and a hint of admiration.

Forget about Lari, Madori told herself. She screamed and charged toward Serin. *I go after the big fish.*

She lunged toward the lord, shovel swinging, as he thrust his sword toward her.

* * * * *

The enemy covered the land, spreading into the horizon, a sea of steel surging forth.

Their catapults swung. Their trebuchets twanged. From the ranks of enemy troops, dozens of boulders hurtled through the air, bristly with metal spikes.

Torin stood upon the walls of his city, hundreds of soldiers stretching to his sides. Protector of Kingswall, he raised his sword and cried at the top of his lungs.

"Archers! Fire!"

Around him, a hundred archers loosed their arrows. Whistles filled the air. A hundred glinting shards flew upward, reached their zenith, then plunged down toward the enemy. Below upon the fields, shields rose. Arrows slammed into wood. Three men fell dead, maybe four. Jeers rose from the enemy troops.

With a rumbling like thunder, the enemy's boulders slammed into the city of Kingswall.

One stone crashed into the wall beneath Torin, cracking the stone. The battlements shook. Another boulder sailed over his head, and Torin looked over his shoulder to see a steeple snap, tilt, and slam down to drive into the street. Other boulders slammed into houses, crashing through tiled roofs.

"Trebuchets, fire!" Torin shouted.

The contraptions of wood, metal, and rope twanged upon the city ramparts. Flaming barrels flew from the battlements of Kingswall, spinning and shrieking, to crash into the enemy below. Magerian troops fell, fire blazing across them.

"Archers!" Torin shouted and more arrows sailed.

Fire crackled in the field. Smoke rose. With a blast of smoke and flame, the buffalo cannon fired. The world seemed to shake.

The cannon ball, large as a boulder, slammed into a turret only paces away from Torin. The tower crumbled. Bricks rained and archers fell. Dust filled the air. The blast nearly knocked Torin off the wall.

Mules grunted in the fields, clad in steel, tugging forth siege towers of wood and metal. Enemy archers stood upon them, firing onto the walls. Arrows flew around Torin, and one slammed into his shield. Another grazed his helmet. He fired his bow, hitting an enemy archer upon a siege engine. A trebuchet swung at his side, slamming its boulder into another engine, scattering wood and enemy soldiers.

One wooden tower reached the wall, and a plank slammed down. Magerian swordsmen rushed onto the battlements. Torin ran toward them, sword swinging, and locked blades with an enemy soldier. With a kick and thrust of his shield, he sent the man tumbling off the wall. More Magerians surged from the siege engine, and Torin snarled as he fought, slaying men, sending them crashing down. His comrades fought at his sides.

"Burn the siege engine!" Torin shouted over his shoulder. Men stood there with torches, lighting the wooden trebuchet projectiles. "Bring fire!"

Men rushed forth, holding torches and pots of oil. Cauldrons tilted over the battlements. Bubbling oil crackled over a siege engine. Torches fell, landed upon the wood, and the wooden tower burst into flames like a pyre. Torin stepped back and shielded his eyes from the heat. Those Magerian troops still in the engine screamed, engulfed in fire.

The tower collapsed but Torin found no rest. The buffalo cannon fired a second time, and another turret crumbled and fell off the wall. More catapult boulders sailed overhead. In the city, roofs shattered and houses crumbled. A domed temple crashed down, scattering bricks. Smoke, dust, and fire covered the city.

Through the screams of battle, shrieks of arrows, and roars of fire rose a deep chant. The voices boomed across the battlefield. Torin's heart sank.

"The mages," he muttered.

He stared between two merlons and a chill gripped him.

The enemy troops parted below like a splitting sea. Down the path rode a hundred black horses, and upon them sat a hundred mages clad in black robes and hoods. At their lead rode the captain of Mageria's forces, the towering Gehena, his four arms raised like serpents about to strike. Swordsmen and archers chanted at the mages' sides, raising their swords and bows, cheering on their champions.

Torin turned back toward his men.

"Archers!" he shouted. "Aim at the mages! Slay the mages!"

He fired his own bow. His arrow sailed toward the mages, burst into flame in mid-air, and disintegrated. A hundred other arrows followed his, only to suffer the same fate.

The mages halted outside the city gates. At their lead, Gehena raised his head, his red eyes crackling like flames, staring straight at Torin. His four hands collected smoke and fire, forging them, coiling them into the shape of a great champion. Behind the captain, the lesser mages added their own smoke to the creation. The creature took shape in the fields—a great buffalo, large as a ship, its horns formed of countless metal shards. The ghostly animal shrieked, an unearthly sound, and charged.

Arrows rained upon the creature, passing through its smoke. The astral horns, each like a battering ram, slammed into the city gates.

The walls shook.

The doors smashed.

The gates of Kingswall shattered.

The mages moved aside. Cheering for victory, the enemy troops surged into the city.

It is lost, Torin knew, looking down to see the enemy racing into the inner courtyard. *The city has fallen. The city will be our graveyard.*

The world became a dream—a nightmare of smoke, blood, wounds, steel, arrows, death. They fought in the streets. They fought in homes, upon roofs, in the ruins of shattered temples. More and more Ardishmen fell, and ever the Magerians stormed forth, filling the streets like poison seeping through arteries. Torin fought for a turn, maybe more, ever falling back as the enemy claimed street by street. With blood, fire, and shattering stones, the city of Kingswall crumbled.

CHAPTER TWENTY-SIX
FLIGHT

We're too slow.

Cam panted as he rode across the countryside, leading three thousand armored riders. His horse foamed at the mouth, the courser's eyes rolling, nostrils flaring, ears lying flat against its head. The other beasts were just as exhausted. Cam knew he was driving them too hard, yet how could he rest?

We're too damn slow.

His family was at Kingswall. Torin was at Kingswall. Hundreds of thousands of his people were at Kingswall.

The serpent heads there now. Serin.

Cam clenched his fist as he rode. He did not doubt Serin's actions now; the man had fooled them, drawn them to Hornsford with his army of straw, leaving Kingswall a fruit ripe for the picking. Cam had sent Nitomi and Qato ahead in their hot air balloon, entreating the dojai to rescue whoever they could. But Kingswall needed more than two Elorian spies; it needed an army. It needed Cam and his riders.

Idar damn it, too slow!

The landscape rose and fell around them, grassy hills to the north, the Sern River to the south. Miles behind, his ground troops were heading east too, but Cam would not wait. In his mind's eye, he could imagine the Magerian horde assaulting the city, toppling walls, storming the streets.

With three thousand riders, I can tear through the enemy, he thought, gazing upon his forces. Every man wore good steel and carried a blade and sword. *We can still save our city. We can—*

Chants rose ahead, interrupting his thoughts.

Cam stared toward the sound and his breath died.

"Idar help us," he whispered.

The enemy covered the landscape, twenty thousand troops or more bearing the Radian standards. Thousands among them rode upon horses. Scythed chariots rolled forth. Men beat drums and sang for victory, and horns—thousands of horns—shrieked like birds of prey.

Behind Cam, his men raised their own horns. The song rose in the wind, the song of Arden, a song for victory. Men aimed lances and took battle formations.

"We will slay them, my king!" cried a lord.

"For Arden!" cried a knight.

The two armies stormed across the countryside toward each other.

We're trapped, Cam thought, a shiver taking him. *Of course*. He howled in rage. *He planned this too.*

He leaned forward in his saddle and drew his sword, prepared for battle—but he knew this was not a battle he could win. This was not a battle on his terms.

He flushed me away from my walls. He trapped me between Hornsford and Kingswall. Now my city stands alone and I'm caught like a sheep between wolves.

The fear—for his family, his friends, his people—stormed through him like an icy torrent.

The enemy roared as they charged, covering the land, thousands of horses and chariots with spinning blades upon their wheels. Thousands of arrows flew. Cam swung his sword, and blood stained the fields of Arden.

* * * * *

Lari grinned and licked her lips as she fired her crossbow, aiming at the filthy mongrel. When her quarrel shattered against the shield of air, Lari stared for an instant, disbelief freezing her.

The mongrel shattered my quarrel.

Lari felt her smile vanish, replaced with a snarl. She screamed.

The damn mongrel thinks she can magic her way out of this.

Growling, Lari placed another quarrel in her crossbow and began to turn the crank, tugging the string back. Crossbows were such crude machines—too slow to load. Weapons for commoners. The Elorians were racing onto the road, swinging their shovels. Abandoning hope of loading the second quarrel fast enough, Lari cursed and tossed her crossbow at the nightcrawlers. The weapon slammed into an Elorian's forehead, cutting a deep groove, and Lari smiled and hissed through clenched teeth.

Good. First blood.

She raised her hands, prepared to fight the way a proper, highborn girl should fight—with magic, cruel and twisting and dark, a force to rip bones out of flesh. Madori would die slowly, Lari decided. A quick blast to the heart was too good for mongrels.

I will coil your bones, pull out your organs, and make you watch and beg me for death. She licked her lips and her nostrils flared, already smelling the mongrel blood.

She took a step toward Madori, gathering the magic in her hands, when the other maggot—the one called Jitomi—swung a shovel toward her head.

Lari sneered and swung her arms, tossing the ball of magic—the one intended for Madori—at the shovel instead. Inches away from her head, the shovel jerked backwards, tugging Jitomi two steps back.

Lightning flashed and slammed into a tree nearby. Lari grinned, raised her palms, and sucked the energy toward her, forming two glowing balls. She smiled crookedly at Jitomi, that piece of nightcrawler filth.

"Toss down your shovel and fight like a mage," she said. "Or are nightcrawlers so weak with magic, you fight like gravediggers?"

Around them, the others were battling—Elorian students dueling soldiers, shovels clanging against swords. Jitomi tugged back his hood and stared at her with blue, monstrous eyes the size of limes. His white hair fell across his brow, and his skin gleamed when lightning struck again. The dragon tattoo coiling across his face seemed to stare too. Never breaking his gaze, he tossed his shovel aside and raised his hands, collecting metallic particles from the air.

Lari leaned forward, tossing her balls of lightning.

He reacted at once, lobbing his projectiles toward her. The balls of lightning crashed and shattered. A thousand bright shards hovered in the air for an instant, then pattered down.

Sneering, Lari chose his boot. She claimed the leather. She tugged and he fell. Quickly she chose the air around a rock, levitated it above the Elorian, and tossed it down toward his face.

Jitomi rolled aside, and the rock thumped into the mud. A blast of that mud showered upward, flying toward Lari, blinding her and filling her mouth.

She held one hand forward, shoving a field of air, and wiped the mud off her face to see him crash backward.

"Better." She spat out mud, smiled, and wriggled her fingers, collecting strands of smoke. "Now we're having fun."

She tossed the smoky ropes at him, the same magic she had used on Madori back at Teel. The murky tentacles spun around him. Lari tugged her arm back, tightening the grip, and Jitomi gasped. She shoved her palm forward, blasting out power and knocking him onto his back. She chose a branch above, claimed the wood, and cracked it. The bough slammed down onto Jitomi, pinning him to the ground.

Lari grinned and chose his foot—not just his boot this time but the flesh within. He lay, blinking, struggling to rise, still wrapped in the magical ropes.

Her grin so wide it hurt her cheeks, Lari tugged his foot, and he screamed. She spun him in the mud, dragging him toward the ditch until he teetered on the edge.

He tried to resist. He summoned a ball of mud, air, and wooden chips; Lari dodged the projectile easily. She stepped forward, pouted mockingly, and placed her foot against Jitomi's neck, smearing the dragon tattoo with mud.

"You dug your own grave, worm," she said sweetly. "Now fall into it."

She kicked, shoving him into the ditch. He fell into the grave and lay, groggy and bleeding. Lari stood above and laughed. She lifted a shovel and began tossing mud into the ditch, covering the Elorian, burying him alive.

"Die in the mud like the worm that you are." She laughed. "Your mongrel friend will join you soon."

She tossed in another shovelful of mud, lightning flashed, and she saw them emerge from the forest across the ditch.

Two figures, a boy and girl, blades in their hands.

Lari sneered.

"Tam and Neekeya." She spat. "The two traitors. So you've come to die too."

The two stepped to the opposite edge of the ditch. Tam raised his eyebrows.

"Hullo, Lari!" he said. "It's always strange meeting a student outside of your school, isn't it?"

Neekeya nodded at his side. "It is! And you know the best part?" She raised her sword with the crocodile-claw pommel. "At the university there are rules. But here . . ." The swamp dweller smiled toothily. "Here I do believe we can kill the girl."

The two lunged over the ditch, flying toward her.

Lari growled and tossed air their way.

Their own magic blasted forth, tearing through her defenses, and they landed before her. Lari leaped back, narrowly dodging Neekeya's blade. Tam swung his dagger and Lari screamed; the blade tore across her cheek, and her blood splattered.

"That," the boy said, "is for what you did to Madori's cheek."

Lari screamed and tossed dark tendrils toward him. Neekeya sliced the magic with her blade, then thrust the sword. The tip nicked Lari's other cheek, splashing more blood.

"And that," said Neekeya, "is for Madori's second cheek." She lunged forward, swinging her blade. "The next cut will be for me."

Lari screamed and stumbled backward. She had never cast so much magic before, and when she tried to claim Neekeya's sword, to heat the steel until the barbarian dropped it, she could not. The material slipped from her mind. She tossed a stone, but the projectile bounced uselessly off Neekeya's scale armor.

"You're nothing but a swamp monster!" Lari screamed. She turned toward Tam. "You're nothing but a pathetic traitor who mingles with scum!"

They thrust their blades toward her again, and Lari fled into the forest, screaming and cursing and clutching her wounded cheeks.

* * * * *

He stood in the tallest tower of Kingswall Palace, staring down upon a dying city.

The Magerian enemy covered the city slopes, clogging the streets with steel. Already the Radian banners rose upon the domes and steeples of Kingswall, capital of Arden. The city gates had fallen. The countryside still swarmed with the enemy, and ever more crossed Mudwater Bridge in the south. Only this palace still stood, a single island in the Radian sea.

Some banners, Torin saw, rose upon humble homes, willingly raised by city folk. Those people—his fellow Ardishmen—cheered along the streets and upon roofs, welcoming the enemy.

"Death to nightcrawlers!" they chanted. "Radian rises!"

More than the corpses at the walls, the enemy surging along the streets, or the dark magic coiling like smoke, the sight of these traitors disgusted Torin. In future tales, would bards sing of an Arden who fought nobly against Serin . . . or a kingdom that welcomed evil?

"Where are you, Cam?" Torin whispered, staring out the window at the ruin of his city. "Where are you, my king, my friend?"

Cam's army—myriads of archers, swordsmen, and riders—could have stopped this assault. But now the might of Arden languished in the west at Hornsford, useless as the capital shattered, as the ancient kingdom fell. When Torin lowered his gaze, he saw Magerian troops stream into the palace gardens, marching toward the gates. Soon they would storm through the throne room, climb the stairs, and finally emerge here into this tower. And it would end.

A hand touched his shoulder. A soft voice spoke.

"Torin. What do we do?"

He turned around. He saw them there and his eyes stung.

Queen Linee stood in the round chamber, her eyes wide with fear. She gripped a sword in her hands, but the blade shook. Beside her stood her son and heir, Prince Omry, his armor cracked and bloodied. He too held a blade, and a bandage covered his brow.

What do we do . . .

Torin looked down at his own blade, a katana of the night. Years ago, the Chanku Pack—great wolfriders of the Qaelish empire—had gifted him this blade. He had fought many men with this steel, yet now . . . now would the blade find another task?

What we do is fall on our swords, he thought. *What we do is die before they capture us. Because the fate they plan will be worse than death.*

He licked his lips, trying to speak those words. Somewhere below, men chanted, wood and stone crashed, and the tower shook.

"They're breaking in," said Prince Omry, eyes grim. "They will be here soon."

Torin nodded, for a moment choking, unable to breathe, unable to speak.

I will never see my wife and daughter again. I love you, Koyee and Madori. He looked around at the chamber—the tapestries on the walls, the jeweled raven statues, the lush rugs, the giltwood tables. It was a comfortable place, a good place to die.

He raised his blade. He spoke gently. "Let me do it. I will be quick. I—"

A cry sounded behind him.

Linee gasped and pointed.

Torin spun around to face the window and his eyes widened. He lost his breath.

Nitomi and Qato, the two dojai, hovered outside the window in a basket.

"Hurry!" Nitomi said, gesturing for them to enter the basket. "Hop on board! Did you know that there's a giant army of thousands of swordsmen and mages and riders and archers outside, and maybe they even have elephants, and they're all over the city, and they're breaking into this palace, and—"

"Yes, Nitomi, we know!" Torin said. He thrust his head out the window and gazed upward. Ropes connected the basket to a hot air balloon; Torin had not seen these vessels since the war in Eloria years ago. When he looked down, he saw Magerian soldiers streaming through the shattered palace gates; countless more spread across the city. A Magerian archer nocked an arrow and aimed up at the balloon; a bolt from Qato's crossbow sent the man sprawling.

Torin pulled his head back into the chamber. He held Linee's hands and guided her out the window and into the basket. The gondola dipped several inches under her weight. The queen stood still, her sword still in her hand, a tear streaming down her cheek as she gazed upon the fall of her city.

When Torin turned toward Prince Omry, the armored young man shook his head. He raised his sword. "I'm staying."

Torin clutched his arm. "No. Omry, you're flying away from here. You are the heir of Arden."

His eyes flashed. "Which is why I go down with this kingdom."

"Your kingdom does not fall this turn." Torin tugged the boy toward the window. "Your father still fights for this kingdom. Your mother will still lead Arden from safety. If you fall with this city—if the hosts of the enemy slay the heir of Arden—that would shatter the spirit of those who still fight. If you live this day, if you speak for Arden from a place of safety, you will bring hope to the hearts of all Ardishmen."

The prince hesitated, sword wavering. The sounds of boots stomped up the tower now; the chants of Magerians rose below.

"Go!" Torin shouted.

Reluctantly, the prince climbed out the window and into the basket. It dipped two full feet; it seemed barely able to stay afloat.

More arrows whistled from below. Two slammed into the basket. Qato leaned down and fired his crossbow, hitting one archer, then another.

"Hurry, Torin!" Nitomi cried, reaching toward him. "Into the basket! Now!"

Torin looked at the small dojai, then back at the chamber. The walls were shaking, and a framed picture fell and shattered. The cries of Magerians rose louder as they climbed the stairs.

The queen and prince must live to inspire hope, he thought. *But I am Lord Protector of this city. I cannot abandon a sinking ship.*

He turned back to the window. "Go, Nitomi! Fly."

Her eyes watered. "Torin, come on!"

Behind her, Linee and Omry cried out too. "Into the basket!"

Torin's eyes stung. "It won't support my weight." He shoved the gondola away from the tower wall. "Fly! I'll find another way."

Tears streamed down Linee's cheeks, and she cried out to him. "Torin, please!"

"Go!" He shoved the basket again and switched to speaking Ilari, a language of the night. "Nitomi, take them to safety. Take them to Oshy. I'll meet you there. Now go!"

Tears streamed down the small assassin's cheeks as she tugged ropes, letting the hot air balloon soar into the air. Linee was still shouting, reaching over the basket to him, as the vessel ascended and glided eastward, arrows sailing beneath it.

Torin stepped away from the chamber, raised his sword and shield, and faced the door just as it shattered open.

Four mages stepped into the room, clad in black robes, their faces hidden beneath their hoods. Their garments revealed only their fingertips—pale, clawed digits. They stepped aside and stood at attention, allowing a towering figure to enter the room—a man eight feet tall, clad in black, his arms spreading out like mandibles. Red eyes blazed from within his black iron helm. A voice like a hiss rose from that helmet, unearthly, deep, echoing, twisting with cruel mirth.

"Torin Greenmoat . . ."

His four blades burst into white flame, crackling, spewing smoke.

"Take him alive," spoke Gehena, field marshal of the Magerian forces. "Lord Serin will break him."

Torin screamed and charged, sword swinging.

The mages raised their hands.

The smoke blasted Torin's way, crashing against him. He swung his sword, cutting through the tendrils. Blackness covered the room, darker than the night. Pain drove through Torin, creaking his bones.

For Koyee. For Madori. For Moth.

He screamed and lashed his sword.

The katana clanged against Gehena and shattered into countless shards. The steel cut into Torin, and his blood spurted, and he fell.

Blackness enveloped him, almost soft, almost warm, cocooning him in deep slumber.

CHAPTER TWENTY-SEVEN
STEEL AND STONE

He stood before her—Lord Tirus Serin, the new King of Mageria, the Light of Radian—the man she must kill.

Screaming, Madori swung her shovel toward him.

His sword slammed into the handle, diverting the blow.

"Again we meet on the road, sweet Madori!" he said, smiling like a wolf at a sheep. "And again you lunge at me. Last time I spared your life. This time your grave is already dug and awaiting you."

The others fought around them—Elorian outcasts battling Radian soldiers. Madori would not spare the battle a glance; here before her stood her only target. She raised her shovel, prepared to strike again, but the wooden shaft caught flame in her hands. She yelped and tossed the shovel at Serin, but it clanged uselessly against his breastplate, then fell to the ground.

"Poor, innocent child." Serin took a step toward her. "Go on, attack me with magic. I see that you want to. I think I will toy with you a little before I—"

Madori screamed and tossed a ball of dark magic toward his face.

An inch away from hitting him, the projectile scattered and fell like ash.

"Good!" said Serin. "Good. You chose the particles in the air around us, formed a perfect missile, and tossed it within a heartbeat." He tsked and shook his head. "But you forgot to form new bonds between the materials, allowing me to easily disperse the projectile." He swung his sword, slicing skin off her arm. "Try again! Every time you fail, I will cut off another piece of you."

Madori yowled. Blood gushed from her arm. She had no time to heal the wound. Instead, she claimed his breastplate and began to heat the metal.

He sighed like a teacher at an erring pupil, shook his head, and transferred the heat from his breastplate into his sword. The blade turned red-hot, and he swung it again, nicking Madori's shoulder. She screamed, the wound sizzling.

"Not good enough!" Serin said. "Why heat armor without sealing the fire within?" He sighed. "Truly you mongrels are pathetic creatures. That is why you will die in our fire, and the true masters of magic—Magerians of pure blood—will rule both day and night. Try again!"

Madori trembled, her wounds dripping, barely able to focus, barely able to muster the strength to stand up. She needed help. She needed her friends. He was too strong. But the others were fighting their own enemies; Madori faced this man alone.

With a scream, she claimed his sword, trying to loosen the bonds within the blade, to bend the steel while it was hot. He responded by claiming the blade himself, curving it into a saber, and nicking her ear. She tried to claim the cobblestones beneath his feet, to tug them free and send him falling. He stepped aside, regained his footing, and stabbed her thigh.

Madori screamed, more blood spilling, and fell to her knees.

"My my." Serin shook his head sadly. "For a year you studied magic, yet you cannot even defeat an old man like me." He stepped closer to her, raised his hand, and blasted a cone of air at her chest. The blow knocked the breath out of her. She fell onto her back, gasping for air, her blood trickling.

He placed a boot upon her chest. His sword tore through her shirt, drawing a line across her chest, and more blood flowed.

"Foul mongrel blood," he said, pinning her down. He spat. "The pure blood of Timandra . . . mixed with poison of Eloria. It disgusts me. I will bleed you now, child—slowly, drop by drop, and you will stare upon me as your life trickles away, then join your subhuman friends in the grave you dug."

She tried to cast her magic; she was too weak. She tried to shove his boot off; he was too strong, crushing her, and she felt that her organs could burst, her ribs snap. Her eyes rolled back. She tried to cry for help, but only a whisper left her throat.

Breath by bre—

Yet his boot pressed deeper, and she couldn't even breathe.

Her eyes rolled back, and she thought she heard her friends calling to her: Tam, her oldest friend, a prince of Arden, a boy she had loved all her life; and Neekeya, her only female friend, a girl Madori loved more than life. How could they be here too? How could she fail, let them die here in the forest with her?

I'm sorry, my friends. I'm sorry, my parents. I love you all so much.

Tears streamed down her cheeks, mingling with the blood and mud.

Serin flipped his sword over, pointing the blade downward. He raised the sword slowly, prepared to drive it down like a tent peg.

No. How can I die here? I spent a year studying magic. How can I fail? She thought back to her professors: little Professor Fen, his mustache bristling as he taught Basic Principles; elderly Professor Yovan, a kindly graybeard who taught her the art of healing; wise Professor Maleen, poisoned by the Radians; and finally, the brightest light among them, Headmistress Egeria, the wisest woman Madori had known, a woman now imprisoned for her resistance.

They believed in me. They taught me to be strong. How can I let them down?

"And now," Serin said, digging his heel into her, "I gut you like a fish and watch your organs spill."

His face changed, turning cruel, delighted, red with bloodlust. He hissed, lips peeled back, and drove his sword downward.

With her last drops of strength, Madori chose and claimed the blade.

As the sword plunged down, she split the blade into two halves—down to the hilt. Each half curled outward like a great, steel jaw opening wide. The two shards slammed into the earth at Madori's sides, driving deep into the mud, missing her body.

She had no more power for magic. She grabbed a rock and hurled it, hitting his forehead.

Serin shouted and stumbled back, blood spurting and filling his eyes.

Dizzy and covered in blood, she tossed his broken sword aside and struggled to her feet. She stumbled a few steps toward a dead Radian soldier; she realized that most of the Radians were dead, and the Elorian outcasts were battling the last of them. Madori tugged the corpse's sword free and swung the blade at Lord Serin.

His sword gone, he tried to parry with his arms, relying on his armor for protection. Madori's blade slammed into his hand, severing a finger. She swung again, hitting the side of his helmet, denting the steel.

He emitted a sound like a butchered animal.

"We'll see who's gutted!" Madori said, stepping closer to him.

Around her, the other Elorians—bloodied, panting, and holding their own claimed swords—stepped forward with her, advancing toward the wounded Serin. Dead Radians lay upon the road around them.

"Father!" rose a voice from the forest behind—Lari's voice, sounding afraid and young. "Father, help!"

Madori lunged toward Serin, swinging her blade.

The mighty lord, the Light of Radian, the King of Mageria—spun on his heel and fled. He raced into the forest, clutching the stump of his finger, calling his daughter's name.

Madori tried to chase him. She wobbled and nearly fell. Arms caught her, and she found herself leaning against Tam.

"She's hurt!" the prince called over his shoulder. "Neekeya, bring bandages!"

Madori tried to free herself, to run into the forest. "We have to catch him, Tam," she whispered, blood in her mouth, blood in her eyes. "We have to kill him. We . . ."

The world spun. She was vaguely aware of her friends placing her down on the road, of Jitomi's warms hands upon her wounds, of Neekeya whispering prayers.

A raven circled above, cawing, the bird of Arden, of her home.

Her eyes closed. She slept.

* * * * *

For a long time Tam stood in the rain, staring down at the grave, his fists clenched at his sides.

"I'm sorry," he said, voice hoarse, as the rain streamed down his face. "My friends, I'm sorry."

He lowered his head. Mud and stones covered the communal grave on the roadside, containing the bodies of Radian soldiers and five Elorian youths, outcast students fallen to Serin's cruelty. The rain pattered against the grave, and Tam wanted to kneel, to dig through the mud, to check again for life signs, to save them somehow. But he only stood, ashamed.

"You came into the lands of sunlight to learn our ways," he whispered. "You didn't distinguish between Magerians, Ardishmen, Daenorians, or any other children of sunlight; to you we were all foreigners. You came into sunlight trusting us . . . and now you lie dead. And now the forces of hatred march across this land."

Tam knew that he wasn't to blame. He knew that he'd done all he could to protect these Elorians. Yet still the guilt coursed through him—guilt for Timandra and the blood staining these lands of eternal daylight.

A hand touched his shoulder. He turned to see Neekeya gazing at him with soft eyes.

"We have to go." She caressed his wet hair. "Serin will be back with more men. We have to leave now."

He looked back at the road. The surviving Elorian students—twenty in all—were back inside the cage upon the wagon. Madori lay between them, her wounds bandaged, still unconscious. Jitomi sat with her, cradling her head in his lap. As the rain fell, the large Elorian eyes stared at him, blue and lavender, gleaming like lanterns.

"We'll take them to Arden," Tam said. "To the city of Kingswall, where they'll find rest and supplies. From there they can continue their journey to Eloria." He lowered his head. "My days at Teel University are over. I will not return there. In this time of bloodshed, I return to my homeland, to my city, to my family."

Neekeya clasped his hand. "And I go with you."

He tucked a loose strand of her hair behind her ear. "But your home lies in the west, Neekeya, in the swamps of Daenor."

She nodded. "And I will return there someday, but not yet. I will not leave you." She embraced him. "The Elorians need us; in the endless day, they are afraid, and they are weak, and they are alone. I will not abandon them any sooner than you would." She kissed him. "And I will not leave you. We'll drive this cart east. We'll bring them to safety."

He held her for a moment longer, never wanting to break apart from her warmth, from her goodness. Cruelty raged across the land, war loomed, his best friend was wounded, and the bodies of five more friends lay underground—but there was some hope in the world, there was some goodness in the pain. There was Neekeya.

They donned cloaks and hoods, hiding their faces. They climbed onto the cart, replacing its fallen driver. The horses began to move. They would not stay on the road for long, only until Madori was well enough to walk; then they would travel through the forest, hidden until they could reach the border.

For now the wagon trundled, and the road stretched ahead between the trees, leading east into lands of water, light, and unknown shadows.

CHAPTER TWENTY-EIGHT
THE JOURNEY HOME

Madori was shivering by the campfire, the dark forest creaking around her, when she remembered the piece of paper.

Headmistress Egeria had slipped the little, folded paper to her turns ago; it felt like years. With all that had happened—the attack in the cloister, the long ride in the wagon, the battle on the road—Madori had forgotten. Perhaps she had wanted to forget. Perhaps the memory of the kindly old headmistress was too painful.

She reached into her pocket now, hand trembling, and felt the paper still there. Small. Folded several times.

A gust of wind blew. The trees swayed and sparks flew from the campfire. Her friends all shivered and huddled closer to the fire. Tam and Neekeya sat pressed together, sharing a cloak.

Madori sat apart from the others on an old log. Cold. Alone. Half her body in the light of the fire, half in darkness, torn even here.

Her eyes stung.

I miss you, Egeria. Teel is so far, and I'm so afraid.

She pulled the piece of paper out of her pocket. She stared at it but dared not unfold it. Were words written here? A farewell? A warning? Madori felt as if cold emanated from this paper. If she unfolded it, would she be releasing a beast she could not tame?

She lowered her head.

I never should have left home, she thought. *I should have stayed in Fairwool-by-Night. With my family. The people I love. I can't fight this darkness. I can't defeat this evil alone.*

She had come here for adventure, come to seek a new life, a new path. Come to grow up. Now, more than anything, Madori wished she could turn back time. Yet perhaps youth was something that could never be reclaimed, not its innocence, not its joy, not the warmth that was but a memory in the cold.

Hands numb, chest tight, she unfolded the paper.

Words were written here in Egeria's delicate script.

Dearest Madori,

I wanted to protect you for a while longer. I wanted to guide you. To teach you. To watch you grow up. I wanted to prepare you for the fire I knew would burn.

Yet perhaps we are never ready for fire. Perhaps we are always but children, afraid and crying out, when the flames burn us. Even the very old and very wise are still as children when tragedy strikes—scared, alone, seeking aid from parents we cannot find.

I will never see you again, Madori, and I don't know if you will ever find aid from another—from a parent, from a teacher, from a friend. I don't know if you will walk the burning paths alone.

But I know that you are strong.

And I know that you will walk them.

And I know that you will survive them.

Our time—the old guardians of Moth—has ended. We failed you. We vowed to bring peace to this torn world and we could not. Now—too soon, too soon!—this torch is yours to carry.

In the light of blazing hatred, carry the light of wisdom. Along the path of swords and arrows, carry hope.

Remember, child. Stars shine in the darkness. Life blooms from ash. The world is dark and cruel but full of goodness too, goodness that is worth fighting for. Fight for it. Always.

Your headmistress,
Egeria

Madori stared at the note a while longer, then folded it and placed it back into her pocket. She left the fallen log where she sat. She moved to nestle between Tam and Neekeya. They wrapped their arms around her, and they sat together, watching the campfire.

* * * * *

They walked up the hill, stood between two oaks, and gazed down at the dead heart of Arden.

Madori's eyes stung. She reached out and clasped Tam's hand.

"So it's true," she whispered. "Kingswall has fallen."

Tam drew his dagger, his face twisted, and he seemed ready to charge downhill, cross the fields, and attack the city walls himself. Instead he fell to his knees, lowered his head, and shook. Madori knelt beside him, pulled him close, and held him tightly. She gazed south with him, the pain like claws digging inside her.

Radian banners rose above the city of Kingswall, replacing the old raven banners. Magerian troops manned the walls, clad in black steel, and marched in the fields. The Magerian fleet sailed upon the Sern River, and more Radian banners rose upon Mudwater Bridge.

"The city's people live," Madori whispered to Tam, squeezing him, trembling with him. "Mageria conquered but did not destroy. Our families are alive."

He turned toward her, his eyes red. "My mother was in that city. My brother." His voice was hoarse. "Your father too."

She dug her fingers into him, baring her teeth. "Your mother is Queen, and your brother the heir of Arden. My father is a war hero. Serin will keep them alive. They're worthless to him dead. They're worth a fortune while they breathe."

The others walked uphill too and stood around them. Neekeya knelt on Tam's other side, stroked his hair, and whispered into his ear. Jitomi knelt by Madori and touched her arm, speaking of Torin being strong and wise, clever enough to escape. The other Elorians, outcast students from Teel, simply stood silently, hoods and robes protecting their skin from the Timandrian sun.

Madori wanted to say more. But her voice caught in her throat, and tears filled her eyes. For long turns, they had traveled through the wilderness, staying off the roads and rivers, hiding in forests and wild grasslands. All over Arden they had seen the remnants of battle: smoldering farms, ravaged towns, and castles now hoisting the enemy standards. For all these turns, Madori had told herself that Kingswall—fabled, ancient city of Ardish might—would withstand the Radian fire. Now she found it too overrun. Now her hope for aid—from Queen Linee, from Price Omry, from her own father—crashed like so many toppled forts.

"Come, friends," she said. "Further back. Behind the trees. We're exposed here."

They stepped back and huddled in a copse between elms, oaks, and pine trees. An ancient mosaic and three fallen columns peeked from the grass, hints of a lost world, remnants of the ancient Riyonan Empire which had ruled here a thousand years ago. Madori wondered if her own kingdom would join the ghosts of Riyona. Tam sat on a fallen column and placed his head in his hands; Neekeya sat beside him, stroking his hair and whispering soft comforts to him. The Elorians huddled together; they had hoped to find rest and aid here on their way back home to the night.

Back home to the night, Madori thought, staring south. The wind played with her hair, scented of old fire and blood. *We come from darkness . . . to the night we return.*

She had thought to find sanctuary behind these sunlit walls, but perhaps her home lay—had always lain—in the darkness.

"Now we must choose our paths," she said. "We fled the lands of Mageria only to find the snake crawling upon Ardish soil too. This land—the river, the city, these plains—is the road to the night. Lord Serin will send his troops into the darkness." She turned to look at the Elorians. "He will send them after your families . . . after my mother. Now we must choose whether we hide or fight, whether we dig hideouts or lift swords and make our stand."

* * * * *

For a long time, Teel's outcasts sat in the grove, whispering, praying, huddling together as the world crumbled around them.

Tam paced between the trees, his boots stepping on pine needles, rich brown soil, and the remnants of the ancient mosaic. The head of a statue rose from the earth, a woman's haloed head. Tam lowered his own head, the pain too great to bear.

My father—trapped fighting a losing battle in the north. My mother and brother—trapped in conquered Kingswall, perhaps dead. My kingdom— in ruins.

He was a prince of Arden, the younger of the twins, never an heir, never one who mattered to the throne. He had fled this realm—to be with Madori, the only one who understood feeling torn, forgotten, afraid. And now . . . now as his kingdom burned, what path did he have? Did he travel with Madori into the darkness, abandoning his home to the buffaloes of Mageria?

The others were huddling together, the Elorians speaking in their language, Madori staring south in silence, the wind in her hair. Tam did not approach them. He needed to walk here, alone, to grieve, to pray. He wore only a tattered tunic and cloak, stubble covered his cheeks, and burrs filled his hair, yet he was still a prince of this land. He had to fight for it—to join his father in the northwestern battles, to sneak into the city, to find aid outside these borders, to lead rebels from the wilderness, to do something—anything—for his home. He had always relied on others for guidance—his parents, his professors, Madori's advice—and now he felt lost, trapped like in his recurring nightmare of racing through a labyrinth, desperate to escape but finding no exit.

Pine needles crunched behind him, and Tam turned to see Neekeya approaching him, her eyes soft, her crocodile helmet tucked under her arm.

Seeing her soothed him.   The breeze played with her black, chin-length hair, and the sunlight gleamed upon her dusky skin and scale armor. When she reached him, the tall swamp dweller took his hands in hers. Her grip was warm, the fingers long, the palms soft.

"I don't know what to do, Neekeya," he whispered. "Those we passed in the wilderness say my father still fights in the northwest, but none can say where. Even if I find him, he lies behind enemy lines. Do I seek him, Neekeya? And if I do, will you come with me?"

She touched his cheek, and her eyes dampened. "No. I return to Daenor, to the swamplands of my home. I will speak to my father; he's a great lord. I will tell him of the Radian menace. I will entreat him to send soldiers across the mountains, to strike at Mageria from the west. We will summon a great council of swamp lords in our pyramid. We are strong in Daenor. We will fight the tyrant."

He lowered his head. "I don't want you to leave me."

She took a shuddering breath and embraced him. Her tears fell. She cupped his cheek in her hand, and she kissed him—a deep kiss, warm and desperate and mingling with her tears. Her lips trembled against his, and their bodies pressed together—his clad in old cotton, hers in steel scales.

Finally their lips parted, and she stroked his hair. "Nor do I. Travel west with me, Tam. Travel into the swamps with me, then return to your land with an army behind you. Return here as a true prince, a true conqueror."

He wanted to laugh, but only a weak breath left his throat. "How would I be a prince among you? In Daenor I would be only an exile, a coward fled from his kingdom as the enemy marched across it. How princely would I seem then, returning here with the hosts of other men?"

She squeezed his hand. "Be my prince then! Wed me in the swamps. Be my husband, and you will not return as an exile but as a liberator. Let us forge an alliance between Daenor and Arden." She smiled through her tears. "When we return here, we will return together—husband and wife, strong, our houses joined, our armies roaring."

He looked into her large, earnest eyes. He stroked her cheek, trailing his fingers down to her chin. She was beautiful. She was strong. She was a woman Tam loved more than life.

"I don't want to wed you for power," he said. "Nor for armies. I will wed you for love. I love you, Neekeya."

She held him close and laid her head against his shoulder. "I love you too—always. Since I first saw you."

They stood together upon the old mosaic on the hill. The leaves glided around them, and in the south the enemy chanted and its horns blew for victory.

* * * * *

Madori walked alone, leaving the others in the grove. Upon the hill, she found the remnant of an old brick wall, only three feet tall, most of it long fallen or perhaps buried underground—a relic of Riyona, an empire lost to time. She climbed onto the wall fragment and stared at the four directions of the wind.

In the west her enemy mustered new power—the forces of Mageria and its corrupt ideology, the cruel Radian Order. When she turned to look north, she saw plains leading to dark forests; beyond them lay the realm of Verilon, a cold land of snow, ice, and pine trees, a realm she did not know, a realm she feared. In the south the capital of her home lay fallen, overrun with the tyrant's forces; even as she stood here, Madori heard the distant chanting of the enemy.

"Are you trapped within those walls, Father?" she whispered, eyes stinging. "Are you chained like I was chained, and are you thinking of me too? Or did you escape into shadows?"

Finally Madori turned to look east. The Sern River stretched across the land, the Ardish plains rolling to its north, the Nayan rainforest sprawling to its south. Mist and light covered the horizon, but beyond them, Madori knew—many leagues away— lay the shadows of Eloria, and that too was her home. There stretched her path, she knew—The Journey Home, like the old song, a journey into darkness.

She returned to the grove and saw the others standing, their packs slung across their shoulders, their eyes somber, staring at her.

Madori spoke softly. "I return to the darkness of night—the village of Oshy in the empire of Qaelin. That land is in danger now; the front line will move to the dusk. There I will make my stand. There I will fight with sword and magic against the tyrant— not in sunlight but in shadows." Her breath shook. "For many years, I thought that I could be a child of sunlight—like my friend Tam, like my fellow villagers, like my father." Her eyes stung. "For many years, I felt the pain of that sun and its people. I sought acceptance at Teel and still bear the scars—on my body, in my heart. Perhaps I've always been only a child of darkness; perhaps in the night will I find my home. My friends, join me there."

Jitomi came to stand by her side. He took her hand in his and squeezed it. The other Elorians, twenty in all, came to stand behind her, robed and hooded. Only Tam and Neekeya, the two Timandrians of their group, did not join her. They remained standing ahead under a pine tree, holding hands.

"We go to Daenor," Tam said softly. "Here our path forks. Here our quartet breaks."

He spoke some more—of forging an alliance with the western realm, of marrying Neekeya in her pyramid, of returning to Arden with a great host of men—but Madori heard little of it. As he spoke, she could only think of losing her friends.

She stepped toward them, her eyes damp, and embraced Neekeya—a crushing embrace, a cocoon of warmth she never wanted to be released from.

"Goodbye, Neekeya," she whispered and kissed the girl's cheek. "Goodbye, my sweet friend."

The swamp dweller smiled, tears in her eyes, and kissed Madori's forehead. "You're my dearest friend, Madori, now and always. We will meet again."

Her cheeks wet, Madori turned to look at Tam, and for a moment she hesitated. How could she part from him—her dearest and only friend for most of her life? The boy she had spent every summer with, had run through fields and gardens with, had daydreamed together with so many times? All her life, Tam had been the beacon of her soul. Now he was traveling away from her, an exiled prince, a man she might never see again.

He pulled her into his arms, and she laid her head against his chest, and she wept in his embrace. He kissed her tears away, and she never wanted to leave him, and when he finally walked downhill, Neekeya at his side, Madori stood for a long time, silent, a hole inside her. She stood there among the trees, watching her friends walk westward until they were only specks in the distance . . . and then were gone from her. Perhaps for years. Perhaps forever. And Madori knew that losing them was a wound greater than any her enemies had given her.

After a long time, she turned back toward the others. They stood silently, wrapped in their cloaks, their eyes—large Elorian eyes like hers—gleaming in the shadows of their hoods.

"It will be a long journey to the night," she said. "And danger crawls upon this land. We hoped to find safety behind brick walls; we will seek it in the shadows. Our road to darkness begins."

She began to walk, leading the way across the hills and valleys, for they dared not travel by road or boat behind enemy lines. Jitomi walked behind her, and the others trailed behind him in single file, slim figures in hoods and robes, outcasts, far from home.

They traveled as the moon waxed and waned, buying food in farms, hunting with magic, gathering mushrooms and berries. Every town they passed displayed the banners of Radianism, and every road they came across bore the soldiers of the enemy. They kept walking, hiding between trees, living off the gifts of the forest. Whenever they rested, Madori thought of those she loved—of her parents, of Tam and Neekeya, of Headmistress Egeria, and sometimes the pain was so cold inside her she couldn't breathe. Jitomi would hold her at those times, stroke her hair, and kiss her forehead, until she slept in his arms.

Autumn leaves rustled in the forests when Madori and her companions reached the dusk.

The village of Fairwool-by-Night lay to their south, Radian banners rising from the library roof. Madori stood between the trees, squeezing Jitomi's hand, staring upon her fallen home. A

Magerian warship stood tethered at the docks, and enemy troops marched in the village square, clad in black armor. Madori's own home, the cottage where she'd been born and raised, stood enclosed in a new iron fence, its gardens burnt, its roof displaying an eclipse standard.

Eyes burning, Madori turned away. She stared east at the great, glowing line of dusk, the border between day and night.

"Into the darkness," she whispered, not trusting herself to speak any louder without weeping. "Quickly."

She walked between the trees, heading into that orange glow. The Elorians walked behind her, silent and grim. Only Jitomi walked at her side, holding her hand tight, and in his eyes Madori saw his compassion; he knew this was her home, and he knew her pain.

The sun dipped behind them as they walked, and shadows stretched across the forest, dark and tall like ghostly soldiers. With every step the light dimmed, turning a deep gold, then orange, then bronze. Their eyes glowed in the darkness, blue lanterns, eyes for seeing in the dark. The trees withered, thinning out, becoming stunted and weak. Soon the sun vanished beneath the horizon and they left the last trees behind. Only sparse grass and moss covered the hills here. Duskmoths rose to flutter around them, tiny dancers, their left wings white, their right wings black, creatures torn like the world. One landed on Madori's hand, and she remembered the duskmoth that had visited her at Teel University, and she wondered if this was the same one, a guardian, a soul that cared for her.

They walked on through the shadows, crested a hill, and there they saw it. The companions froze and stared.

"The night," Madori whispered. "Eloria."

The land of her mother rolled before them, cloaked in shadows. Lifeless black hills rolled into the distance, and the Inaro River snaked between them, a silver thread. The moon shone above, a silver crescent, and starlight fell upon Madori for the first time in a year.

"Eloria," Jitomi whispered. "Our home."

Your home, she thought, looking at him. *Your home,* she thought, looking at the other Elorians. *Yet what home is mine? Will I find any more of a home in darkness than I did in the sunlight?*

She kept walking.

They traveled across a valley and climbed a hill, and there above it loomed: Salai Castle, a pagoda with three tiers of blue, tiled roofs, the fortress named after Madori's grandfather. A golden dragon statue stood upon its topmost roof, and guards stood clad in scale armor at the gates, katanas at their sides. Their long white hair flowed in the wind, and their blue eyes gleamed. Below the hill nestled the village of Oshy, its lanterns bright as the stars, its junk boats floating in the river.

"We'll be safe here, friends," Madori said, turning toward her companions who stood upon the hill. "This is where we make our stand. In the darkness. War will come here too, and the cruelty of Serin will pour into these lands." She clenched her fists. "And we will fight it."

The castle doors creaked open. A gasp sounded. Madori spun around to see a slim figure emerge from within.

"Madori!"

Koyee rushed toward her, her white hair streaming, her lavender eyes filling with tears.

Madori's own tears fell, and suddenly she was trembling, and all the strength she thought she had—of a warrior, a leader, a mage—vanished like rain into a river, leaving her only a girl, so afraid, so hurt.

"Mother!"

She ran toward her mother, and they crashed together in an embrace. Their tears mingled.

"I'm home, Mother," Madori whispered. "I'm home."

* * * * *

They rode into the village in the chill of autumn, their horse's hooves scattering fallen leaves. Upon his mount, Lord Serin stared around in disgust and spat.

"A backwater," he said. "A sty. Barely worth the trouble."

His daughter sat beside him upon a white courser, a furred hood shielding her head from the wind. "Her home. A place that was dear to her." Lari sneered, turned her head around, and shouted toward their men. "Burn it! Burn it all down."

A hundred riders stormed down the hillside, clad in black steel, visors hiding their faces. Their banners rose high, streams of red against the gray sky like blood trailing along a corpse. Their torches crackled, raising columns of smoke.

"Slay them all!" Serin shouted. "Loot what you crave and burn the rest!"

The riders thundered between the cottages of Fairwool-by-Night, torching the thatch roofs. Children ran across the village square, crying for their mothers, as riders tore into them with blades. Villagers emerged from homes, the tavern, and the brick library, begging for life, praising Serin, chanting of Radian's might.

They begged and they died.

Serin sneered, riding his horse toward a young woman shielding a boy in her arms. He thrust his spear, skewering them both. At his side, Lari laughed as she trampled over a dead man, her courser's hooves snapping bones. Soldiers stormed into the library, tugged out books, piled them around the maple tree rising from the village square, and burned them all in a great pyre.

"Here's her house!" Lari said, pointing at a cottage. The word "Greenmoat" appeared upon the door. Lari laughed. "This little chamberpot of a cottage." She raced inside, then emerged holding a rag doll—perhaps a toy Madori had once played with.

Lari spat. "The vermin are gone. The mongrel and her mother fled. Of course they did."

Serin handed her a torch. "Burn the house. This one is yours."

He watched, pride swelling within him, as his daughter set fire to the cottage, as the smoke and flames rose from the home of their enemies.

Blood stained Fairwool-by-Night, red as the fallen maple leaves. Bodies lay crushed and broken. Homes and fields burned. The autumn leaves fell upon nothing but death.

Serin withdrew his men to the hill. They gathered around the old stone watchtower, gazing down at the flaming ruins. A thin smile stretched across Serin's lips, and he wiped blood off his sword.

"The nightcrawlers will see this flame," he said. "The smoke will rise above the dusk, and the stench of death will carry on the eastward wind. The vermin are watching, my daughter. I do not doubt that the mongrel is among them."

He dismounted his horse and helped Lari dismount as well. They entered the watchtower, climbed its spiraling staircase, and emerged onto the battlements. A lone boy stood there, trembling, a youth barely old enough to shave. The lone survivor of Fairwool-by-Night, he made a clumsy attempt at some last honor, firing an arrow at Serin. The projectile missed the lord by two feet.

"Lari?" Serin said, raising an eyebrow.

She grinned, stepped toward the trembling boy, and slashed her sword across his belly. He fell, gasping, dying, his innards spilling.

Serin approached the eastern battlements and leaned forward between two merlons. Lari came to stand at his side, the cold wind billowing her hair and reddening her cheeks. Before them spread the dusk, the shadowy no man's land separating day from night. And there in the distance they saw it: the great shadow, the land of endless night. Eloria.

A castle rose in those shadows, perhaps a league away, a pagoda with three tiers of roofs. As his men emerged onto the tower top, raising a great Radian banner, Serin stared toward that pagoda, and he imagined that he was staring into her eyes.

"Hello, Madori," he whispered, stroking a merlon as if stroking Madori's head. "Do you see this fire? Do you smell this death? We will muster here, mongrel. We will raise an army like the world has never seen. We are coming for you." He licked his lips and caressed the stump of his finger—the finger she had removed. "Soon you will burn too."

Lari leaned against him, and Serin slung an arm around her. They stood watching the night, savoring the smell of victory.

THE END

NOVELS BY DANIEL ARENSON

Misfit Heroes:
Eye of the Wizard (2011)
Wand of the Witch (2012)

Dawn of Dragons:
Requiem's Song (2014)
Requiem's Hope (2014)
Requiem's Prayer (2014)

Song of Dragons:
Blood of Requiem (2011)
Tears of Requiem (2011)
Light of Requiem (2011)

Dragonlore:
A Dawn of Dragonfire (2012)
A Day of Dragon Blood (2012)
A Night of Dragon Wings (2013)

The Dragon War:
A Legacy of Light (2013)
A Birthright of Blood (2013)
A Memory of Fire (2013)

The Moth Saga
Moth (2013)
Empires of Moth (2014)
Secrets of Moth (2014)
Daughter of Moth (2014)
Shadows of Moth (2014)
Legacy of Moth (2014)

KEEP IN TOUCH

www.DanielArenson.com
Daniel@DanielArenson.com
Facebook.com/DanielArenson
Twitter.com/DanielArenson